Hungry Mother Creek

Heather W. Cobham

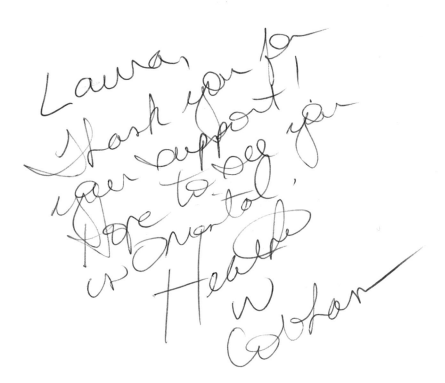

Published by 2nd Star Online Publishers

Cover and Author photo by Alan Welch

ISBN: 978-1495936418

This book is dedicated to my women's circle,

with my deepest respect and all my love.

Acknowledgements

I spent many hours alone with a pen and legal pad writing *Hungry Mother Creek*, but would have never completed the novel and gotten it published without the encouragement and support of so many. I am deeply grateful to the following: Gaye and Ann, my writing friends, who read my first scenes and provided critical feedback throughout the process, but mostly I thank them for their friendship and unending support and inspiration. We are writers! Lynn York and Zelda Lockhart, workshop leaders whose teaching helped me grow as a writer; Alice Osborn for her editing skills and enthusiastic support of my writing; Alan Welch, a wonderful photographer who captured the spirit of *Hungry Mother Creek* in the cover photo; Alan and Leigh Jenkins of Second Star Publishing for their patience and expertise in formatting my manuscript and designing my author webpage; Mepkin Abbey, a monastery along the Cooper River in South Carolina, for providing a sacred sanctuary under the live oaks where I finished *Hungry Mother Creek*, and then returned to work on final edits; Elizabeth Harris, for reading my manuscript and providing the perspective of an Oriental resident; Tracey Lantz, for taking time out of her busy family and work schedule to read the final version of my novel; My goddess group, for teaching me to focus on what I want to achieve and not my fears; Tracy Pollert, a lifelong friend, whose love and belief in me kept me motivated and who was the first to read the entire unedited version of *Hungry Mother Creek;* Melissa Ockert who always believed in me and never doubted I would finish my novel; Julia Brandon for her rich friendship and encouragement to push my limits; My father, the other writer in the family, for his love, support and high expectations; My mother for her unconditional love and exceptional grammatical editing; My sister for always understanding and listening and for being one of my first readers; My husband, Bobby, for his love and unwavering support from my first declaration that I was going to write a book to the moment we held *Hungry Mother Creek*, in our hands. I am a better person because of you. And of course, Maya, my rescued yellow lab and muse who lay curled at my feet while I wrote almost every word of this novel.

Prologue

Friday August 26, 2005, Bay St. Louis, Mississippi

Maya pressed the accelerator a little harder and raced to catch Steven before he left for his guy's weekend. After talking with her co-workers, Maya felt they should be taking this storm more seriously. Several of the women who worked with her in the medical records department were heading out tonight. They were going to stay with friends or family who lived out of the direct path like in Houston, Shreveport and Tallahassee. Her sister Kate in Raleigh was begging her to leave first thing in the morning to come to North Carolina. She had called her three times already today.

Maya lifted her left leg to push in the clutch and shift into fifth gear. She could feel her slip sticking against her legs courtesy of the Gulf Coast humidity so she pulled her skirt and slip up around her knees to cool off. Maya occasionally wore skirts to work because it was cooler than pants, but outside of work she lived in her running shorts and sneakers. She was an avid runner which kept her fit, and looking younger than her 37 years, but the primary purpose of her runs was to provide an escape from Steven's unpredictable moods.

The wind from the open car windows blew Maya's shoulder length brown hair into a crazy swirl. She grabbed it with one hand and twirled it around her fingers as she drove down Drinkwater Boulevard, beautiful historic homes off to her left. Maya remembered the first time she came to Bay St. Louis to see Steven. It was a month after she had met him on vacation in Key West and she'd been thrilled that their long distance telephone relationship had culminated in an invitation for her to visit. Steven had the long weekend perfectly planned with a picnic lunch on the beach by the Gulf, dinner in a historic café, dancing and gambling at a casino in Gulfport. Steven was spontaneous and self confident and when she was with him, Maya felt so alive and in the moment. No one had ever made her feel as special as he did that weekend, and she hadn't wanted that feeling to end. It didn't at the beginning of their marriage, but over the last couple years things had changed as Steven pulled away emotionally and his focus turned towards his friends and partying. Maya kept the hope alive that the Steven she had fallen in love with was still within reach. Occasionally her hope was rewarded with an evening where he once again made her feel special. They would cook dinner at home and talk about their frustrations and dreams. A couple of times they even talked about starting a family with both of them declaring they would be different from their own parents, more loving, more attentive.   Maya wondered if these infrequent times when they connected emotionally and physically should be enough.   She had watched her parents lead mostly separate lives, coming together only occasionally for some event she or Kate had or when it was a mandatory family gathering such as Thanksgiving dinner or Christmas morning.   Growing up, she and Kate had always said they would never have a marriage like that, and Kate had been able to create a much happier marriage, but why hadn't she?

Maya turned down St. George Street toward the yellow bungalow she and Steven had rented since they married six years ago. Her heart pounded in anticipation of either confronting Steven and asking him to stay home for the weekend or finding him already gone, leaving her and Doodle Bug to fend for themselves. Their house came into view and Steven's car was still in the driveway. Maya pulled in beside him, leapt out of her Saturn and raced towards the house.   She pushed the screen door open and almost tripped over Doodle Bug, her two-year-old yellow lab, wagging and waiting for a greeting. Maya scratched her behind the ears and then hurried back to the bedroom.

She hoped he hadn't starting drinking yet and screwed up her courage to confront him. Steven was standing by their bed with his back to her, folding several shirts to take with him. His physical presence always unnerved her. He was tall with broad shoulders that tapered down to a trim waist, although that waist had softened in the last year with more time spent in bars than at the gym. Steven, sensing her presence, turned and as his green eyes locked into hers, she felt her stomach tighten and she took a breath.

"Steven, haven't you watched the news today? You can't go to New Orleans for a guy's weekend now. One of the largest hurricanes we've ever had is heading our way and everyone at work is evacuating."

"My God, Maya, why are you even listening to those women at work? There's no way I'm going to miss out on this trip because of a warning for a hurricane that won't even happen. When I was a kid we wasted money on gas and hotels and would come home to only a few branches down in the yard. I don't have the time or money to waste on this storm. It'll probably blow on out to the ocean. Now, move out of my way!"

Maya was leaning against their dresser and Steven pushed her to the side to grab a wad of underwear out of the drawer and then stuffed it into the gym bag he was using as a suitcase. Maya's eyes filled with tears. She felt anger rising at him for how he treated her, and at herself for letting him. It hadn't always been like this.

"I'm worried this time. What will I do if it gets bad? I can't believe you would leave me and Doodle Bug here while you go off and get drunk with your friends. You just went out with them on Wednesday night, anyway. Can't you postpone this for a few weeks?"

"Come on. You and that mutt will be fine. If you get scared you can always go over to Zoe's house next door for company. Worst case scenario you can go to one of those shelters at the school and besides, I deserve a break. I've worked my ass off this week and need to blow off some steam."

Maya's eyes darted out the bedroom window, over to Zoe's driveway and she didn't see her car. She's probably already at her parent's house 40 miles inland, Maya thought. She also knew she couldn't go to a shelter because dogs weren't allowed and she would never leave Doodle Bug alone in a hurricane.

As Steven zipped his bag, Maya caught sight of a roll of twenty dollar bills. Where in the world did he get that? She kept a running balance of their checking account in her head and knew that was more than they had. She held back, knowing her questions would only fan his anger, but made a mental note to check their credit card balance. Steven swung his bag over his shoulder and grabbed his keys and wallet off the night stand as he headed out the bedroom door.

Maya followed him silently out to the kitchen, torn between her unease of being alone in the hurricane and her relief at being alone without his anger. Steven grabbed a Samuel Adams from the fridge and poured it into a large plastic cup Maya had gotten in her goody bag when she ran the New Orleans marathon last year. Maya sat down at the kitchen table with a sigh.

"Don't even say it. I can drink one beer and drive, no problem. I'm running late and don't want my boys to get ahead of me."

Maya bit her tongue. They'd just finished paying off the lawyer who got him out of his second DUI a few months ago. She knew one beer wouldn't affect him much but she also knew he probably had a cooler behind the seat of his car with a twelve pack in it. He would drink three or four more on the 45-minute drive to New Orleans.

"Maya, I'll be back sometime Sunday night, but don't wait up. I'll definitely be back in time to be at the car lot by ten Monday morning."

"Where are you staying? Did you pack extra insulin? Will you leave your cell phone on in case I need you?"

"You worry too fucking much. I won't get stranded and I can live without my insulin. You know I've gone days without taking it before. Just let it go! You'll be fine too. You won't need me for anything. We haven't decided where we're staying yet but I'll leave my phone on. Of course, it's hard to hear if we're in a bar." Steven leaned down and gave her a soft kiss on the lips. "Have a good weekend. Everything will be fine and on Monday night we'll go get a pizza at The Sycamore House." He always did this, seduced her with soft kisses and promises of things to come. It infuriated her but at the same time she knew it kept her hooked into the relationship.

Steven turned and headed out the back door to the driveway. Maya walked to the front of the house and watched him pull away in his used BMW 325. You won't need me for anything Steven had said. You won't need me for anything. For once he actually spoke the truth. Maya really didn't need him for anything. So why did she stay? Her sister and Zoe had asked her this in the past few months and she had no good answer. She just felt she didn't have the energy it would take to leave him. She was exhausted; drained of energy from trying to make her marriage work, trying to seem happy at work, trying to live with the disappointment in her life.

Not liking her train of thought, Maya plopped down on their couch and turned on the Weather Channel. Doodle Bug jumped up beside her and they watched the latest projected path of Katrina. The hurricane was headed straight for them. She could only hope that Steven was right and Monday night they'd be eating pizza at The Sycamore House, but the sinking feeling in her chest told her otherwise. Her cell phone rang. It was her sister again. Maya let it go to voicemail.

Chapter 1

Saturday April 14, 2007   Oriental, North Carolina

Maya watched Travis' strong, tanned arms flexing as he lifted the kayaks onto the trailer attached to his jeep. A local kayaking guide recommended by the B&B where Maya and her sister Kate were staying, Travis was taking Maya on a half day kayak trip down Beards Creek. His jeep was parked in front of the Neuse Paddle Company, located directly across from the town dock where sailboats, power boats and a couple large trawlers were moored. They'd be driving to a more secluded creek known for its cypress tress with Spanish moss, fish nurseries and osprey nests. Maya was looking forward to some time out in nature, something she hadn't had since living in Raleigh where she'd moved after Katrina, and Steven's death. For the past two years she'd kept herself distracted with her medical records job at Wake Med Hospital during the day and her personal training clients in the evenings and on the weekends. She'd focused on paying off the debt she and Steven had acquired and had little free time. Perhaps that was more of a blessing than a regret.

Maya and Kate were having a girls retreat in Oriental, North Carolina. They had decided a weekend away was in order since Maya had just become debt free for the first time since the early years of her marriage to Steven and Kate only had six weeks until her due date. It would be a while before they would have sister time again. Oriental was a quiet town of about 900 residents located where the Neuse River empties into the Pamlico Sound. It used to be a fishing village, but now it's the homeport for the best East Coast sailing and the sailing capital of North Carolina. Besides the sailors, Oriental was also sustained by a population of retirees from across the United States, but from the accents Maya had heard, it seemed like most were from the North. And then, there were the folks looking for a quiet waterside retreat, like she and Kate.

"Have you ever been kayaking before?" Travis asked, bringing Maya back to the present. She realized the jeep was packed and ready to go.

"No. On the Gulf Coast I was close to lots of paddling options but never tried. I guess I stuck to running by the water or swimming. I usually had my yellow lab, Doodle Bug with me and couldn't fathom her sitting quietly in a kayak." Maya had left her back in Raleigh with Kate's husband, Rob. This was the first time they'd been apart for longer than eight hours since Katrina. She knew Doodle Bug would be fine as she had grown fond of Rob while they were living with him and Kate immediately after Katrina, but Maya still felt a little lost without her sidekick. Travis motioned for her to get in the passenger side of the jeep as he started the engine.

"So you're a dog person?" Travis asked.

"Well, not always, but after getting Doodle Bug about four years ago, I became a card carrying member of the certifiably crazy over their dog club," Maya smiled. "She's more faithful then some people have been in my life." Maya tensed, realizing she divulged more than she had meant to. Luckily, Travis didn't seem to notice and continued with the topic.

"I know how you feel. Elvis, my hound dog mutt, is my best buddy. He's great company and always listens to me. Sometimes I wonder if I'm going crazy cause I talk to him so much."

"No. I think that is totally normal," Maya said with a smile and then sat back against the worn, brown leather seat. Her right arm hung out the window and the warm late April air blew through her hair. She loved this time of year when the air was beginning to warm and the trees were aglow with golden green buds. As they continued their drive down deserted country roads to reach Beards Creek, the smells of spring filled the jeep, the earthy smell of freshly plowed dirt and then the sweet smell of the wisteria that decorated the trees along the road.

Out of the corner of her eye, Maya watched Travis as he maneuvered the jeep and trailer with kayaks down the winding road. His face was tanned from many hours out in the eastern North Carolina sun and had a shadow of a beard which just added to his outdoorsy look. Maya guessed he was close to her age and without thinking, her eyes traveled to his left hand. No ring and no suntan mark, so most likely he wasn't married.

As they reached the final turn down to the boat ramp, Travis moved his feet to depress the brake and clutch and Maya couldn't help but admire his quads as they flexed and strained against the fabric of his shorts. Maya blushed when she realized what she was doing but was relieved that Travis was oblivious as he backed the jeep down towards the water. This was the first time she'd really paid attention to a man in a long time. She had felt numb after Steven died and hadn't thought about men or dating much since then. She also struggled with conflicted feelings about his death and their relationship. Why hadn't she had the strength to leave him on her own? Why did it take a natural disaster to propel her into a new life? Maybe if she had left him, he wouldn't have gone to New Orleans before Katrina and would still be alive today. Maya could feel her thoughts begin to race and didn't want them to ruin her afternoon so began focusing on the present. This was helped when Travis slammed his car door. She was jolted back to the boat ramp, on

Beards Creek in Oriental, North Carolina, miles and miles away from Bay St. Louis and her former life.

Travis jumped out and started untying the kayaks from the trailer. "Grab your water bottle and snack and head over to the ramp. I'll bring everything over."

Maya could tell Travis had done this many times and in just a few minutes they were in the water of Beards Creek, heading north.

Maya's athleticism made her a quick study of the balance and strength needed to kayak. With just a few pointers from Travis, she was moving swiftly through the water, dark from the bark of the cypress trees lining the bank. The knobby knees of the cypress trees stuck out of the water like her grandmother's knees used to when she took her evening bubble bath and Maya would sit on the toilet and talk with her. Maya smiled at the memory and felt gratitude for the summers she and Kate had spent with their grandmother at her home on Kerr Lake in Clarksville, Virginia. They both basked in the love and attention from an adult and were always sad to see summer's end. Maya and Kate had canoed on Kerr Lake those summers but now Maya was enjoying the new sensation of being in a kayak. She felt almost like she was part of the water, with only a thin layer of fiberglass separating her from the tea colored water that occasionally bubbled with schools of small bait fish.

The rhythm of her paddle strokes comforted Maya. She and Travis paddled for about twenty minutes in silence. Even without words, there was plenty to listen to from the entry of her paddle in the water, the call of the kingfisher searching for fish and the gentle rustle of the river grasses that grew on the bank. Maya sighed, leaned back, and let her body be rocked by the undulations of the kayak. Suddenly, tears sprang to her eyes as the power of the moment hit her. This was the first time since Katrina that nature had comforted her rather than be a source of tragedy. She had always found joy in nature, especially on her daily morning runs, the waxing and waning of the moon, the seasonal changes of the morning light or deer feeding at dawn all provided her with inspiration. The death and destruction she witnessed in Katrina had been a sharp contrast to her usual experience of nature.

A tear slid down her cheek and Maya felt her heart crack open just a bit and warmth spread across her chest. She tilted her face up to the sun, forgiving nature for her power to destroy and grateful for all her gifts. But maybe she should also be grateful for the destruction. Wasn't that a part of life's cycle? Hadn't some good come to her life from the devastation of Katrina? Oh, there was the guilt again, working its way to the front of her consciousness but Maya stopped it by focusing on the gentle caress of the breeze on her face. She floated with the current of the creek until a scraping noise startled her when her kayak's bow hit the shoreline.

"You all right?" Travis called.

"Yes. Yes." Maya said as she opened her eyes to see what she had hit. "I got so relaxed that I wasn't paying attention to where I was going."

"Well, sometimes just going with the flow is the best option. Are you planning on visiting Miss Hazel?" Travis asked.

"What do you mean?"

"You just beached yourself on the property of Hazel Underhill."

Maya's eyes lifted from the shoreline and she saw a beautiful nineteenth century farmhouse facing the creek. There were wraparound porches on the first and second floors both decorated with ferns in hanging baskets. The house was white with colonial blue shutters and was surrounded by huge hydrangea bushes that were starting to fill out with new bright green leaves. A worn path in the grass led from the house down to the boathouse and dock. The dock had three boat slips, one empty, one with a small motorboat and one with a 30-foot sailboat, showing its age with peeling paint, green algae and barnacles growing where the boat met the waterline. As Maya looked at the Underhill property she could imagine family picnics in the yard and children fishing off the dock and catching blue crabs with the bones left over from fried chicken.

"Does anyone live there now?"

"Miss Hazel still lives there in the big farmhouse. She's in her late 70s and somehow manages the upkeep inside her house, but sometimes I'll help her with small repairs outside and yard work."

"So she's there all alone, in that big house?"

"Yep. I don't think she'll ever give up this place." Travis' kayak now drifted up the shoreline beside Maya. "Her grandmother was born in this house and Hazel grew up here. I think she lived in Raleigh for a long time but then came back to Oriental after her husband died. I was a teenager, so that must have been about twenty years ago. My grandparents are from here and my grandmother and Miss Hazel were in the same women's circle at church so they knew each other quite well. In the summer when I would stay with my grandparents, Miss Hazel would sometimes take me out in her sailboat. I thought I was something when she would let me take the wheel out in the middle of the sound."

"Does she have any sisters or brothers? I wonder if she ever gets lonely in that big house without any company." Maya couldn't imagine being old without her sister around.

"She's never mentioned a brother or sister but I see her at church and around town so she must have somewhat of a social life.

She's fun to be around. I always try to get her talking when I go to help her. She has some interesting life stories and knows a lot of the history of this area."

Maya used her paddle to push her kayak off the bank and back out into the creek. Travis followed her lead and then stopped. "Well, look at that. Maybe Miss Hazel is getting lonely. She's finally put a 'For Rent' sign up in her boathouse. I helped renovate it into a one bedroom cottage a few years ago but once it was finished she seemed hesitant about someone actually living there."

Maya's eyes rested on the small boathouse. It was painted in the same color scheme as the house and she could see Travis had added a small porch on the back that looked out onto the creek. Maya could imagine herself sitting there reading while Doodle Bug swam in the creek. She wondered if she lived here if she would feel as peaceful as she did now or if that was just a vacation fantasy everyone has, dreaming about moving to the place you're visiting. Any place can seem idyllic when you don't have any responsibilities. The phone number, 779-0831 was written in purple magic marker at the bottom of the For Rent sign. Maya, living out her vacation fantasy, made a mental note of that number.

***

Maya slid out of Travis' jeep at Oriental's town dock. As she shut the door, she could feel soreness in her upper back.

"I noticed a little grimace there. Are your back muscles sore?" Travis asked as he began to untie the kayaks from the trailer.

"Yes. I can't remember when my upper body felt this tired. Usually it's my legs that are sore."

"If you keep this up you'll get used to it. Have you thought about buying a kayak? I know of several places near Raleigh to kayak and you could always come back down here."

"It was great today but probably need to kayak a few more times before I invest in one of my own."

"I have an idea," Travis said. "When are you and your sister leaving?"

"Sunday, after lunch. Why?"

"I think you should try a sunrise paddle to experience kayaking again before you leave. After seeing the sunrise over the Pamlico Sound from a kayak, I know you'll be hooked. I'll check with Pat, my boss, but I'm sure she'll be fine with me leaving the kayak for you around the corner at Town Beach. In the morning, you can walk over, slip into the water and watch the sunrise."

This was very thoughtful but Maya wondered why Travis was so interested in her becoming a kayaker. Well, maybe he gets a cut of the profit if she buys a kayak or maybe he's just being nice, sharing his enthusiasm for something he loves. Maya realized over the last few years she had become more cynical and looked for ulterior motives instead of believing in their inherent kindness.

"Thanks, Travis. I'll take you up on that offer. I'm an early riser anyway and love to see the sunrise over the water. I don't think I've seen that since I left the gulf after Katrina." As the last sentence slipped out, Maya silently cursed herself. She didn't usually share that she was a Katrina survivor. It often brought lots of unwanted sympathy and questions. Maya looked up at Travis, now leaning against his jeep. The wind ruffled his hair and he had a streak of gray mud from the creek across his cheek. He was pretty close to Maya's age, but seeing him now, Maya could imagine him as a seventeen-year-old with lots of energy and mischief. Travis' eyes held hers for a few seconds.

"You've been through a lot. We've had hurricanes here, though nothing on the magnitude of Katrina. I don't think anyone could understand what it's like without experiencing it. I'm just glad you made it out okay."

Maya silently thanked him for not asking any questions.

"I'll leave the kayak on the left side of the Town Beach for you to use tomorrow morning. Pretty much no crime here, so it will be fine overnight. I'll have Pat pick it up tomorrow afternoon as I'll be tied up."

"Travis, thanks so much for such a wonderful afternoon. The creek was beautiful and I just loved the kayaking."

"No problem. Glad you enjoyed it. Make sure to let Pat know. It always helps for the owner to know my customers are satisfied."

For a second Maya had forgotten she had paid for this trip. She and Travis had such a nice rapport that she felt more like friends. Well, she guessed that was part of what he was paid for, to make people feel comfortable. Even if she did have to pay for it, it was fun to hang out with a guy for a change. Since living in Raleigh, Maya had mostly spent time with her sister, her personal training clients and the women she worked with in the medical records department.

"Can I drop you off at The Captain's Quarter's?"

"No. It's not far and I need to stretch my legs a bit before dinner." Maya turned and began heading up Water Street. She could feel Travis' eyes on her back and then heard his jeep starting.

***

It was almost five thirty when Maya pushed open the door to the room she and Kate were sharing at The Captain's Quarters. She paused in the doorway when she saw Kate asleep on the twin bed by the window, a fleece throw keeping off the spring breeze coming in the open window. Kate was lying on her back and Maya smiled at her protruding belly which was in marked contrast to her otherwise thin frame.

Kate was only two years younger than Maya but seemed to have settled into her life more easily than she had. She and Rob had been married for five years, and in six weeks would welcome a new baby into their family. Maya remembered Kate talking about the type of mother she wanted to become as they drove down to Oriental, and like most new mothers, her goal was to be totally different from their own mother.

Kate and Maya's parents loved them and provided for all their physical needs, but there was always some emotional distance. Their father maintained his distance in a physical sense by spending long hours at the bookstore he owned near the grounds of the University of Virginia. At night he drank glasses of Merlot to take the edge off. Usually this led to an impassioned speech on his favorite author of the moment with little time for his daughters to share their day with him.

Their mother was always physically present, taking them to and from school each day. She taught kindergarten so had the same schedule as Kate and Maya. At home, she would retreat to her study to read or go out to her "animal" garden where she had flowers with animal names like snap dragons, tiger lilies and lamb's ear. One whole corner of the backyard was filled with lavender bushes that in

June would be harvested and made into wreaths, lavender wands and sachets to be sold at the farmers' market.

Maya sat in a chair by the door, letting Kate continue to sleep. She remembered when she was about eight, watching her mother out the window in her lavender. She and Kate sat at the kitchen table with their snack of milk and mint Girl Scout cookies that their mother had just prepared before grabbing her gardening gloves and heading outside. Maya studied her mother kneeling by each bush, sprinkling fertilizer around the base and gently sculpting a mound of fresh mulch. At that moment, Maya wished, with all the wishing power of an eight-year-old, to be a lavender bush and to bask in the love and attention her mother seemed to reserve for her garden and her books. The saving grace for Maya and Kate was their relationship.

They shared the small details of their day, a test score, a mean look from a popular girl, their latest crush. They often talked long after they went to bed about their dreams for the future. At least Kate did. She was clear that she wanted to teach and be a mother. Maya had less clarity but many ideas, a writer, a news reporter, a ranger in a state park. They were lucky that unlike other siblings, they had little rivalry. They both were smart and always made straight As. Their interests were different with Kate preferring ballet and piano and Maya soccer and cross country.

They both chose to go to the University of Virginia, not so much to be close to their parents, but to be close to one another. Their first separation came when Kate graduated and moved to Raleigh to work in the Wake County School System teaching third grade, following Rob who had gotten an IT job in Research Triangle Park. Maya, who had taken a job in the medical records department at UVa medical center, remembered the empty feeling the day she watched Kate leave. Her best friend and life long support would now be four hours away. It was only a few months after that when she had met Steven in the Keys.

Thinking of him startled Maya. Since the kayak trip, the thoughts of Steven had retreated. Maybe it was being in a totally new place and spending time on the water. As she continued to watch her pregnant sister sleep, Maya wondered if Steven would have ever come to a town like Oriental, or would it be too quiet for his tastes? Would they have started a family like her sister has? Maya felt her thoughts beginning to pick up speed. Occasionally this happened as she contemplated what life may have held if Steven had lived. Maya took a deep breath like her counselor instructed her, stopped her cascading thoughts and brought herself back to the room with her sleeping sister. She tried to ignore her rising guilt at the sense of relief she felt as she returned to the present moment without Steven as a part of her life.

Kate stirred, moving her hand unconsciously to rest on her belly. Her eyes slowly opened, weighted with the heaviness of a good sleep.

"Did you have a good day?" Maya asked.

"Ahh. It was perfect. I walked around town after we had lunch, read a little and have slept about two and a half hours," she said as she glanced at her watch. "How was your kayaking trip?"

"Fantastic. It was relaxing being on the water in the kayak, very peaceful like that Sunday morning quiet time before you've finished your first cup of coffee."

"So how was your guide? He was a cutie," her sister said playfully.

"He was fine," Maya replied looking at her sister with unblinking eyes. "He showed me the basics of kayaking and told me a little history of the area. He really seemed to want me to like kayaking. He said he'd leave me a kayak at Town Beach down the street so I can take a sunrise paddle tomorrow morning."

"Is he going with you?" Kate asked with a smile.

"No, Miss Smarty Pants. He's busy tomorrow morning. Anyway, I think he wants me to become enamored with kayaking so I'll buy one and he'll get the commission."

"Oh, Maya, always the cynic lately. Maybe he saw how much you enjoyed your time and wanted to give you another opportunity to experience that feeling."

"Well, maybe. Right now, let's talk about where we are going to eat dinner. I'm starved."

***

Maya awoke at 5:45 a.m., just five minutes before the alarm, like she almost always did. For the most part she thought of this trait as a blessing, waking up naturally, and not being blasted from her sleep by the shrill alarm or worse yet one of Madonna's hits from the 80s on the clock radio. She rolled over in the twin bed and moved the curtain to look out the window. It was still dark, but the stars she saw let her know the skies were clear. Maya pulled the comforter up to her chin, her body warm from its own heat captured under the covers. It would be easy to stay right here and drift back to sleep, Maya thought, but the sunrise promised by Travis and the memory of that peaceful feeling of being on the water lured her out of bed.

Maya carefully closed the front door of the B&B making sure the antique and rusting door knob slowly clicked back to its resting place. As she walked east down Church Street, Maya could see a soft pink glow on the horizon. She estimated she had fifteen minutes or so till sunrise, so she picked up her pace to a jog. She passed a mixture of one story bungalows, two story Charleston style homes and a new three story condo unit that seemed out of place next to the homes built when Oriental was a fishing village.

Town Beach was only a half mile from The Captain's Quarters and after a couple minutes, Maya was there. Calling this area a beach seemed to be a stretch. The sandy area was about the size of her mother's lavender patch, but it was sandy and did meet up with a large body of water, so technically met the definition for a beach.

The kayak was easy to spot, pulled over to the left side of the beach like Travis had promised. The sky was slowly turning from pink to a pale yellow. Maya pulled the kayak down to the water's edge, threw on the PFD Travis had left in the cockpit and pushed herself out into the Neuse River.

This was a totally different experience compared to yesterday's creek. Travis had told her that at this point the Neuse River was five miles wide. It created a much more expansive feel than the narrower creek she'd been on yesterday. A slight breeze lifted Maya's hair and she zipped up her windbreaker against the cool morning air. She turned her kayak straight out towards the ever brightening eastern horizon and paddled steadily.

The top crescent of the sun burst into sight and with surprising speed it grew and presented its full orb to Maya. Like yesterday, she floated without paddling, the first rays of the sun warming her face. The kayak gently rocked with the pulse of the water and she felt suspended in time, so fully present in this moment that no intrusive thoughts of the past or worries of the future entered her mind. Once again her heart was filled with gratitude for the ability to feel this sense of contentment in nature again and about life in general.

As the sun climbed higher, Maya's stomach began to growl, ready for the gourmet breakfast of quiche, fruit and blueberry muffins she soon would have at The Captain's Quarters. What a perfect way to start the day. Travis had been right, Maya thought as she began paddling back to shore. Without realizing it, Maya found herself reciting the phone number that had been written on the For Rent sign at the boathouse she had seen yesterday.

Chapter 2

Saturday August 18, 2007

Maya set the stained glass sailboat she'd bought yesterday at the farmers' market on the small end table. She sat back on the couch and looked out the double windows to Beards Creek, the late afternoon sun still full of intensity. The windows were closed against the heavy heat and humidity of late August. The window air conditioning unit hummed almost constantly to keep the small boathouse at 78 degrees. Now what? Maya thought.

Maya had been in Oriental exactly a week now. It felt surreal that she was sitting inside Hazel Underhill's boathouse looking out onto Beards Creek when just three months ago she'd been outside in a kayak looking in. After that weekend with her sister, Maya's thoughts often returned to the feeling of peace she had experienced in Oriental. Her mind continued to repeat the phone number on the For Rent sign on Hazel's boathouse and finally one day she just called. After that call and a trip to Oriental to meet Hazel, Maya began making plans for the move. She'd had some trepidation before moving because she had no concrete reason why she should move, just a knowing in her body that this was the path to follow. She'd had these feelings of knowing before but mostly hadn't listened to them and did what she thought was expected of her or what she thought would make others happy. So far that way hadn't brought much joy to her life so she was ready to follow a more internal compass.

Maya had unpacked, organized and decorated. She'd already discovered that she would be driving at least monthly to New Bern to buy staples and non-perishable items since the small local grocery store was quite expensive. She had found a yoga studio, a vet for Doodle Bug, stopped by the fitness center for a tour and already created four, six and ten mile running routes from her boathouse. Maya also had purchased a used kayak from the rental fleet at the Neuse Paddle Company. Travis had met her there and helped her select an easy to handle, touring style kayak. It was bright blue and only weighed 40 pounds so she would be able to lift it up onto the new roof rack of her Saturn.

Maya leaned forward to pick up the weekly local newspaper, her red cotton tank top sticking to her back in spite of the air conditioner's best efforts. Doodle Bug, sleeping directly in line with the airflow from the air conditioner, raised one eyebrow, looked at Maya and then fell asleep again. She had sold some of her furniture before moving because the boathouse was smaller than her apartment in Raleigh. That money combined with the small savings she had managed to accrue gave her the luxury of not rushing to find a job. Hazel had hesitated in offering her the $325 monthly rent, like that may have been too much! Maya perused the classified ads and was grateful for her diminished living expenses because she didn't see many jobs that would support the cost of living up in Raleigh, but they would most likely be sufficient for her simpler life here in Oriental.

Finding a job was the next step Maya knew she should take but, feeling no urgency, she folded the paper and lay it down again, not ready to jump into something. She had given herself another week to get to know the village, meet a few people and reflect on what type of job would make her happy. She worried that if she didn't take this time, she'd end up right back in her comfort zone commuting to New Bern for a medical records job at Craven Community Hospital.

Swinging her legs up onto the coach, and leaning back against a pillow, Maya looked towards her cell phone on the coffee table and thought about calling her sister. She remembered that Kate and her perfectly beautiful new nephew, Worth, were most likely napping. She picked up her latest self-help book, *The Power of Intention*, flipped it open to her bookmark and then closed it again. She had no inspiration for much of anything and laid her head back against the pillow. The synergy of heat induced lethargy and the lack of urgency to be anywhere put Maya right to sleep, her breath almost synchronized to Doodle Bug's.

Maya's eyes flew open and she quickly looked around. The room was filled with long shadows as the sun lowered and a quick glance at her cell phone told Maya it was 6:05 p.m. She wondered what had awoken her so suddenly. She stood to look out the window by the front door when she heard a light knock at her door. Who in the world was coming to visit? She had just casually met a few people while at the Farmers' market yesterday. Surely one of them wasn't at the door.

When she made it to the window by the door, she could see Hazel standing patiently with what looked like a casserole dish in her hands. Maya had the advantage of being shielded by the chintz curtain so she took a moment to study Hazel. Hazel had told her that she was 79 but she looked closer to her mid 60s. Her worn khakis were rolled several times forming a thick cuff around her ankles. Maya smiled and imagined Hazel did that rather than going to the time and effort of hemming them. On her top half she wore a pink, long sleeved oxford shirt un-tucked and rolled up to her forearms. She looked cool despite the heat and Maya imagined she must smell of talcum powder. On someone else, this outfit may have looked disheveled, but Hazel pulled it off and managed to look almost regal with her pearl necklace and earrings. With the third knock, Doodle Bug began barking and ran to the door.

"Hi, Maya, I hope I'm not disturbing you, but I wouldn't be a true southern girl if I didn't bring you a casserole to welcome you to Pamlico County." Hazel smiled, making it obvious she didn't take herself too seriously. "I hope you like tuna casserole," she said, handing the glass casserole dish over to Maya.

"How thoughtful. Thank you so much. It'll be perfect for dinner since I was trying to figure out what I was going to eat tonight. Would you like to come in and see how I've decorated?" Maya asked as she stepped back from the door, allowing Hazel to walk in.

Hazel walked into the small living room, stopping to pet Doodle Bug who was again lying directly in front of the flow of the air conditioner. "Hazel, I'll be right back. I'm just going to put this in the fridge."

Maya walked to the small kitchen area just behind the living room. She smiled to herself as she placed the casserole on the bottom shelf and wondered what type of condensed soup Hazel used to make this. She guessed it must be Cream of Mushroom, a southern staple she had used many times while helping her grandmother make Thanksgiving and Christmas meals.

As she turned back towards the living room, Maya's heart lurched when she saw Hazel was holding the decorative urn she thought had been discretely placed, but it must have caught Hazel's eye. "Maya, this urn is beautiful. I love the yellows, blues and greens in the pattern. Surely you didn't find it here in Oriental? It's so well-made."

Maya's pulse quickened and she felt the color drain from her face. She stood frozen not prepared for this discussion and unsure of how much of the truth she wanted to share.

"Maya, are you okay? You look like you might faint." Hazel placed the urn on the coffee table and hurried to Maya's side. She placed her hand in the small of Maya's back and led her over to the couch. Hazel's hand was small, but very strong and her touch comforted Maya as she lowered herself down to the couch. She had a flash of insight that said she could trust Hazel and as she regained her composure, Maya decided to be truthful.

"Sorry if I scared you, Hazel. It's just that this urn is much more than a decoration. It contains the ashes of Steven, my husband who died two years ago because of Hurricane Katrina."

Well, it was a lot easier than Maya thought it would be, sharing this truth, although not the whole truth, with the first person outside her family. It actually wasn't that hard talking about the ashes. The hard part would be answering the questions that may follow.

"Steven has a brother who wasn't able to come to Mississippi after his death," her words tumbled out, "and everything was in such a state of destruction and confusion I didn't feel right about spreading the ashes in Mississippi. I've just kept them with me since then."

As Maya was speaking, Hazel sat down beside her on the couch, her hands folded neatly in her lap as she listened. Maya and Hazel's eyes met and Maya could see Hazel's eyes were moist with emotion. She reached over and took one of Maya's hands into hers.

"Oh, honey," Hazel started, her southern accent drawing the syllables out. "I am so sorry. Losing your husband is one of the most difficult things to endure. My husband died when I was just 50 and it took me a while to make sense of my life, not having him in it. At least we'd already had 25 years of marriage and a son. You and Steven still had so much left to do together." Hazel's eyes filled again as she squeezed Maya's hands.

Maya turned her head to look out the creek window. She was embarrassed by her lack of emotion and didn't want Hazel to see her dry eyes. What was wrong with her? Why couldn't she even muster up a couple of tears for Steven? When he was alive he made her cry easily. Now a lump did form in Maya's throat.

She felt his grip tightening on her upper arm as he dragged her out into the parking lot of Sherlock's, the pub a couple of miles from their house. When they were away from the entrance, he said, "Don't you tell me I've had enough to drink ever again! Do you hear me? You embarrassed me in front of my friends." He shot the words at her through clenched teeth and she physically recoiled, shrinking as his grip on her arm tightened. He yanked her arm for emphasis and continued, "I can't help it if your lame ass is wasted after three or four beers but I'm fucking fine so leave me alone. If you can't hang anymore then maybe you should just go home."

He released her arm, turned and strode into the pub without looking back. Maya instinctively began rubbing her arm. The emotion she had been holding in her chest erupted and tears rolled down her cheeks. She knew she couldn't go back inside and since Steven had the car keys, so began the walk home, her body weighted by shame.

Hazel squeezed her hand and Maya turned back to look at her, the urn prominent in her peripheral vision. "Well, at least you found his body and knew for sure what happened to him. I've heard of so many people who are still searching for their loved ones who most likely got washed out to sea."

Maya's face flushed knowing she wasn't being fully truthful, but she wasn't ready yet to talk about the real cause of Steven's death.

After a few seconds of silence, she said, "Thanks for understanding. You're the first person I've told outside my family."

"Well, Maya, please know you can talk with me any time about Steven, and for extreme circumstances I can always make you another casserole." Maya smiled, appreciating Hazel's humor and the change of topic.

"I know I've already said this, but I'm so happy you decided to rent my boathouse. I grew up here with my mother and grandmother but have been alone for the past fifteen years so it feels good to have another woman on the property."

"It feels good to be here. When I visited in April something just told me this was the place to come. I'm looking forward to meeting more people, getting a job and creating some happy memories here." Maya smiled, feeling very comfortable sitting next to Hazel. Maybe one day she would tell Hazel the whole story.

"I better get on my way so you can heat up that casserole for dinner. Good luck with your job search and I'll let you know if I hear of anything." Hazel stood and walked to the door, Doodle Bug following at her heels.

Hazel's hand rested on the doorknob just a millisecond longer than necessary. Maya waited for her to turn back and say something else. Hazel never turned but opened the door and stepped out into the humid early evening. The sound of cicadas filled the air.

"Thanks again for the casserole. I'm looking forward to having it tonight," Maya ventured, buying time for Hazel.

Hazel turned, "It was my pleasure, dear. I always enjoy cooking when it's for someone else. Have a good night." Hazel took a few steps and then stopped, turning back towards Maya who was still standing in the doorway. "Maya, you remember Travis, the kayak guide who works for the Paddle Company?" Maya nodded yes, wondering where this was going and how Hazel knew she had gone kayaking with Travis.

"Well he's very handy and helps me keep this place up. In fact, he renovated this boathouse into a cottage. I've asked him to stop by this evening to check in with you and make sure everything is ship shape so to speak. Feel free to let him know if anything needs repair or adjustment to make things more comfortable for you."

"That's very thoughtful, but you didn't have to do that. Everything is just perfect."

"You can let him know that. I imagine he's already on his way. Maybe you can share some of the casserole with him." Hazel turned and continued walking up the worn path to her house, but not before Maya caught a sly smile on her face.

Maya took a deep breath as she felt her pulse quicken. She couldn't believe Hazel was trying to set her up with someone after only being here a week. She wasn't ready to date and have to deal

with a relationship. This was just too soon. Maya's thoughts were
beginning to spin. She became aware of this as she walked back to
the couch and sat down. She continued to take deep breaths and
focused on petting Doodle Bug. Maybe she was blowing this out of
proportion. She imagined that Travis was just doing this as a favor to
Hazel. Maya looked out the creek windows, using the water to calm
her thoughts and couldn't help but remember Travis' strong arms
lifting the kayaks off the trailer back in April and the patience he had
shown just a few days ago helping her pick out her kayak. Before her
mind could wander any further, there was a knock on her door and
her heart flipped, which was unusual given how heavy it had felt over
the last couple of years.

Doodle Bug jumped up and beat Maya to the door, ready to
greet the second guest of the evening. Her tail was wagging as
quickly as Maya's heart was beating. Maya watched Doodle Bug's
enthusiasm for what lay behind the door and wished she could have a
similar attitude, always ready for something new and always expecting
the best outcome.

Maya took a quick peek out the window by the door. Travis,
in sharp contrast to Hazel, took up almost all the space on the small
front stoop. He fit the image of a kayak guide, tanned, in khaki
shorts, a Columbia shirt and Teva sandals. He shifted his weight
from foot to foot as he waited for Maya to open the door. She barely

opened the door and Doodle Bug barreled out to greet Travis, who squatted down and gave Doodle Bug a good rub on the belly in exchange for a slobbery kiss.

"Hey, Maya," he said as he stood from his canine greeting. "Hazel asked me to stop by and make sure everything is okay for you in the boathouse. I'm not the best electrician so hope all the switches and plugs are working."

"Everything seems perfect. I haven't found any defects yet. Why don't you come in and see your finished product," Maya said as she stepped away from the door. She figured that it was the least she could do in return for all his help. After all, if it wasn't for the kayak trip with Travis, she may never have ended up in Oriental.

As Travis walked into the living room, Maya's eyes saw the urn sitting right in the middle of the coffee table where Hazel had left it. She silently hoped he would focus more on the structure of the boathouse than the interior decorating.

"Everything looks great, Maya. It really has a homey feel." Travis walked right past the coffee table and headed to the creek side windows. Maya exhaled. "Did you notice these windows are hurricane impact resistant? We rarely get hurricane force winds here, but when we do these windows will hold up fine."

As Travis finished the sentence and his words registered, a flush crept up his neck. "Oh. Sorry. I didn't mean to bring up the topic of hurricanes. After what you've been through...."

"That's all right, Travis." Maya said, " It's been two years and even though I'll never fully get over the destruction I saw in Katrina, I do have to think about the possibility of being in severe weather since I'm living by the coast again. I feel safe here on Beards Creek though, compared to living just a few miles away from the Gulf of Mexico like I did in Bay St. Louis."

Maya's stomach growled loudly and she moved her hand to muffle it. She suddenly became self conscious as it registered that she hadn't showered since she worked up a sweat organizing things in the living room, her hair was pulled carelessly back in a ponytail and her tank top and gym shorts left vast expanses of bare limbs exposed. Well, it was too late now to change.

"Was that your stomach, Maya?" Travis asked smiling. "I haven't eaten either. Want to run over to Toucan's for dinner?"

Maya, halfway prepared for this after Hazel's prompting, said, "Hazel just brought over a tuna casserole. Why don't I heat that up and throw together a quick salad and you can be my first official dinner guest?"

"Sounds perfect," Travis said as he followed her towards the kitchen.

Maya opened the fridge and pulled out two Coronas. "Would you like a beer?"

"Sure. I believe that will make a fine pairing with tuna casserole," Travis said with a grin as he took the cold beer from Maya. Travis sat down at her small café table and relaxed back into the chair as Maya put the casserole in the oven.

Maya, her back to Travis, focused on slicing the tomatoes for the salad and realized that her heart had returned to its normal rhythm and she actually felt relaxed. She couldn't remember the last time she had felt this at ease with another man, the last year with Steven she'd been walking on egg shells. Every decision she made was weighted against how he might react to it.

"Maya, let me know if I can help. Being a bachelor the past few years, I've become quite competent in the kitchen."

"Thanks. I'm good right now. So, what brought you to Oriental?" Maya asked, consciously steering the conversation away from her.

"Well, there is a long and short version to that story. The short version is that my marriage ended and I needed a change. My grandparents were from here and I always loved visiting Oriental in the summers so it felt like the right place. In fact, my grandmother grew up with Hazel."

"Sounds like you've come full circle, back to your family's roots. Where does the rest of your family live?"

"My parents have retired to Asheville and I have a younger brother in Texas and an older sister in Charlotte. My grandfather died when I was in high school and my grandmother died five years ago. They both are buried in the cemetery of the First Baptist Church here. I'm living in their small cottage downtown now."

Maya placed the salads on the table and handed Travis the napkins and silverware so he could set the table. The smell of canned tuna and cream of mushroom soup wafted through the air.

"You mentioned your grandmother, and smelling this casserole reminds me of mine. When I was little, tuna casserole was one of her staples. Almost every other dinner at her house would be tuna casserole, green beans and homemade biscuits. Wow, haven't thought of that meal for a while."

Travis raised his bottle to toast and as Maya clinked his Corona he said, "To our grandmothers."

"To our grandmothers!"

Conversation flowed easily during dinner. Several times while eating Maya felt like she was having an out of body experience. Here she was in Oriental, North Carolina having dinner with a kayak guide in her renovated boathouse home. It felt like worlds away from her one bedroom apartment in Raleigh surrounded by parking lots, highways and debt. As she looked down on the scene, she felt a lightness that had been absent from her life for many years and a feeling of anticipation of what might come. Maybe she was becoming like Doodle Bug.

Travis glanced at his watch and said, "Well, I better get going. Thanks so much for sharing your tuna casserole. It hit the spot." Travis stood and took his dishes to the sink. "Can I help clean up?"

"Oh, no. Just a couple of dishes. It won't take me but a minute."

"Hey, thanks again," Travis said as he walked into the living room towards the front door. Maya held her breath again as she watched from the kitchen. He passed the coffee table and this time Travis spied the urn Hazel had left there. He stopped and picked it up and Maya felt the tuna casserole inching up her throat.

"This is a beautiful vase. I love the colors. Did you get this when you were living on the Gulf Coast?"

Maya, better prepared after her encounter earlier with Hazel, did not visibly show her unease. "I did in fact get that just after the hurricane, before I left." Well, there was no subtle way to say the rest. Maya walked over and sat on the couch.

"Travis, this is not a vase. It's an urn that contains the ashes of my late husband. He died because of Hurricane Katrina."

Travis paled with this revelation. He hurriedly replaced the urn on the coffee table and came over to sit by Maya. Maya watched him and he appeared more distraught than she was. This was starting to become a pattern.

"Sorry, Travis. I didn't mean to catch you so off guard with all this information."

Travis continued to appear flustered as his eyes darted between Maya and the urn.

"Maya, it's just that, well, I'm so sorry about your husband. What a huge loss for you. Quite frankly I'm feeling very uncomfortable sitting here next to the ashes of his body. It just doesn't feel right. Why didn't you bury him properly and have a funeral?"

Now Maya was reeling. This seemed like a different Travis. She suddenly felt like he was judging her and why was he so concerned about a funeral anyway? "Travis, there are several reasons why I didn't have a funeral, but I don't want to go into them all now. It was just such a disaster down there and I was in a state of shock. I did the best I could." For the first time that evening, Maya's eyes welled with tears and she felt her chest tighten as she remembered the call about Steven from the Red Cross. They said he had survived the hurricane, but was found in a diabetic coma under a bridge outside of New Orleans. He was dead before rescuers could get him to a hospital. She identified the body several days later and then was all alone trying to make the right decision about what to do.

"I'm so sorry. You certainly don't owe me any explanations. I just hope your husband's soul is at peace." Travis glanced at his watch again and said, "I really do have to leave. Thanks again for dinner. Maybe we can get together in a couple days."

Maya stayed seated on the couch as Travis let himself out. Doodle Bug jumped up beside her and put her head in Maya's lap sensing her need to be comforted.

I hope his soul is at peace. Where did that come from, Maya thought? Why was Travis all of a sudden concerned about funerals and souls? It didn't seem congruent with the jovial man who only ten minutes ago was drinking a Corona and sharing his favorite kayaking spots. She'd had such a nice evening with Travis and then Steven's ashes changed the whole atmosphere. She felt her anger towards Steven rising. He was negatively impacting her life even after his death. She spent a few minutes mentally blaming Steven for ruining the evening but then realized the responsibility lay with her. After all, if she'd been able to make peace with her marriage to Steven, she probably would have scattered the ashes by now so there would have been no urn to start the conversation. She was clinging to those ashes just as she had clung to the marriage. Why was this bond so strong when their relationship hadn't been? Maya's stomach tightened and then she knew the answer. Having emotional distance was normal to her. Even thought it caused her pain, it was what she had been used to growing up and somehow she'd never accepted the fact she deserved better. Staying connected to the ashes now continued to keep her from being available for a healthier, more intimate relationship. Maya wondered how she was supposed to fix this. How to you feel worthy of unconditional love. She leaned back on the couch and stared out the windows to the creek, watching the fireflies ignite themselves against the darkening sky. The small window air conditioner maintained its low hum.

***

Maya awoke slowly, enjoying that fuzzy feeling of only being half awake, only aware that she was in the bed with a new day ahead but her brain not fully engaged so there was no internal chatter. Just peace. As Maya began to wake up, she thought that this quiet mind was what she had read about in several of her self-help books. Since Katrina, and Steven's death, Maya had put herself on a self improvement quest and always had a book on hand to assist with this endeavor. Well, at least now she had an understanding of what she was shooting for, not that it helped. It only made the goal feel more unattainable. To feel this level of peace when her mind was fully aware would be next to impossible. She was always thinking about Katrina, Steven, how she was moving along the path of her mourning, how she would adapt to Oriental, how she missed her sister and now, after last night, she was running over her interaction with Travis, re-playing their conversation about the ashes, wondering what she could have said to have made it less uncomfortable. Well, she'd only been awake for five minutes now and already her mind was on the racetrack.

Maya leaned up to look at the clock, 7:30 a.m. She was really sleeping well. This was late for her. It was Sunday and her day off from running. She looked out her bedroom window facing the creek. She had kept the curtain opened so now she could see the sun cresting above the pine forest on the other side of the creek. Maya turned to her side and watched the shadows move as the sun inched higher.

Honk! Honk! Maya heard the blue heron and then saw it fly low across to the other side of the creek, disturbed from its morning fishing spot near Hazel's dock. Then she heard a splash soon followed by, "Hot damn!" Who was out there shouting on a Sunday morning? Surely you couldn't do that till after noon, like buying alcohol, Maya thought with a smile.

She slid over to the window and looked towards the dock, just 100 feet or so from her boathouse. There, was a short, gray haired and gray bearded man in an old Carolina Skiff, throwing out a net. She guessed it must be for shrimp based on the talk she heard at the farmers' market yesterday. From his exclamations, Maya could

only imagine he was having success. She watched him throw the net

which floated through the air in a perfect circle, then landed in the

shallows near some river grass. The man quickly pulled the net in,

which was now more in the shape of a bubble. As he released his

catch into a waiting bucket, Maya could see large, white shrimp

hopping around like kernels of corn that had just popped. The man

looked up towards her window and she stepped back, remembering

she was naked. Cussing and nudity on a Sunday morning, maybe the

day was off to a good start. Since being in the boathouse, Maya had

stripped her sweaty clothes off each night and lay on top of the sheets

naked to fully appreciate the breeze from the ceiling fan. She had

never slept in the nude before, even with Steven, but it felt like the

thing to do right now.

Maya glanced back out the window and to her horror, the

bearded man in the boat waved hello and then motioned for her to

come outside.

My God. He must have seen me, Maya thought. Well, he

was far enough away that he wouldn't have been able to make out

details. Hopefully he just thought she had on a beige shirt.

Maya was intrigued by this man who looked like the

Gordon's Fisherman minus the yellow rain suit. She threw on her

clothes from yesterday that were left on the floor by the bed and headed to the front door, grabbing a baseball cap on the way out to complete her Sunday morning ensemble.

She walked across the wet grass and pushed through the wall of humidity towards Hazel's dock. The coolness of the grass felt good on her bare feet. Doodle Bug ran straight into the water, danced a couple of happy circles and then stood in six inches of water, tail wagging with her eyes glued to Maya.

"No fetching now, girl. Come on with me."

Splash. The Gordon's Fisherman threw his net and Doodle Bug was off in an instant looking for the source of the sound out in the water.

"Doodle Bug, come! Stay away from the net."

"Hey there," the man called, "don't worry about the dog. I'm done with this spot anyway. Caught enough shrimp for today. I'm Buster. You must be Maya."

"Yes. I am. How did you know who I was?" Maya was now at the end of the dock even with the fisherman's boat.

"Oh, I'm friends with Miss Hazel and I saw her in the grocery yesterday buying the ingredients for a tuna casserole. Said she had a pretty young lady who was renting her boathouse, so I knew that was you."

"Wow. Not many secrets in this town."

"There are a few, but with only 900 residents, most of who are retired, not much goes unnoticed."

"So, Buster, are you from here? You look like a natural with that net."

Now that Maya was close, she could see the sun weathered face and hazel eyes whose corners pleated like a school girl's Irish kilt when he smiled. She guessed he must be in his late 60s.

"Yeah. Born and raised here in Oriental. My granddaddy taught me how to throw a shrimp net before I could even read."

Despite their age difference, Maya felt immediately comfortable with Buster, like she knew him already. Later she would realize that it was his complete comfort with himself that put her at ease.

Maya watched as Buster reached into his back pocket, removed his billfold and plucked out a dollar bill, waving it in the air and saying, "Wasn't sure if you required a tip for your window peek." He smiled and leaned back to laugh. "You should see your face, Maya, red as those geraniums on your back porch. Don't mind me, I just love to tease. I didn't see anything I haven't seen before, but I would close your curtain before a fleet of boats show up each morning filled with Viagra enhanced retirees." With this Buster began laughing again, leaning over to hold his stomach and then sitting on the small seat in his skiff. He wiped the corner of his eyes, damp with happy tears.

Maya stood frozen watching his delight in teasing her, not sure if she should be offended. She had been conditioned by Steven to always be on guard for an attack. Luckily Maya inserted a millisecond between Buster's words and her instinctual reaction of fear and defensiveness and reminded herself this was not Steven. She took a breath to regain her equilibrium and to her surprise her exhale came as a combination laugh and snort, which then sent her into a fit of laughter. The more she laughed, the funnier the situation became to her. The laughter built upon itself, growing in intensity much like her guilt did at times, but this was so incredibly fun.

Finally, weak from her bout of hilarity, she sat down at the edge of the dock, her pink toenails just able to dip into the water. Kicking her feet, she sent a fan of water towards the skiff.

"Well, Buster, I am looking for a job around here. At least I know I have a back-up option in case I don't find any respectable employment."

They sat in silence for a moment listening to the lap of water on the boat and the rustle of the river grass. Doodle Bug lay down beside Maya, plopping her head on Maya's thigh. She absently stroked Doodle Bug's damp head. She looked back to Buster who was taking a deep drag of his freshly lit cigarette. Their eyes met and she smiled, knowing she had made a friend here in Oriental.

Chapter 3

Tuesday August 21, 2007

Maya's paddle dipped into the tea colored water. She could have driven over to meet Travis at the Bean, but it was quicker to kayak and way more beautiful. It was a gorgeous morning. The night before, a cold front had come through bringing with it some less humid air and a manageable 70 degrees. Maya almost put on a light jacket, but decided against it so she could fully absorb the cooler temperatures. Travis had called early Sunday evening to invite her to coffee and offered to show her some of his favorite creeks in Pamlico County. She was curious to see how things would be with him after the awkward ending on Saturday night.

Maya could feel her arms were getting stronger from all her recent paddling. Over the past few weeks, she had spent lots of time in the bright, blue touring kayak she had bought over at the Paddle Company. She now slid effortlessly through the water, passing a trailer park community located close to where Beards Creek entered the Neuse River. This neighborhood looked like it had been there for at least twenty years and the trailers with waterfront property now clung to the creek bank edge, time and erosion having swallowed their backyard. Rudimentary decks made of mismatched boards sagged and a loose screen door opened and closed gently in the morning breeze.

The trailers brought Zoe and Bay St. Louis to mind and Maya wondered how she was doing. It had been a few months since she had spoken with her and she was still in a FEMA trailer then. Almost two years in a trailer, unbelievable. Luckily Zoe's new home should be ready at the first of the year. Of course thinking of Zoe opened Pandora's Box in her mind and Maya couldn't help but think of her own bungalow that was next to Zoe's. She wondered if her landlord had rebuilt it. Without warning, Maya began to relive the night of Katrina, water seeping under the front door, the wind so loud it sounded like a 747 landing in her yard. Her heart began to race faster than her kayaking required.

"STOP!" Maya yelled out loud. Over the past two years, with conscious effort, she'd been able to stop the Katina flashbacks which helped reduce the chance of a full blown anxiety attack.

Maya was reading *The Power of Now* as her latest self-book, so the last few weeks had been trying to follow the path of mindfulness to help her anxiety. She brought her attention back to the present and noticed the sun had risen above the bridge spanning the creek.

She looked at her watch and saw 8:50 so she only had ten minutes to be on time to meet Travis.

She increased the cadence of her strokes passing under the bridge and veering towards town. On her left was Oriental Marina which had over 100 boat slips filled with large sail boats, none appeared to be less than 30 feet. Maya heard the halyards clanking against the masts in the wind. As she aimed her kayak towards the dingy dock, someone called out, "Good morning, young lady." Maya saw a couple in their mid 60s, silver haired and tan, enjoying coffee on the deck of a sailboat moored in the harbor. Maya waved but kept focused on getting to shore.

Her kayak skidded to a stop on the soft sand just beside the dingy dock. There were only a couple of minutes to make it by nine, so she jogged down the empty side street over to The Bean. She had no need to worry about traffic on the weekdays in Oriental as most people walked, bicycled or boated where they needed to go. At nine on a Tuesday, The Bean was really the only place to go anyway. The front porch was already full with four men in their 60s and 70s talking about the latest in politics and rating how well the boats moored at the town dock, directly across from The Bean. Maya pulled the door open, looking for Travis as she walked into the cramped coffee shop.

"Hi, Maya. You want the regular?" Carl, the owner of the

shop asked.

"Sounds great." Maya was amazed at the friendliness of a

small town. She had gone into the same coffee shop for two years up

in Raleigh, and they never remembered her. Today was only her

fourth time in The Bean and already they knew her name and how

she liked her coffee. It only took a minute for Carl to prepare her

medium half caff black coffee.

Travis hadn't arrived yet and for some reason Maya didn't

feel like sitting down. She slid past a table of ladies who she assumed

to be the wives of the men on the porch, in an animated discussion

about grandchildren. She stopped at the shelves which had large glass

jars filled with different types of coffee beans. She lifted several of the

lids inhaling the aroma of breakfast blend, fog lifter, and hazelnut.

She heard the door open and turned to see Travis entering. Her

heart jumped and the glass lid for the hazelnut beans slipped from her

hand and clattered back in its spot. She was just meeting Travis for

coffee to learn some new creeks to paddle on. No reason to feel

flustered, she told herself.

It only took Travis two strides to get from the door to the

counter where Carl had his large coffee ready. He turned and caught

Maya's eye.

"Maya, grab us that table by the window." When Travis spoke, the four ladies momentarily stopped their conversation to look admiringly at him in his jeans and snug black t-shirt. Maya and Travis reached the table at the same time and he threw a map down in the middle of it.

The walk to the table helped Maya regain her composure and she pulled the small wooden chair away from the table and sat down. She thanked him right away for meeting her here.

"No problem. It's the least I can do after you shared your tuna casserole with me. And, by the way, I'm sorry for rushing out like that. It just caught me off guard that you would have an urn of ashes in your home. Growing up Southern Baptist, I'm used to a coffin being six feet under within a few days of a death, so that was a new experience for me."

Maya opened her mouth to respond but Travis kept his head down, stirring sugar into his coffee, and continued talking, "Anyway, you'll enjoy these smaller back creeks in the fall and winter cause there's hardly any wind and it's warmer than being out on the bigger water."

Travis began unfolding the Pamlico County map and as Maya reached over to help spread the map out on the table, her right hand and Travis' left hand intersected. The millisecond of contact sent a tingle up Maya's arm. Travis, focused on the map, didn't seem to notice and began describing the put-in point for a paddle trip up Crescent Creek.

***

Maya and Travis pulled their kayaks up onto the edge of the creek and sat on the sand and dirt creek bank. She was thankful for the shade of the cypress tree, protecting them from the 90 degree heat. Good thing they'd begun their paddle at 7:30 a.m.; it was only 9:20 and already felt steamy.

After their talk at The Bean yesterday, Travis had invited Maya to explore Crescent Creek. She had an interview at a chiropractor's office on Thursday but was still free today to go. As they made these plans, she had wondered how Travis made enough money to live on because he rarely mentioned his work as a kayak guide or handyman and always seemed available. Well, he probably wondered the same thing about her. It seemed a lot of people in Oriental were able to get by with seemingly little effort in the work department. This morning they had met at The Paddle Company and put both kayaks on Travis' jeep before driving twenty minutes to the put-in point. So far the paddle had been pretty with scenery similar to Beards Creek.

Maya unzipped a small insulated bag she had filled with water and some trail mix. She could be counted on to never leave home without a snack. She took a water bottle for herself and handed another to Travis.

"Thanks, Maya. I always seem to be well fed when I'm around you," he said, reaching into the Ziploc bag with the trail mix.

"No problem. There wasn't much food after Katrina, so now I overcompensate."

Maya surprised herself with how openly she talked with Travis. She hadn't really gone into such detail with anyone but her sister about her ordeal in Katrina. Except for his reaction about Steven's ashes, he was a calm and non-judgmental presence. He was a great listener and didn't press her with questions she wasn't ready to answer. Maya was also aware of his strong physical presence. They were sitting only a foot apart with the trail mix between them, but she was aware of where his skin ended and hers began. It felt like an electrical charge down the left side of her body, just like when their hands touched in The Bean yesterday. Maya tried to ignore this feeling and focused on watching the pelicans diving for fish out in the creek. She could feel Travis glancing at her out of the corner of his eyes.

Suddenly she was transported back to the Lamplight Cinema when she was fourteen. She was out with a group of friends, but Henry Montgomery had made sure he was sitting next to her. During the first 30 minutes of the movie, she could feel him working

up his nerve to put his arm around her. When he finally did, he was
so nervous that he yanked off her earring as he was making his move.
They ended up bumping heads as they both reached to the floor to
pick it up. She had the same feeling now, but imagined Travis would
have better moves then a fourteen year old. Wait a minute! Did she
actually want him to kiss her? Her body gave her a definite yes as she
tingled all over.

She turned to look at Travis to get a read on what was going
through his mind. He used this opportunity to move his right hand
up to the side of her face and began moving his face towards her.
Maya was too shocked to move. She thought maybe he'd reach for
her hand or put an arm around her shoulder but here he was going
straight for the kiss. Well, he wasn't fourteen years old like Henry so
she'd guessed they didn't have to start at first base, like then. She
didn't move away and tilted her head upward just a little to meet his
lips more squarely. When their lips did meet, it felt as if a fire ignited
and raced outwards through the dry branches of her body. She
reached up and put a hand around his neck and drew him closer to
her as their lips parted and tongues met.

Good God. Her body responded more passionately then it
had the last year with Steven. Was she so attracted to Travis or was
her 38-year-old body just so deprived of sex? She certainly hadn't
had any sex in the past two years since Katrina and the last few years

with Steven the sex had become infrequent and mechanical, nothing like she was feeling now.

Suddenly Travis stopped and pulled away. "Oh, God, Maya. I'm so sorry. I didn't plan that, but something just hit me when you turned to me and without thinking, I kissed you."

"No need to apologize. I could have said no but I think my response speaks for itself."

Travis smiled. "We both did seem to enjoy it. Let's not let this ruin anything. We don't need to rush and still need to get to know one another better."

"That sounds good, so why don't you tell me more about yourself? I only know your grandparents lived here and that you do some handyman work and work as a kayak guide. Isn't there more?"

Travis grabbed another handful of trail mix and in between chewing asked, "What would you like to know?"

"Well, tell me about your life before you came to Oriental?"

"As I mentioned the other night, I used to be married. I was twenty-three when I married my college sweetheart the summer after college graduation. We were happy for a couple of years but then began to grow apart. She wanted to start a family and buy a bigger house. I didn't feel ready and had some wanderlust that needed to be satisfied. She wasn't interested in seeing the country and wanted to put down roots in Southern Pines where she was from. We ended up separating after five years when I was twenty-eight."

"I'm sorry. That must have been hard."

"It was, but now that some years have passed, I know it was the right thing. Neither of us would have been able to follow our true path if we had stayed in the relationship."

"How long ago was that?"

"Eight years ago."

Maya quickly did the math to calculate Travis' age at 36. A younger man. That was a first. Usually she was attracted to men at least a little older then she, but at this point in her life two years didn't make much difference.

Maya and Travis sat on the creek bank for another 30 minutes as the sun and temperatures rose. Travis talked more about his marriage and then his adjustment to single life. Maya listened, asking lots of questions in hopes she could avoid going into more detail about her marriage to Steven. She could only imagine that Travis assumed they had a healthy and satisfying relationship and that she was bereft about his death. Maya did keep up her end of the conversation, talking about her sister, brother-in-law and nephew.

Travis reached over and held Maya's left hand. Those electrical charges fired up again, radiating from her hand out to the rest of her body. She took a deep breath to slow her heart that suddenly jumped into high gear. "It's after ten and getting hotter. We should head back. Maybe we can grab some lunch from Toucans."

"Sounds good to me." Maya gave Travis' hand a squeeze and stood to walk to her kayak.

They paddled back to the jeep with steady strokes and little conversation. Maya was just ready to get out of the heat. The sun was high now and there was no shade out in the middle of the creek. The humidity was so thick you could see a haze along the horizon. Their silence was comfortable. Maya was actually thankful for it. It gave her time to process the morning. What did the kiss and hand holding mean? Were they "a couple" now or was it just a moment that occurred on a hot summer day and didn't really mean anything? Well, she wouldn't know what it meant to Travis till she asked him, so no point wasting her time trying to read his mind. What she could do is figure out what it all meant to her. She reviewed the things she knew for sure in her head. One, she liked Travis and felt comfortable with him. Two, she was definitely physically attracted to him. Three, she had fun when they were together and four he treated her with care and respect. These were all positive aspects but when she tried to think of her and Travis in a serious relationship, waking up naked on a Sunday morning and making love before breakfast, she just couldn't picture it. Something didn't fit.

No need to jump so far ahead, Maya thought. Just stay focused on this moment and as long as it continues to feel good, I'll keep moving forward. She still wondered what was going on in his mind though.

Back at The Paddle Company, Travis and Maya unloaded her kayak and put it on top of her Saturn. "So, do you still feel like having lunch?" Maya asked.

"Of course. I'm thinking of a fin on a bun with homemade chips."

"Sounds good to me." Maya was starving; she had gotten up at five so she and Doodle Bug could get in a five mile run before kayaking.

Maya and Travis walked past a couple of boats tied up at Toucan's marina. From the inscriptions on their sterns, Maya could see one was from just up the river in New Bern and the other two, who must be traveling together, were from Maryland. She loved looking at the names of the boats and wondering what they meant to the owners. *Topsy Turvey, Moon Dancer* and *Carlie May* were the three docked today. Maya's boat musings were interrupted by Travis talking hold of her hand. Funny, she had gotten so absorbed in the boats that she had almost forgotten he was beside her. She guessed that was normal after several years of being mostly alone. His touch took her right back to their kiss on the creek bank and caused her stomach to flop in a pleasant way, like at a high school dance when the cutest guy is walking towards you and you know it is you he wants to dance with. Still holding her hand, Travis stopped in front of *Carlie May* and turned her towards him. "I just wanted to say what a great morning I've had with you."

Before she could say anything, Maya saw Bay Witherspoon out of the corner of her eye watching them. Maya rolled her eyes and then hoped Travis hadn't noticed. Bay was such a busybody and was probably about to head their way to try to determine what was going on between her and Travis. Bay was about Maya's age and married to an older man who was retired. Maya had seen her at the gym a couple of times but never shared more with her then a few general pleasantries. Their lives were too different and Maya didn't see the point of trying to get to know her. Bay began to make her way over towards them. Then her much older husband, Holden, came out of The Bean with some coffee and called her back to their car, a dark blue BMW of some sort.

Maya brought her eyes back to Travis now that Bay was safely headed in the other direction. "I've had a great time too. It's been a long time since I've had a friend to talk to and do things with."

She caught the word, friend, just as it was leaving her mouth. Surely she thought more of him than that because of how she felt when they kissed? It was early on and she realized she probably needed to do more processing of Steven's death before she could let herself open up enough to be in a romantic relationship.

Travis seemed unfazed by the word and swung her arm as they started walking again. "Come on. Let's eat before we melt out here in the sun."

Chapter 4

Friday August 31, 2007

Doodle Bug lay in the middle of the kitchen in her post run repose. Her eyes followed Maya as she darted back and forth, rearranging the flowers in the vase on the kitchen table, fluffing the pillows on the couch again and then walking to look out the window. It was ten o'clock Friday morning and her sister and three month old nephew were on their way down from Raleigh for a visit. Maya was thankful that her new job at the chiropractor's office didn't start till Monday.

Because Maya moved here only a couple months after Worth was born, her sister hadn't been able to see her place yet. She was so excited to see them both. She had spent most evenings and weekends with them just after Worth was born but hadn't been back to visit since she'd been in Oriental. Finally, with too much energy to stay inside, Maya went out her front door and sat on the single step of her front stoop waiting to see the flash of sun reflecting off her sister's car as she turned down Hazel's driveway.

Her sister had asked a few weeks ago about coming today and
spending one night. Kate didn't mentioned why, but Maya knew it
was because it was just a few days after the second anniversary of
Katrina and Steven's death. Last year this time had been very
difficult for her. She ended up calling in sick on August 29 because
she had trouble keeping all the images from flooding her mind—the
loneliness and fear of sitting on her couch with only Doodle Bug,
watching the impending hurricane approach, the sounds of the wind
lashing at her small cottage, hurling branches, yard ornaments and
hanging baskets of flowers flailing at her windows and later the water
rising and rising and no way to contact anyone. She remembered the
destruction of her neighborhood after it was all over. Entire houses
gone with nothing left but their foundation, the trees stripped of
their leaves, the railroad track a few blocks away buckled like a piece
of ribbon candy.

She remembered reporting Steven was missing a couple of
days after the hurricane, not sure if he truly was or if he had chosen
not to call her or come home. Those first days after the hurricane
Maya had been immobilized by not knowing what to do or where to
go. Thank God she had Doodle Bug so could focus attention on
caring for her.

Most of that day last year, she and Doodle Bug stayed inside.
Maya cried often and turned the TV off and on, not sure if she

wanted to watch the news shows that were commemorating the first anniversary of Katrina or if she wanted to be left alone with her own images. Finally her sister was able to get there after school and listened to the stories she'd heard before, made dinner and helped Maya focus on what was happening now in her life and how far she'd come in a year. That night was also when she gave Maya the number for a counselor. Kate thought she had PTSD and needed professional help to move her through this. Maya felt hers was a normal response to an extreme situation and she would move through it on her own. Just to satisfy her sister, she had agreed to go to the counselor at least once.

As Maya remembered her mental state this time last year, she understood why her sister was concerned about her being down here alone. Since being in Oriental, she felt like her anxiety had been taken down a notch or two. Bad weather and anything that made her think of Steven seemed to be the biggest triggers of her anxiety attacks, but luckily, looking at the date on the calendar was innocuous this year. Maya was glad anyway that her sister and nephew were coming so she could show them her new home and town and her sister would be able to envision her new surroundings whenever she thought of Maya.

Maya saw the glint in the sun she'd been waiting for and jumped up just as her sister's hunter green Subaru Outback pulled

around the corner of Hazel's driveway. Maya ran up the slope
between her house and the driveway and directed Kate to where she
should park.

Kate jumped out, gave Maya a quick hug and then hurried to
unlock Worth out of his infant car seat. "Maya, what a gorgeous old
home. So this belongs to Hazel whom you've told me about? It
looks like the mistress of the house could come floating out in a long
gown and parasol and offer us a mint julep."

"You're right on one front, Kate. The house is old. It was
built over 100 years ago, but I doubt anyone in Hazel's family were
drinking mint juleps on the front porch." Maya thought that no one
lounged around in those days: most all the men in Hazel's family
were probably hardworking fishermen and were gone a good part of
the year and the women stayed home taking care of the house, the
garden and the children. "Let me grab some of your things and we'll
go down to my cottage."

Kate popped the wagon's "trunk" to begin unloading.
Maya's eyes widened at all the stuff. They were only staying one
night but it looked like she had enough things for a week. Well, she
only had Doodle Bug to care for and didn't know much about
children. Evidently they require a lot of supplies.

Maya grabbed the Pack 'n Play and said, "I'm so happy to
have you here. I've missed you." It was strange for Maya to live

somewhere without memories of her sister. "Hey, maybe this will become a regular trip for you and when Worth gets older he can spend a week or two here in the summers."

"Maya, he's only three months old. No need to age him too quickly. Based on what you just said though, it sounds like you're planning on being here for a while."

As they walked down to her boathouse, Maya thought about her sister's comment. It seemed natural to think she would be here until Worth was seven or eight. Maybe this would become her permanent home. She certainly felt an immediate attachment to the place. Mentally she tried to picture her future here. Would she buy a house, marry again, keep the same job?

"Hey. What are you thinking about?" Kate asked as she lugged Worth in his car seat and a large suitcase down the hill. "You seemed a million miles away."

"Sorry. I was mentally trying to picture what my life might look like here in Oriental in eight or ten years."

"Could you see anything in your crystal ball, O Psychic Maya?" Kate asked playfully.

"No, smarty pants. Now put that bag down and come in to see my home."

Kate left the suitcase at the front door and Maya gave her the grand tour. They spent the rest of the morning on Maya's small back porch talking about the details of Maya's new life in Oriental and Kate's new life as a mother. Kate knew of Travis and Maya told her about their kiss a few days ago and Kate shared her relief that she could take a year off from teaching to stay at home with Worth.

At this moment, their lives were the most different from one another as they had ever been but their relationship remained strong nonetheless. They had always cheered each other's successes and provided support with their challenges no matter what. There was no competition or rivalry, just an earnest desire for the other to be happy. Maya knew she was very lucky to have this relationship with Kate. So far in her life, Kate had always been there for her. They both had learned early on that their parents were too busy and emotionally unavailable to provide what they needed so they intuitively stepped up to meet each other's needs and continued to do so today.

Maya, Kate and Worth in his car seat, ate lunch at the deli overlooking Oriental marina and meandered through some of the art galleries where Kate bought Maya a lovely painting by a local artist. It was of an old row boat tied up at a small dock under some live oaks back in a creek. The blues, greens and browns matched Maya's colors in the boathouse and the picture would look perfect in the kitchen.

The time passed quickly when they were together, and before they knew it, it was 7:30 p.m. and Kate was putting Worth down for the night in his Pack 'n Play crib. While Kate had been readying Worth for bed, Maya had been cooking dinner for them. "Come on little Momma, sit down for some dinner."

Kate pulled out a chair and plopped down. "Maya, this looks wonderful. You don't know how long it's been since someone has cooked me dinner. Since I'm staying home now, I feel obligated to always prepare the meals. I guess I feel I should earn my keep, but some nights I'm just exhausted from caring for Worth."

Kate took her first bite, "This is delicious. Everything always tastes so much better when someone else cooks it and especially when it's so fresh."

They were having sautéed flounder that Buster had given Maya, fresh corn and green beans from the farmer's stand down the road and some seven grain bread Maya had bought at the farmers' market that morning before Kate arrived. Maya and Kate ate for a few minutes in silence and savored the flavors of the food that they had paired with a crisp Chardonnay.

"Maya, we haven't talked about this, but I'm sure you know part of my reason for coming was to make sure you were doing okay on this second anniversary of Katrina. It seems like you must be since you haven't even mentioned it yet."

"I do feel good. Right now I'm trying to stay focused on the present and creating my new life, so that helps. When I was back in Raleigh, it felt like I was cleaning up the past, trying to pay off the debt Steven had created and now I feel like I have a fresh start. I can tell you though it's easier being here with you since you aren't asking lots of questions. The hardest part has been when Hazel and Travis have asked me about Steven. Actually neither asked specifically about him but they saw his urn and commented on that which meant I had to tell them something. I try not to think about that unless I have to. I may be in denial but like you said earlier, I'm doing well so it must be working. So, are you ready for dessert?"

"Don't change the subject. We've had this conversation before. You need to make peace with your marriage and Steven's death and do something with those ashes. I don't see how you can really put that all behind you until that's done."

Maya stood to begin clearing their dishes feeling frustrated that this lovely day was going to end with a discussion of Steven. "I know, Kate. I'm just sick of thinking about that and want to forget it and move on."

"I agree with the moving on part, but you know as well as I, you can't just forget about your marriage. Somehow you have to come to terms with what happened and your feelings about that."

Maya's throat began to constrict and her mouth was dry. Interestingly, it was her mouth and throat that were symptomatic. Maybe these symptoms would be relieved if she would speak her truth about her feelings. "Kate, I appreciate your concern and I will take care of it in my own time. Can we just change the subject now? I don't want to end our evening this way."

Worth let out a scream and Kate rushed to him, unbuttoning her shirt on the way. Maya smiled. Her nephew must be on her side and knew exactly when his mother needed to be distracted. Kate breastfeed Worth on the couch and Maya finished washing their dinner dishes. It was a wonderful sight. Both Kate and Worth had looks of pure contentment on their faces. Just watching them helped Maya let go of her aggravation with Kate for bringing up Steven. She knew Kate was right and she also had to admit to herself she was putting on a good show of being perfectly adjusted so her sister wouldn't bring that topic up. She should have known Kate wouldn't let her get away with that. She also knew she shouldn't let herself get away with the denial either, but she was getting so good at it.

***

Hazel stood at her living room window, watching Maya and her sister loading Worth into the back of the car. She knew they were going over to The Bean for a cup of coffee so Kate could see the morning crowd. Maya had invited her to go but she declined. She did have a meeting at nine which could have been changed to ten or eleven but she couldn't bring herself to be around the baby. Her heart hurt now like a thousand bees had stung it, just watching them from a distance.

Over the years she had become adept at keeping herself away from newborns. It had been so long she should have worked through it by now. Of course, if she had ever talked about it with someone that would have helped. Hazel knew she had sacrificed living an authentically happy life because she kept these feelings inside, but she wasn't sure what the answer was. She felt the full force of her anger, remorse, grief and emptiness would wash her away so instead she only let it out in small increments before damming it up again. Like water, her emotions over time had eroded her capacity for true joy. She had settled for a life of neutrality.

Oh, it wasn't all horrible. She did have days when the sun reflecting off the water and the breeze across her skin would overwhelm her with their beauty or a gathering of her women's circle would make her laugh and feel appreciated. But many days she awoke feeling empty and alone. On those days she would get some relief with a visit from the UPS man or a scheduled meeting. These things helped to push down those uncomfortable feelings for a while anyway. She knew it wasn't healthy but....what could you do?.

Hazel watched Kate's Subaru head down her driveway for The Bean and then stop as it met a silver Hyundai that had just turned in. The Hyundai backed up to let Maya and Kate out and then headed down Hazel's driveway. On cue, the distraction had arrived to turn Hazel's attention away from her emotions. She turned from the window and hurried down the hall to her office in the sunroom at the front of the house.

Out her office window, she saw a tall middle aged black man dressed in a suit unfold himself from the passenger seat of the small rental car. She imagined he must be stiff, cramped in that car all the way from Raleigh. Out from behind the steering wheel popped a short round woman with graying hair and sensible laced up shoes. They certainly were a contrasting pair. Hazel opened her roll top desk and took out the proposal they had Fed Exed to her a couple of days ago. She watched their progress and was relieved when they came straight to her office door on the driveway side of the house as she had instructed. The sweeping front porch was inviting and used to welcome her grandparents' guests, but Hazel hadn't let anyone in that door for many years. In fact, she wasn't even sure she could get to that door anymore.

She opened the door to her office before they had a chance to knock.

"Mrs. Underhill?" the black man asked as he held out his hand.

"Yes, Yes. That's me." Hazel said as she shook his hand. "And you must be Mr. Lafayette and Ms. Simpkins. Did you have any trouble finding your way?"

"No, not at all," Ms. Simpkins said. "We're just so happy you agreed to see us and are considering our proposal."

"Do come in." Hazel said as she stepped back from the door and motioned them to the two chairs across from her desk. "I was impressed with your proposal and just have a few more questions."

Just a little over an hour later, Hazel was waving to Mr. Lafayette and Ms. Simpkins as their car headed down the driveway. Everyone was all smiles. Hazel even thought she saw the two of them high five each other just before they rounded the corner of her driveway and out of sight. That made her smile even bigger. She closed the door and sat down at her desk to file the proposal. The sting in her heart had gone and, even if only for a short while, she felt happy and connected to a higher purpose. Hazel glanced at her calendar and saw her next appointment was two weeks away. Hopefully this feeling could sustain her mood till then. She knew it probably wouldn't but she could always hope.

***

As Maya and Kate turned left off Highway 55 onto the road where Hazel lived, they passed the silver Hyundai again as it was about to turn onto the highway and head out of town. "There's that car that was pulling into Hazel's as we left." Kate said. "They didn't visit very long."

"I'm not sure what the deal is with Hazel's visitors. This is the third time since living here that I've seen people coming to visit her. I don't recognize them as local. They're usually dressed up and sometimes carrying briefcases and they never stay long. She told me she's a retired English teacher from Meredith but never mentioned any other business."

"Well, it's just nice she has people coming by. At her age, I imagine a lot of her friends have already died, so she may be lonely."

"You're right. I should make more of an effort to spend time with her. She's a lovely woman and very caring. Did I tell you about the tuna casserole she brought me my first night here?"

"You did and how she asked about the urn and how she got teared up when you talked about Steven. She sounds very sweet."

"Speaking of tuna casserole," Maya said, wanting to change the subject, "Remember how Granny would make that at least once a week? Seems like every other time we had dinner with her she'd cook that."

"Yep. It always tasted great and she would serve it with biscuits and green beans. That was comfort food. I haven't had that meal since she died. Have you?"

"No, not that exact combination. I think I know what the next meal will be when you and Worth come to visit."

Kate pulled the Subaru up beside Maya's Saturn. Before getting out, she grabbed Maya's hand. "That would be perfect. I look forward to coming back soon. I've been so happy to be here with you. I've missed you since you left Raleigh."

"Me too, Kate. Come on. Let's get my nephew his morning snack and down for his nap before you have to leave."

Maya unsnapped Worth from the car seat base as Kate followed with his diaper bag. Maya's heart swelled with love for this little person who was part of her sister and part of her. She swung his fifteen pound body and seven pound car seat, working her right arm muscles. Kate came up beside her and put an arm around her waist. They didn't say anything but Maya knew they were supporting each other again through major life transitions, Kate into motherhood and Maya, maybe finally into a life all her own. As they walked into the boathouse Maya saw the urn sitting, or rather glowering on the end table, a reminder that her life was not yet fully her own.

***

Tropical Storm – Thursday September 6, 2007

Doodle Bug was behaving just as Maya felt. She had as much of her doggie surface area in contact with Maya's body as possible. She shivered and whimpered with each thunderclap. Maya tried to maintain her composure. I need to be an adult about this, she thought. Francine is only a tropical storm and the worst of this will be through by midnight. She tried to distract herself with reading, but it wasn't working.

She jumped up suddenly and pulled back the lace curtain that covered the creek window. Each flash of lightning illuminated the pier and creek. Hazel's 30-foot sailboat and small inflatable dingy danced and bowed to the left and right on top of the boiling creek water. Hands clenched and her breath coming in short gasps, Maya turned from the window and her eyes immediately went to the front door to look for the stealthy creep of water. She was overcome with the fear and panic she had felt during Katrina. She remembered the water level in the house rising and watching her furniture float as she and Doodle Bug went upstairs. Then the terror as the water continued to rise up the steps, saturating the upstairs carpet. How Maya got a 70-pound lab up the accordion steps to the attic she will never know, but at least they had stayed dry and safe up there.

Maya's heart was pounding against her chest and she felt sweat prickle around her brow line. She needed someone to talk to so her thoughts would stop racing. Maybe her sister had been right about her needing support. It was just she needed it now and not a week ago on the Katrina anniversary. She picked her phone up to call Travis, but couldn't get a signal. Not able to sit still Maya walked to the front window and looked up to Hazel's house on the hill. She saw the back porch light flick on and thought Hazel must be looking out towards the creek in the storm.

I've never gotten past her porch before, but I really don't want to be alone tonight, she thought. Surely Hazel will understand. In a swift moment of decision, Maya grabbed her raincoat and threw it on. "Come on, Doodle Bug. Let's run over to Hazel's."

The rain was coming down so hard that each drop felt like a tiny electric shock on her skin. Doodle Bug was right on her heels as they ran through the slick grass. Maya could feel her running shoes sinking into the soft earth but she high stepped it up to Hazel's back porch. Doodle Bug shook several times as Maya caught her breath. She knocked on Hazel's door, suddenly feeling self conscious that a grown woman needed comfort during a storm. Hazel opened the porch door wearing her usual outfit of khakis and an oxford shirt with pearls. Her gray hair was pulled up in a loose bun on the back of her head. Hazel did not step away from the door, somehow managing to block the view inside with her diminutive five foot frame.

"Maya, what on earth are you doing out running during the storm?"

"Umm, I wasn't running. I just was looking...for...ahh...you." Maya's throat tightened and her chest felt heavy. "This storm, well, it's making me think too much about the night of Katrina and I can't sit still or think straight. I thought having someone to talk to would help."

Maya watched Hazel who appeared to be mulling this over. She glanced nervously over her shoulder into the house and then back at Maya. Hazel, looking smaller than her five feet now, stepped aside and motioned for Maya to come in. Hazel's face was pinched, her shoulders rounded and she appeared distressed. Maybe we should just go home, Maya thought. She doesn't seem too happy to have us.

As Maya's eyes adjusted to the light, she took in the narrow foyer and living room just off to the right. She caught her breath and suddenly understood the source of Hazel's discomfort. There was only a small pathway from the front door into the living room and nowhere to sit once you got there. Every available surface was covered with papers, magazines and clothes. There were half-opened UPS boxes sitting everywhere with various tools, kitchen gadgets and jewelry peeking out the top. The air was thick and Maya could smell the mold that must be growing somewhere under those piles.

In one corner of the living room the face of a beautiful grandfather clock was visible but the rest was obscured by a mound of stuffed animals of various sizes. They ranged from the Beanie Babies so popular in the early 1990s to a huge giraffe that might have been won years ago at a county fair. Some of the animals were yellowed with age and all were covered with dust. Maya could only imagine what creatures were deep within the pile making a home and gnawing away at the artificial fur, stuffing and plastic eyes.

Maya took a deep breath to let all this sink in as Doodle Bug tried to find a space large enough to lie down. She kept circling to the right and then to the left like dogs do before lying down, but never found a spot so just leaned against Maya's left leg. All this time Hazel had stood silently by the front door, watching Maya's appraisal of her home. Her downcast eyes came up to meet Maya's and Maya could feel Hazel's plea for compassion and non-judgment without her saying a word.

After several deep breaths, Hazel regained her composure. "We can talk about this," Hazel swept her arm around her head, indicating the piles, "some other time. But for now let's go back to my office and I'll make us a cup of tea."

Hazel led Maya down the hallway with a walkway just wide enough for her small frame. Maya kept her arms close to her body so as not to disturb the precarious piles on either side. She hoped Doodle Bug was cautious with her tail and wouldn't knock a juicer or nail gun down on her head. As they passed the kitchen on their right, Maya peered in and wondered exactly how this tea would be prepared since there was no clear surface in the kitchen, including the stove.

Hazel stepped into the kitchen and instructed Maya to continue to her office at the end of the hall.

Maya and Doodle Bug followed Hazel's instructions and safely arrived in the office, without tripping over anything or knocking something from its perch on the piles lining the hall. Maya stepped into the office and was shocked by the contrast to the rest of the house. This room looked as if it had been added to the side of the house as an afterthought. There was a door that opened outside to Hazel's driveway and windows on the three other walls making it feel like a sun room, but the furnishings were definitely of an office. There was an antique roll top desk against the wall with the window that looked across her small front yard into the woods, now illuminated every few minutes by lightning. Across from the desk, two wing back chairs upholstered in a blue and yellow paisley print angled toward one another with a small drop leaf table between them.

Everything was clean with no clutter in sight. Maya's eyes went to the opened desk and saw envelopes in one of the cubby holes, paperclips in an old silver ashtray and one neat stack of papers in the middle with a pen lying diagonally across it, waiting for Hazel to complete. Maya wondered why this room was so neat and orderly while the rest of the house looked like a distribution center for the Home Shopping Network.

The wind picked up again throwing a branch against the window and Maya involuntarily jumped. Doodle Bug pressed closer to Maya's legs and was shaking. Maya walked over to one of the wing back chairs and sat down, perched on the edge, the roar of the wind making it impossible to relax. In the kitchen, she could hear the whistle of a tea kettle over the thunder and rain. She expected to smell smoke from a stray stuffed animal lying near the stove, but instead got a whiff of toast.

Maya continued to look around the room, having trouble processing the stark contrast it made to the rest of the house. As her mind raced for explanations, she remembered the silver Hyundai she and Kate had just seen here on Saturday morning. One morning a few weeks ago, she had also seen a strange car and saw a man in his early 50s, dressed in a business suit, walking towards the house with a briefcase in hand. Now, seeing the inside of the house she knew he had been heading to Hazel's office. At that time she just thought it was Hazel's attorney but now she questioned that. Maya looked over at the pile of papers on Hazel's desk, wondering if they held any explanation for the visitors and this neat room.

Hazel walked into her office carrying a tray with two tea cups, a tea pot, a plate of cinnamon toast and a bowl of sugar cubes, complete with sterling silver sugar tongs. Maya admired the rose bud pattern on the tea service and wondered what magic Hazel had used to create this in the disorderly kitchen. Hazel placed the tray on the table between the chairs and sat across from Maya. Doodle Bug, now lying on the floor, raised her head, her nose twitching as she caught the smell of the toast. This is how I had imagined Hazel, Maya thought as she watched Hazel pouring the tea into the antique cups. It was hard to reconcile the contrasts in this gentile woman preparing the tea and the clutter and mess in the rest of the house.

Hazel plopped two cubes of sugar into one of the cups and handed it to Maya whose eyes had wandered back to the neat stack of papers on Hazel's desk. Before picking up her own cup, Hazel leaned forward and pulled down the cover of the desk with one swift and graceful movement of her left hand while her right hand offered Maya the cinnamon toast.

***

Hazel walked down the front hall to her living room. She glanced at her grandfather clock and was surprised it was already

10:30. She and Maya had spent over an hour talking back in her office. Hazel looked out the windows of the living room. The lights from her back porch and the dock allowed her to see Maya and Doodle Bug walking around the corner of the house and then down towards the boathouse. Doodle Bug seemed invigorated now that the storm had passed and ran around Maya in happy circles. Hazel had let them out her office door rather than enduring the humiliation of Maya walking through her cluttered home again. It was something Hazel tried to ignore, spending most of her time outside, in her office or out in town. Now that someone else knew her secret, it was harder to pretend there wasn't a problem.

Hazel sat on top of a box by the window. She wasn't even sure what was in the box but it was sturdy enough to hold her 105 pounds. She looked down towards the creek and saw a light in the boathouse come on and Maya pulling closed the curtains. Despite the initial humiliation, it had been nice to have another woman in her home. Hazel had enjoyed the ritual of having tea, something she had done often with her grandmother when she was young and then with her mother when she'd moved back here after Bill had died. She looked around the living room trying to imagine how it must have looked to Maya. She could remember ordering some of the items, but others looked unfamiliar. She felt anger rising as she surveyed all these things. How had she let this happen?

Hazel didn't want to dwell on that thought and rose from the box, now sagging in the middle. She turned and scurried down the narrow pathway to her office, her mind focused on the proposal sitting on her desk. In her haste and the dim light, Hazel didn't notice the ab roller that Doodle Bug must have knocked from its perch with her tail. Hazel's left foot caught in it and threw her off balance. She pitched forward and grabbed at the piles on either side to slow her fall. She landed with a thud accompanied by the clatter of a canister set she knocked from one of the piles. Hazel sat up and scooted back to rest against a box. She felt no sharp pain indicating a break, just a dull ache in her right hip that would most likely flower into a blue black bruise overnight.

As Hazel caught her breath, she realized she was holding something in her left hand. She must have grabbed at it on her way down. Now she opened her hand and held the object to the light coming down the hall from the kitchen. A wave of nausea filled her as she saw what was in her hand. The one thing she should have thrown out she had kept.

Hazel held a 3 x 5 picture frame in her hand. It was silver with blue glass stones embedded around the edge. One of her students had given it to her at the end of her senior year. The frame had sat in the right hand corner of her desk at Meredith. On the surface, the picture was of two colleagues enjoying a spring day on the grounds. A yearbook photographer had come upon her and Hay

having a picnic lunch on a warm April day in 1967 and snapped

their picture. Luckily they looked appropriate as if they were

discussing a mutual student or their plans for the approaching

summer. Only Hazel saw the small smear of lipstick in the right

corner of her mouth and noticed the loosening of the scarf she had

worn tied around her neck that day, and only she knew why her right

hand was resting protectively below the waistband of her shirt dress.

Hazel leaned back against the wall, the tears flowing freely as

they always did. When will the pain ease? She cursed herself for the

millionth time and her self-loathing made her feel as if she could

throw up. How can I make peace with my decision 40 years ago?

She had spoken with her Baptist minister who assured her all her sins

were forgiven if Christ was in her heart but she wasn't so sure.

Maybe she should take this to her women's circle at their equinox

gathering in a few weeks. She had toyed with this idea for years but

never had the courage. Maybe the women in her circle and the

Mother Tree would help diminish her pain. Hazel lay there until the

early hours of the morning. Her small body crumpled in a pile

amongst the piles of things that crowded her house but never filled

the emptiness.

Chapter 5

Wednesday September 19, 2007

Maya cradled her coffee cup with both hands absorbing the heat from the mug. She lifted it to her nose and inhaled the strong aroma of the fog lifter blend she had purchased from The Bean. It was nine in the morning and she closed her eyes, appreciating the warmth of the sun on her face. She slid back in the rocking chair on her small back porch overlooking Beards Creek, her muscles pleasantly fatigued from her six mile run this morning. Doodle Bug was lying at her feet, her eyes intently watching a kingfisher swooping down to the water for its breakfast. Maya was thankful it was Wednesday, her day off during the week, for this September morning was pristine. She had begun working as the office manager for Dr. Allen's chiropractic center in Alliance, just ten miles away. So far she enjoyed the work but especially appreciated the fact she got a day off in the middle of the week and still made enough to live on.

As she contemplated the day, she knew she wanted to get out in her kayak and not waste this perfect weather. The last few weeks,

she and Travis had gone kayaking together on Wednesday, but today
he had an errand to run in New Bern so he couldn't come. Not in
the mood to load her kayak up on her car and drive to another spot,
she decided to go west on Beards Creek and explore a branch off it
called Hungry Mother Creek.

A few weeks ago she and Travis were kayaking when he
pointed out where Hungry Mother split off from Beards Creek and
he highly recommended she explore it. That day they were paddling
to the very end of Beards Creek so didn't have time for a side
excursion. Maya blushed as she remembered their picnic lunch on a
small spit of land at the end of Beards Creek.

After eating, she had lain back in the sun to take a quick nap
when Travis leaned down and kissed her. She was still amazed at
how her body responded to his touch. Things continued to progress
until a powerboat came by, looking for bait fish at the back of the
creek. She'd been thankful for that jolt back to reality as things may
have gone further than she had intended without this interruption.
But what if she wanted things to go further? They were both single,
consenting adults, right? But, somehow, Maya felt hesitant and didn't
know why. Thankfully Travis never pushed this issue either.

Maya, not wanting to spend the morning analyzing her
relationship with Travis rose from her rocking chair with Doodle Bug
close on her heels; the Doodles knowing something was up. Inside,

she filled a water bottle and grabbed a granola bar for a snack. Doodle Bug watched her closely, her tail wagging.

"Sorry, girl. I'm going in the kayak this morning. You stay here and sleep for a few hours." Doodle Bug seemed to understand and curled up on her favorite spot on the couch as Maya left the boathouse.

Maya slid her kayak into water and headed upstream. She was familiar with this part of the creek as she had paddled it almost weekly since moving in. Her thoughts, lulled by the steady cadence of her paddle strokes, reflected on how much her life had changed over the past two years. This time two years ago she had just moved to Raleigh, was living with Kate and Rob and still reeling from Steven's death and the destruction of Katrina. Now she was back living by the water, debt free and a widow. A widow. This was not a label she could identify with. Technically she met the criteria, but her emotions didn't match what she thought a widow should feel like. Maya thought back on her conversation with Hazel, who even after 28 years, still teared up when she talked of her husband's death.

Maya wasn't sure how much progress she had made in processing Steven's death. She stayed so busy while living in Raleigh, working two jobs, helping her sister prepare for the baby and running with Doodle Bug in her free time. She rarely allowed herself to think too much, which frustrated her counselor to no end. She

had called that counselor her sister recommended to see if she could
help with the panic attacks she frequently had. Shortly after moving
to Raleigh, Maya had her first attack one night while trying to get to
sleep. Her mind began racing about how she would pay off her debt,
where would she live, what would her future hold. As these thoughts
intensified she felt her heart race, her breath become short and
labored and her chest tighten. She had never felt her body so out of
control and it scared her. This happened several more times, once in
a traffic jam and then that time on the first anniversary of Katrina.

It seemed being by the water was better than the counselor's
chair because since moving to Oriental, Maya had been able to think
about Katrina and Steven's death without the same emotional
intensity. As her strong strokes pushed her further up the creek,
Maya allowed her mind to dwell on Steven.

She wondered for the hundredth time why he chose to go to
New Orleans and leave her and Doodle Bug that weekend. What was
the reason he drank so? Steven rarely talked of his parents and
childhood but Maya knew that had something to do with his
drinking. She asked about his parents and he would cut her off,
saying they were out of his life and he didn't want to talk about it.
They hadn't even come to the wedding and she'd never talked with
either one on the phone. In fact, Steven only talked to his mother a
couple of times a year and never to his father. Just the mention of his

father's name would cause the vein across Steven's forehead to thicken and pulse. He would look into the distance, his eyes sometimes more sad than angry, but he never seemed comfortable expressing this sadness.

Why wasn't her love enough to make him happy? This was the question she always returned to. At one level she knew his drinking was unrelated to her, but another part of her took responsibility and she tried to think of what she could have done differently to make him happier. This was the same dance she had done in childhood. Thinking there was some lack in her that was the cause of her parents' emotional distance. It was exhausting always trying to figure out what other peopled needed you to be so they would love you.

STOP! Maya yelled to herself in her head. She didn't want to go down this road and heard her sister's voice reassuring her that she was not responsible for Steven's drinking and the poor choices he made that weekend. After all, she'd asked him to stay home and had reminded him to take extra insulin but he didn't listen to her. As her counselor had taught her, Maya brought herself back to the present. She felt the pull of her paddle against the water, the tightness in her arms as she reached for another stroke and the warm morning sun on her back. With her attention now in the moment, Maya realized she was approaching the turn off for Hungry Mother Creek.

What a name. Travis wasn't sure how it got its name but it made Maya smile. She veered her kayak off to the right, looking forward to exploring new territory. This creek was narrow and had more cypress trees than on the main part of Beards Creek. They grew in an arch and met overhead creating a canopy. Maya could hear the breeze rustling the leaves and the buzz of insects, still active on this warm fall day. She brought her paddle into the boat and closed her eyes to drift, take in the moment and quiet her thoughts. Lulled by the creek sounds, Maya's eyes become heavy. Someone needs to invent a way to lie down in a kayak for a nap, she thought.

The sound of her kayak sliding onto sand aroused Maya from her meditation. She opened her eyes to see that her kayak was on a small sandy beach. That was unusual as most of the creek banks around here were either several feet above the water line and not easily accessible by kayak or looked deceptively like solid ground but engulfed your foot in mud when you took a step out. Maya stepped out of her kayak onto the hard sand and decided to take advantage of the beach and take a quick potty break. Her two cups of coffee had caught up with her. She began looking for a tree to hide behind but then laughed when she realized there wasn't a soul around to see her.

Before getting back into her kayak, Maya studied the beach area. It would be the perfect place to return to with a picnic, blanket and good book. The beach was framed by two cypress trees, both decorated top to bottom with Spanish moss. Just past the sandy beach there were several saw palmettos, their ancient heritage giving the beach area a timeless quality. The woods beyond the beach were not as thick as in some areas and Maya walked past the palmettos for a better look. About 50 feet past the sandy beach was a small clearing. Maya stepped into the clearing and was surprised by what she saw. The clearing had only soft grass or bare dirt and no scrubby underbrush that was usually on the forest floor. As she surveyed the area, Maya saw that rocks about the size and shape of sourdough loaves were purposely placed around the edges of the clearing creating a defined circle.

What was this place? Maybe some type of burial ground for the Indians that once lived here or maybe nothing so dramatic and just a favorite camping spot for the Boy Scouts. It didn't feel like just a camping area though. Standing here felt similar to how Maya had felt in some of the cathedrals she had visited while on a college trip to France. She sensed peace and reverence for life standing in this simple circle in the trees.

Maya decided to sit for a minute and enjoy this pristine spot. She sat just inside the stone circle with her back towards the creek. Now at ground level, her eyes were immediately drawn to the base of a large live oak directly across from her in the circle. There were six candles in front of the tree. Some looked relatively new and others were almost gone, their wax having melted into a pool around the wick.

What was this spot? Who brought these candles and what purpose did this place serve? Maya sat cross legged in the circle and continued to contemplate the candles around the oak. Her eyes began to move up from the base of the tree to the massive trunk. The tree must be several hundred years old. Suddenly Maya's eyes widened. About two feet above the ground, the grooves and curves of the tree's bark made two eyes. Maya blinked and continued her study of the trunk. Slowly she discerned what could be the bump of a nose and a mouth slightly curved upward. This face was not wide eyed and toothy like a carved pumpkin, but gentle, subtle and feminine. She felt as if the eyes were regarding her with acceptance.

Maya jumped up, suddenly uncomfortable with this whole situation. Why would people come here and put candles at the base of a tree that seemed to have a feminine face in the trunk? It now did appear that this stone circle was created for the purpose of gathering around the tree. But who came here and why? Was it some weird pagan cult? She wasn't really sure what a pagan cult was, but growing up around Southern Baptists it was always implied that they were evil.

Maya, still standing across from the tree wreathed in candles, took in a deep breath. This spot had nothing to do with evil. It felt too peaceful and safe. She sat again and focused on her breath as she gazed at the eyes on the trunk. Maya did not pray much but silently sent up a prayer of gratitude for this beautiful spot. She closed her eyes and fully immersed herself in the moment. She could feel a small pebble that was under her right hip but dismissed that minor irritation and came back to her breath. She heard a squirrel rustling in the leaves as he ran on the forest floor. A kingfisher called further up the creek, fishing for her breakfast. A breeze ruffled her hair and she felt a wisp of it sticking to her neck. Maya's meditation was interrupted when her stomach growled, a good indication it was late morning and approaching lunch. She did want to see more of this creek before heading home, so she stood to walk back to her kayak. Before stepping out of the circle she looked back at the face in the bark of the live oak and promised to return.

Maya continued to head up Hungry Mother Creek, grabbing bites of her granola bar in between paddle strokes. At noon, Maya had not reached the end of the creek, but her growling stomach, not satisfied with just a granola bar, coaxed her to turn back to home and lunch. Maya laughed to herself and wondered if everyone left Hungry Mother Creek hungry. She kayaked past the beach area with the stone circle in the woods and again made a mental note of its location. As she neared the intersection with Beards Creek, Maya wondered who she could ask about the stone circle and tree. She felt

Travis would have mentioned it if he knew of the spot. Maybe Hazel

had been there since she had lived around here most of her life. But

Hazel went to the Baptist Church every week. She didn't seem like

the one to ask about a sacred feeling spot in the trees.

As she rounded the last bend on Hungry Mother Creek,

Maya saw a wooden kayak coming from the other direction. The

kayak was gorgeous. The hull was a combination of dark and light

wood in a beautiful design. It looked as if the darker wood was

chocolate sauce poured over the lighter wood. Before Maya's eyes

could focus on the paddler, she was bowled over by the paddles

themselves. They were also made with the same light and dark wood

and the design made each paddle look like a feather. All of a sudden

her electric blue, plastic kayak felt like an eye sore on the water, like a

Wal-Mart in the middle of the Grand Canyon, whereas this kayak

blended right in with the natural surroundings. The two boats were

almost side by side and Maya saw the paddler was a woman, probably

in her mid 50s. Her black hair was thick and curly and pulled back

into a pony tail. Maya back paddled to slow her progress.

"Hi," Maya said. "What a beautiful kayak. Did you make

that yourself?"

"It was a gift but is a handmade kayak from an artist in

Connecticut. I'm Lilith. I don't think I've seen you out on this creek

before."

"Sorry. Your kayak is so beautiful, I forgot my manners. I'm Maya. This is my first trip up Hungry Mother Creek but I've been up and down Beards Creek almost weekly since moving here in August. I'm renting the boathouse on Hazel Underwood's property."

"Oh, so you're that Maya. Hazel has mentioned you. Welcome to Oriental! I've lived here for about ten years now. I usually kayak up this way once or twice a month. What brings you to Oriental?"

There was that question. "I guess I came here for a fresh start. I lived on the Gulf Coast and relocated to my sister's in Raleigh after Hurricane Katrina. My sister and I came down here for a girl's weekend in April and I just fell in love with it."

"I've heard that story before. It's similar to mine."

Maya knew their stories actually couldn't be that similar because of Steven's death. She couldn't imagine anyone else going through something like that. Maya's stomach growled again. "Well, I better let you go; it's getting around lunch time."

"I hear ya. I'm hungry too," Lilith said. "I've packed a lunch to eat at a nice beach area on Hungry Mother Creek. Did you see it when you were that way?"

Maya's ears perked up when she heard this. "This was the first time I've ever been on Hungry Mother Creek but I think I stopped at that beach. What a beautiful and peaceful spot." Maya

left it at that, hoping Lilith would volunteer something more.

"There are others of us that feel the same way. I try to get

there several times a month, weather permitting. The sacredness of

that circle helps to keep me balanced."

Sacred. That seemed like the right word Maya thought. "I

did notice the stones and candles," Maya said. "What do people use

that spot for?"

Lilith's blue eyes looked deeply at Maya and then down

Hungry Mother Creek. "Women have been using that area for over a

hundred years. Since you felt the peace there, I would say you

already have a connection to that piece of land."

"You're right. I definitely want to go back there." Maya

wanted to return and practice some of her mediation there. Hungry

Mother Creek made her feel connected to something.

Maya and Lilith were holding onto the other's kayaks to keep

themselves beside one another in the breeze that was picking up with

the day's warmth. They moved as one unit towards the south bank

of Beards Creek with the direction of the wind.

"Maya, I know we've just met, but I have a good feeling

about you and I already know Hazel thinks you're great. There is a

group of women who still meet at that sacred spot. Would you like to join us? Our next meeting is just in a couple of days, Saturday morning. We'll get started right at sunrise."

Maya was intrigued by this at many levels and immediately accepted, mentally noting that she would have to do her long run on Sunday this week. Maya and Lilith said their goodbyes and paddled in opposite directions, Maya home to her hummus and cucumber sandwich and Lilith to her picnic on Hungry Mother Creek.

***

Maya threw her purse on the coffee table and plopped down on her couch as she leafed through some junk mail that was in her mail box. Thursday and Friday had passed uneventfully as Maya anticipated her Saturday morning on Hungry Mother Creek. The work at the chiropractic office was not mentally challenging but Maya enjoyed the people she worked with and there was always plenty to keep her busy. It was different working as the office manager with just the receptionist and Dr. Allen. Maya had been used to working in large medical records departments with several layers of management between her and the medical records director. This was so much simpler and more personal. In the hospitals, Maya never laid eyes on the patients but here she was able to meet them personally and had even begun to develop a relationship with a couple of the regulars. Dr. Allen was very easy to work with. He was in his late sixties and not very computer literate so was thrilled with

Maya's knowledge and experience. She pretty much had complete autonomy to run the office as she felt was best. He didn't even mind that she brought Doodle Bug to work a couple days a week. As long as they had run five or more miles that morning, Doodle Bug would rest under her desk, rising occasionally to greet a new patient.

I need to get out of these work clothes, Maya thought, as she went to her bedroom and quickly changed into her standard post work uniform of gym shorts, T-shirt and bare feet. The mid September evening was still warm and she wanted to take advantage of this beautiful weather before there was a nip of fall in the air. Maya grabbed a Corona from the fridge and went out to the porch overlooking the creek. She leaned back in the rocking chair and propped her legs up on the porch railing. Doodle Bug followed her out and ran off the porch to chase a squirrel.

Maya nursed her beer, enjoying the taste after drinking water all day. She wondered who would be at the gathering tomorrow morning. What was the purpose for meeting at that place and why meet at sunrise? She hoped she would fit in with the group of women. Maya had never really had a group of friends before. She had one or two friends from different parts of her life, work and running mostly, but never a larger group that shared something in common. She didn't know what to expect with this group but based on how she felt at the sacred circle and with Lilith, she had a good feeling.

***

The clock read, 5:55 a.m., just five minutes before the alarm was set to go off. Maya felt her stomach flip in anticipation of her adventure this morning. She hoped she had timed everything right. The sunrise was at 7:04 so if she left in her kayak by 6:30 she should be at the beach on Hungry Mother Creek by 6:50 or so. She rolled over in bed and threw the sheets off. The cool morning air from the open window felt good against her bare skin. She threw on her khaki shorts, Jimmy Buffett T-shirt, fleece vest and baseball cap. Doodle Bug, who'd been sleeping beside her bed, opened one eye as if to say, "Why aren't you putting on your running clothes?"

"Doodle Bug, I'm going for a kayak this morning instead of a run. I'll do my long run tomorrow." Doodle Bug closed her eyes again and rested her head on her paws, content to sleep a little longer. As she walked through the kitchen, Maya grabbed a banana and quickly filled her water bottle.

Her kayak slid quietly into the calm water. There was no breeze and the air temperature was probably around 62 degrees, which felt perfect. The morning was clear and Maya could still see the brightest stars twinkling. Dawn was just a faint glow in the east

and it cast a soft gray light over the creek. Maya turned up Beards
Creek and began paddling.

As she neared the turn off to Hungry Mother Creek, she
heard the steady sound of paddles dipping into the water behind her.
She stopped her own rhythm and looked back, eastward down Beards
Creek. The horizon was turning from gray to the color of fresh
cantaloupe. A kayak was fast approaching Maya, but in this light she
could not make out the paddler.

"Good morning," a young woman's voice called out.

"Good morning. You're out early," Maya said.

The woman's kayak slid beside Maya's and Maya was
immediately struck by the woman's beauty. She was probably in her
mid to late twenties. She had shoulder length honey blond hair
secured in place with a sapphire blue headband that almost perfectly
matched her eyes. Maya immediately felt self conscious as she
remembered her own reflection in the mirror when she was brushing
her teeth.

"I'm heading up Hungry Mother Creek to meet some friends
for the sunrise," the woman said. She had no trace of a southern
accent but didn't sound like she was from the North either.

"Really? That's where I'm going too. Are you going to meet
Lilith?" Maya asked.

"Yeah. Did she invite you too?"

"Yes. I met her on Wednesday in almost this same spot. We talked a little and I told her how moved I'd been by the sacred circle just off the beach area on Hungry Mother Creek. She invited me to come this morning at sunrise. I'm not sure what to expect."

"Well, let's keep paddling and I can fill you in on what I know. By the way, my name is Ella."

"Nice to meet you, Ella. I'm Maya."

"We're meeting this morning because it's the fall equinox. This group of women always meets at the equinoxes and solstices and sometimes we just meet if we feel the need. The best way I can explain it is we use this time to reconnect to nature, to our spiritual lives and to one another. I first came last winter to the solstice gathering."

"Hmm, that sounds interesting. I've never done anything like this before. How will I know what to do?"

"Don't worry about that. Hazel, our elder, will explain a little of the history to you since you are new, like she did to me last winter. Then, she will review the ritual. This will be my first fall equinox so, like you, today will be my first time with this particular ritual."

Maya didn't say anything, but she was taken back when Ella mentioned Hazel. Maybe it was a different Hazel, but how many older Hazels in Pamlico County could there be and Lilith had also mentioned that she knew her, come to think of it. Hazel didn't seem like the type that would come to a circle of trees for a ritual. After all, she was the one who went to the Baptist Church each Wednesday and Sunday. It didn't make sense to be singing a hymn one day and sitting in the woods with some women another. She'd find out soon enough.

During the course of their conversation, Maya and Ella reached the beach area of Hungry Mother Creek. Lilith's kayak was already there and she quickly came out of the woods. Maya had only seen Lilith in her kayak and hadn't realized she was so tall. She was probably about 5'10" with a strong build. She wasn't fat by any means, but she was solid and there was no risk of the wind knocking her down. She was barefooted and wearing a long sleeved T-shirt that had been washed so many times Maya couldn't even read it. Maya smiled and thought she had at least gotten the dress code right for this gathering.

"Hey, you guys. Glad you're here!" Lilith said.

"Lilith, you always manage to get here first. How is that?" Ella asked.

"This time, I camped out. Since I wasn't going to be at the farmers' market this morning, I took yesterday afternoon off from making bread and came here. It was a gorgeous night."

Maya listened to the exchanges, not knowing what to do next when she realized she was still holding her paddle and had on her PFD. She busied herself with securing her kayak while waiting to be told what to do. She had that awkward feeling she sometimes felt in church, like not knowing when to sit or stand, but this also felt so much different than conventional church.

The hum of a motor interrupted her thoughts and the three women on the beach looked up the creek to see two small skiffs racing their way. As the boats neared, Maya recognized her landlady Hazel as the driver of one. That was a good explanation for why she saw a light on this morning up in Hazel's bedroom. The other boat held a woman and man who looked to be in their mid sixties. As their boat slid up on the beach, the man, whose head was rimmed in silver, leaned down and kissed the woman and then held her hand as she stepped off the bow to the beach. There was an easy loving way about them that made Maya's heart ache for a moment. She and Steven had never had that kind of feeling between them.

"Maya, so glad you're here." Maya turned upon hearing Hazel's voice. Even in the morning light, she could see the glint of Hazel's pearls around her neck. Today she had on a white oxford and blue jeans rolled well above her ankles so they wouldn't get wet as she sloshed through the water to get ashore. Maya noticed her bare feet and the grace with which she moved across the sand towards her. It was obvious she was comfortable here, a sharp contrast to her demeanor a few weeks ago when Maya went to her house during the tropical storm.

"Lilith told me yesterday she had invited you and I was thrilled. I was going to suggest it to the group today but if Lilith felt good about you, I knew it would be okay. Lilith can get a good read on someone's energy and knows immediately if they will fit with our group. I trust her judgment implicitly. That's how we got sweet Ella in our group too."

"Maya, I'm Violet," the woman from the other boat said. Her voice dripped with a sweet southern drawl similar to Hazel's. She was Maya's height and had a pretty face framed by short gray hair. She was pleasantly plump in a grandmotherly sort of way and was wearing a floral wraparound skirt, white Izod shirt and was starting to put on some white Keds now that she was on dry land. Like Hazel, she looked well put together even though she was out in nature.

Lilith looked to the east and saw the pink orange glow of dawn spreading further along the horizon. "Okay, ladies. Let's make our circle. The sun is about to rise."

Maya followed the four other women back to the circle in the trees she had visited just a few days ago. No one had told her anything about what was about to happen. She felt nervous to see what would come next. As they entered the circle of trees, they formed a semi circle in front of the "Mother Tree." Hazel began by pulling small white votives out of the L.L. Bean canvas bag she had been carrying. She placed them in the sandy area at the base of the tree. The ground there appeared to be worn, as if this had happened many times over the years.

The women sat down, Hazel and Violet to Maya's right and Lilith and Ella to her left. She felt comfortable sitting on her cushion of pine straw. The breeze rustled the leaves on the cottonwood trees which were brown at the edges, awaiting the fall. The morning light was long and low and a stream of sunshine made it into the center of their circle. After positioning the votives, Hazel remained standing and faced the group.

"Maya, as the elder of this group, it falls to me to officially welcome you to our circle. There has been a circle of women gathering in this place for over a hundred years. I was first brought here by my grandmother when I was twenty-four, fifty-five years ago. She was introduced to this spot by, Chapawee, a woman from the Neusiok tribe, the people who first inhabited this area. My grandmother was the first white woman to be included. The Neusiok women were slowly dying off and the younger ones were moving away, marrying whites and didn't seem interested in the traditions of their ancestors. The Neusiok elder women wanted to continue this tradition and set out to find some local white women they felt a kindred spirit with. Chapawee told my grandmother that her ancestors felt the gentle face of the woman in the tree was a representation of God the Mother and used this place to honor the strength, beauty, and courage of women. The traditions and rituals at this spot have evolved over the years to meet the different needs of the women in each group. Since my grandmother's time, we have come here to celebrate the solstices and equinoxes and to use these cycles of nature to bring clearer intention and purpose to our lives."

Hazel continued, "Maya, I'm sure you're wondering exactly what we'll do today and Ella you may be too since you haven't participated in this ritual yet. We're here on the fall equinox and tomorrow we will begin to have more darkness than lightness in the day. We'll start by lighting the twelve candles I brought. Each of us will share something that has come to light for us in the long days of summer since we celebrated the summer solstice. After that we will share what issue, thought or desire we need to take with us into the darkness as the nights lengthen and we'll finish by blowing out two candles. At our winter solstice gathering we will discuss the result of our focus on this issue."

Maya listened intently as Hazel shared the history of this circle of trees. She felt honored to be here and to have a connection to the other women who had come here years ago. When Hazel began explaining what they would do this morning, Maya began to panic. What exactly was she talking about? Something that has come to light? What the heck did that mean and taking an issue into the darkness? What was that about? Am I supposed to go sit in a closet and think about something from now till Christmas time? Maya was beginning to feel a little uncomfortable. What in the world was she supposed to talk about? She usually just talked about work, running, family but never this deep touchy feely stuff. It reminded her of *Fried Green Tomatoes* when the women sat around and looked at their vaginas in a mirror together. That may have been easier than this coming into the light and going into the darkness thing.

A look of panic must have been on Maya's face because she felt Lilith's hand squeeze her left knee. She leaned down and whispered, "Don't worry. You can go last and hear the types of things we say or feel free to pass since this is your first time. We're just glad you're here."

Maya smiled at Lilith, thankful she had read her thoughts, or maybe it was her energy she read like Hazel had alluded to earlier. She relaxed, tried not to worry about what she would say and watched as Ella lit the twelve votives.

Violet said, "Let's begin with twelve breaths to center ourselves in this sacred spot and then we can begin sharing."

Breathing, I can do that, Maya thought. Ever since Katrina her breath would bring her back from the grip of fear and anxiety to the present. The five women sat silently, the sound of their breath mingling with the early morning call of the red winged black bird, the breeze in the trees and the crunch of leaves by a frenetic squirrel looking for breakfast. Maya's body felt heavier with each breath, her sitz bones pressing firmly into the earth, her breath deep and even. She had done this many times alone but this time she could feel the energy of the other women radiating out towards one another. She felt safe and secure, as if being hugged.

After twelve breaths, Maya opened her eyes and watched the other women bringing their focus back to the circle. She, Ella and Lilith were sitting cross legged on the ground, and Violet and Hazel each had a small camping chair that was low to the ground. Maya guessed after a certain number of years you deserve to have a little comfort.

Violet reached down into Hazel's bag and brought out a beautifully carved statue of some sort. She held it up and catching Maya's eye said, "Maya, this is our talking stick. It was made by Chapawee's mother and has been used here by women ever since. Whoever holds the stick has the attention of the group and no one else is allowed to speak until the stick is passed to her. Since I have it now, I will go ahead and begin."

Maya felt a swarm of butterflies move from her stomach up into her heart. She wasn't exactly sure what was to come but it felt like nothing she had ever experienced before. Violet passed the stick back and forth between her hands for a moment and then held it gently with both hands.

"What has come to light for me over the summer? I spent a lot of time with my grandchildren this summer. We were at the beach, the pool, taking them to camps and I see how much fun they have and I have when I'm with them. I realize this makes me feel young and energized and as the kids return to school and the weather gets cooler, I still need to focus on bringing more fun into my life. It is my intention to do just that." As Violet finished she pulled a small container of bubbles from behind her chair and blew several times through the wand. She laughed and her eyes sparkled like the bubbles as they floated into the sunlight in the middle of the circle.

Maya relaxed, even more as she laughed with the group. Maybe this didn't have to be as heavy and deep as she imagined. Violet continued to hold the talking stick. "Besides having more fun in the shorter days, I will take into the darkness the fear of my husband's death. I know it will happen, but lately I've had feelings of panic when I think of life without him. I'll get overly worried if he is the least bit late or I can't reach him on his cell phone and I think he may have had a heart attack or stroke and driven off the road. My mother became a widow at 65 which is the age I am now, so I think that may be why it's on my mind. I want to keep my focus on enjoying our time together not fretting about the future." As Violet finished this last sentence, she placed the talking stick in the middle of the circle. She went to the base of the Mother Tree and blew out two of the candles. Once she sat down, there was silence as if to honor her words and then Ella reached for the talking stick.

"What has come to light for me over the summer is that I need to make more friends my age. I travel during the week with my job and then on the weekends just hang out with my parents and their friends. Part of it is laziness because I know it takes such effort to make new friends and a part of it is staying in my comfort zone and not risking being rejected by someone I may try to befriend. So on that note, I will take into the darkness my fear of rejection and try to figure out where it comes from and why I'm letting it hold me back from opening up to people my age." As Ella shared this, her eyes filled with tears. "I love being with you all when we gather, but sometimes I'm lonely and just want someone to go to the movies with, go shopping with, and talk about what's happening in our lives."

As Maya listened, she found it hard to believe that this gorgeous young woman found it difficult to make friends. She just assumed that if you were beautiful, life was easy and people would naturally be attracted to you. Ella wiped her eyes and put the talking stick back in the center. After blowing out two of the candles, she sat back in her spot and Maya noticed Lilith reaching over to hold her hand. Maya wondered if Lilith had any children as she certainly had a motherly and comforting way about her. Lilith released Ella's hand and took the talking stick from the center of the circle.

She spent some time running her fingers over the carvings, her eyes focused on the face of the Mother Tree. After a few minutes, she spoke. "What has come to light? Well, this summer has been wonderful for my business. The New Bern Farmers' Market was open twice a week and I got quite a following. Many people would arrive early to make sure they could get a loaf of my bread. The farmers' market is closing in mid October and I would like to expand my breadmaking business. I want to supply restaurants and local stores with my bread. I thought my entrepreneurial days were over but I'm feeling a spark of desire to expand. I've already signed a deal with The Chelsea in New Bern to provide ten loaves of my sourdough each Friday and Saturday night."

Maya almost yelled out congratulations but then remembered the talking stick and just smiled at Lilith as the others were doing.

"Now, what I want to take into the dark. That would be Paul, my partner. The last few years have been a little slow in the sex department. With menopause, the adjustment to living down here, and both of us growing older we haven't made the effort and have just gotten out of the habit. So as the nights lengthen I plan to make good use of them." Lilith's eyes twinkled mischievously as her hands massaged the talking stick seductively. Everyone laughed and Maya could feel a flush creeping up her neck to her face. She'd never been around someone talking so openly about sex. She was being exposed to many new things this morning. In fact, she was beginning to feel closer to these women than to any other friends she'd ever had. Of course to reciprocate, she would need to open herself up to them too. She began debating with herself if she should speak and what she should say. Before she could get too deep in conversation with herself, the laughter died down and Hazel reached for the talking stick. She was still smiling from Lilith's antics as she sat back in her chair.

"First, I want to say how lovely it is to be here with you, ladies. At 79, I never take for granted that I'll be back at our next gathering so always feel blessed to be here. Like Violet, I've been spending some time the past week reflecting on my summer and what has come into the light for me. The biggest event this summer was having Maya move into my boathouse. Ya'll know I'd had that renovated a couple of years ago and never actually put it up for rent till this spring. As life usually goes, the perfect person saw that sign and has come into my life and my boathouse. What I realized is how much I had missed the presence of another woman on my property. I grew up living mainly with my mother and grandmother and then when I moved back to Oriental after Bill's death, it was me and my mother. If feels wonderful to have Maya now. Even though we don't see each other every day, her presence makes my heart feel warmer."

Hazel caught Maya's eye and smiled warmly. Maya flushed again, this time at the compliment. It felt good to be appreciated. Even her own mother had never said anything this loving. She would tell Maya and Kate she was proud of them or they'd done something well, but she never remembered her mother just being happy she was there like Hazel was.

There was some silence after Hazel finished as the group waited for her to continue. She looked down at the talking stick in her hands and seemed hesitant to go further. Maya could see Hazel's hands begin to shake. "What I need to take into the dark with me is actually something I've kept in the dark for over 40 years. I want to share it with you all and then finally try to make some peace with it. When I was 39 and married to Bill and Wynn was about twelve, I had a brief affair with another professor at Meredith. He was a history professor, very handsome and smart and he began coming by my office at lunch to talk. Hay was also married, so things began very innocently. If it was a pretty day we'd take our lunches outside

and talk about literature and politics. Soon we were talking more
about our lives and our dreams. Bill was traveling a lot with his work
and Wynn didn't want anything to do with Mom. Hay was the only
one at that time in my life that I felt really "got" me and I found
myself falling in love. We started an affair that lasted six months. It
ended when I found out I was pregnant. I knew it must be Hay's
because Bill and I rarely had sex, maybe only a couple times a year. I
had trouble dealing with my emotions after finding out I was
pregnant. I loved Hay but couldn't imagine how both of us could
extricate ourselves from our marriages to be together. Bill and I had
grown apart but the thought of a divorce and raising a newborn and
an adolescent on my own felt impossible too. Back then people
didn't get divorces as much as they do now. I ended the affair and in
desperation had an abortion. It was the hardest thing I've ever done
and I regret it to this day." Hazel's voice cracked and tears flowed
down her cheeks. Her body seemed to shrink in her chair and her
face was contorted with pain.

Maya's heart ached as she watched Hazel. How brave she was
to share this. She must have felt safe and unconditionally loved to
talk about something like that. Without any directions or discussion
the other women stood, and Maya followed their lead as they
enveloped Hazel in a hug. The group rocked together in a rhythmic
way pouring love out to Hazel. After a few minutes, with wet checks

and red eyes, the women went back to their spots within the circle. Hazel continued to hold the talking stick.

"You all know I love my son but always wanted a daughter. It never happened with Bill and sometimes I think that baby may have been a girl and I lost my chance." Hazel stifled a sob and began to cry again.

"I feel like I just can't forgive myself. Even that day it happened my heart told me it was wrong, but I did it anyway, thinking I was protecting Bill and Wynn." The group remained quiet, giving Hazel time to regain her composure. "Anyway, I want to finally make peace with this part of my life so it's not always in the back corner of my heart stealing a little of the joy from each day." Hazel squeezed the talking stick and laid it gently in the middle of the circle. The group remained silent as Hazel blew out two more of the candles and Maya could feel each woman sending healing thoughts to Hazel, who stared intently at the Mother Tree.

Suddenly, Maya realized it was her turn if she wanted it. She felt the weight of the silence around her. Would she take the stick or just sit quietly and wait for them to realize she wasn't going to participate? How long would they wait? It already felt like five minutes. Maya silently began rehearsing what she might say. She was feeling a pull to say something. After all, the others had shared so easily and deeply. If she was going to be a part of this group she should give it a try.

Maya leaned forward and took the talking stick from the center of the circle. She sat back and felt the eyes of the group on her, but not in a judgmental way. She looked up at the face of the Mother Tree whose calm gaze steadied her. She began with a wavering voice, "I'm so honored to have been asked to be here and be a part of this group. I've never done anything like this before so I hope I do it right."

Maya mentally reflected over the summer again before she continued. "What has come to light for me is that I'm independent enough to establish myself in a new place, without a husband, parents or sister close by to provide support. I've been here since the beginning of August and feel more content then I have in a long time even though I'm mostly alone." Maya paused. That was the easy part. She felt a lump rise in her throat and had to clear it before she could continue. "I think what I need to take in the darkness is my husband's death. He died two years ago in Katrina and I still haven't dealt with it. In fact, his ashes are still with me in the boathouse." Maya felt her heart rate pick up and a bead of sweat formed on her upper lip. She brushed it away. The only way to make this work is to be honest she thought. But was she? Was his death really what she needed to deal with or was it the fact she had stayed in the relationship and let herself be treated so badly?

Maya was aware that the talking stick in her right hand was feeling warm so moved it over to her left. She felt tears well in her eyes and the familiar weight of shame on her shoulders. She lifted her eyes to the Mother Tree and knew this was what she needed to talk about.

Lilith, Hazel, Ella and Violet all waited patiently for her to continue. A couple of tears slid down her cheek. "I've just realized it's not so much Steven's death I need to deal with but the reasons why I stayed with him. I should have been long gone before Katrina ever hit. I'm ashamed I didn't have the strength to leave sooner, that I let myself be treated so badly and that it took his death for me to create a new life." Maya had never said these words out loud before. Not even to her counselor or sister. She watched the women in the circle but did not feel any judgment.

"Like Hazel said earlier, I just want to make peace with this part of my life and move on." Maya sat with the talking stick for a moment. She was emotionally drained but had a sense that sharing her story in this sacred space and being totally accepted by the other women was a good way to begin her healing. Maya blew out two of the votives and placed the talking stick back in the center of the circle as the sun crested at the tops the trees.

Chapter 6

Saturday October 13, 2007

Maya bit into her fish sandwich, her taste buds rewarded with the crunchy fried breading followed by the moist flounder, a worthy reward after her Saturday long run of twelve miles. So far, Toucans was one of her favorite places to eat in Oriental. She sat at her regular table by the window, looking out onto the small marina and town dock. Since it was a beautiful fall Saturday, the marina was crowded. Sailboats cruising the Intracoastal Waterway were tied up beside large fishing boats moored until Sunday afternoon.

"Tell Fred the fin on a bun is extra good today," Maya called across the restaurant to Kayla, her usual waitress. Maya turned her attention back to the golden fried flounder sandwich and French fries. Suddenly she heard that voice.

"Kayla, be a dear and get me a chicken salad plate to go."

Maya watched Kayla trudge off to the kitchen, rolling her eyes to the ceiling.

Bay Witherspoon was able to order people around with ease as if she were doing them a favor by asking. Maya kept her eyes focused on her sandwich and a book she had brought to read, not wanting to give Bay a chance to catch her eye.

Maya and Bay had met briefly at the fitness club. They had little in common except their age and running and Maya didn't feel like engaging in conversation with her. Maya briefly looked up and Bay caught her eye, so now it was too late to pretend she didn't see her.

"Maya Sommers," Bay said striding over to the table leaving a trail of Chanel No. 5 behind her.

Maya groaned inwardly but smiled and said, "Hi, Bay. How've you been? I haven't seen you at the club lately."

Bay swept her hand up to run her perfectly manicured nails through her perfectly colored blond hair. Her charm bracelet jingled as it slid down her arm. "Well, Maya, Holden and I just got back from two weeks in Europe to celebrate our fifteenth anniversary. We went to Paris and Barcelona and had a fabulous time. I'm on my own this weekend because Holden is back in Raleigh to go to his grandson's soccer game. Can I join you for lunch?"

Without waiting for a reply, Bay waved her hand at Kayla, "Bring my chicken salad plate here. I'm going to eat lunch with Maya."

Maya closed her book, turning the cover over, suddenly feeling self conscious to be reading *Heal Your Life* in the middle of a busy marina restaurant now filling with hungry sailors and fishermen. Maya could feel Bay's eye on her lunch and knew what she was going to say before she ever said it.

"Oh, Maya, you're lucky to be able to eat all that fat and grease and not get as big as a barn. I have to stick to the chicken salad plate so I can fit into my bathing suit."

Maya kept her thoughts to herself, but it was obvious looking good in her bathing suit was a top priority for Bay. She was in the gym everyday and the massage therapist they both shared had told Maya that Bay's perky 36C's had been financed by her wealthy husband.

Maya wondered if the other diners noticed the contrast between her and Bay. Maya was in her favorite pair of faded jeans topped by her Jimmy Buffett T-shirt and a worn UVa sweatshirt around her shoulders to throw on if the October breeze picked up. Bay looked as if she had just stepped from the pages of a Talbot's catalog, with beige slacks paired with a beige and white striped sweater set. Good Lord, Maya thought. Why am I worried about what I look like and analyzing outfits like one of those makeover shows?

Bay interrupted her thoughts, "Maya, so tell me more about yourself. I only know you love to run and live in the boathouse on Hazel Underhill's property. What brought you to Oriental?"

Maya stared back at Bay. Her stomach knotted and she could feel the muscles tensing in her upper back. She had shared parts of her story with Travis and the women's circle but was still processing everything and certainly wasn't ready to share the intimate details with Bay.

"My sister and I came here from Raleigh for a girl's getaway and I fell in love with the place. I was ready for a change so decided to move here for a simpler life." Maya held her breath hoping that would satisfy her.

"I've mostly seen you with your lab and a couple times with that good looking kayak guide. Are you married? Is your husband back in Raleigh working?"

Maya took another bite of her sandwich, chewing slowly, her mind frantically searching for the right words. She quickly came up with several options for her response. She could follow the example of some of the northern women, aka Yankees, she had met here and be direct, "Why, Bay, we've only just met. Why is my marital status so important to you?" But that wasn't Maya's style so she moved onto option number two which was to spill the whole story with all her sorrow, conflict and guilt, like she had done in the circle. Most likely she would end up crying and Bay, true to her southern upbringing, would re-tell the story, ending it with "Bless her heart." Maya rejected option number two as well. She looked up from her sandwich and saw Bay staring at her intently, her fork poised to retrieve another scoopful of chicken salad. "Bay, that's a story I don't have time to get into right now. I actually need to get on home to let Doodle Bug, my lab, out."

As Maya spoke Bay took a bite of chicken salad. Before she had a chance to swallow and respond, Maya threw a ten dollar bill on the table and hurried out. Maya slowed her pace after descending the steps from Toucans' outside deck. She glanced back through the window and could see Bay shifting in her chair and looking around nervously. Maya felt a pang of guilt for leaving Bay, who now looked quite uncomfortable at the table all alone.

***

Before she even entered the house, Bay dropped her to-go box of chicken salad in the trashcan sitting beside their garage. She walked around to the front of the house overlooking the marina and entered through the front door. It always made her feel better to come home through the front door if she was having a bad day. As she stepped onto the hardwood floors in the foyer, she took a minute to admire the circular staircase to the second floor and an exquisite chandelier she and Holden purchased on their trip to Italy. She could hardly believe this house was hers and usually it filled her with a sense of satisfaction, but today she was unimpressed.

Holden had gone to Raleigh for the whole weekend to visit his daughter and grandchildren, leaving Bay alone for the first time in their new home. Theirs was one of the first homes built in an exclusive new community outside Oriental. River Dunes had been written up in *Coastal Living Magazine* and rumors were that Oprah was considering building there. The prestige and beauty of her living environment did little to comfort Bay now, at 2:00 p.m., on a Saturday and 28 more hours alone. She was deflated after her efforts to have lunch with Maya ended when Maya stormed off in a huff after an innocuous question about her husband.

What should she do now? Bay thought. She'd had her nails done on Monday, went to New Bern for a cut and color on Thursday and had already worked out this morning. The cleaning woman took care of the house and the yard was maintained by the community, part of their monthly homeowners' dues.

Bay threw off her Kenneth Cole sandals and walked barefoot across the Oriental rug in the middle of the foyer, through the formal living room, and pulled open the screen door to the porch. She flopped onto an oversized chair covered in a peach colored shell chintz and swung her feet on the ottoman. Flipping open her cell phone, she hit the number three to speed dial her mother and then snapped it shut. Ever since she had married Holden, their

relationship was strained. Their lives so different now with Bay, not

working, traveling with Holden and decorating her home and her

mother still working 40 plus hours a week on the factory floor at

Caterpillar in Sanford. Their lives had little in common except for

the fact they both were married to men in their early 60s. Bay sat

back and looked out at the marina full of expensive, empty boats that

were rarely used, closed her eyes and hoped she would feel better after

a nap.

***

Maya was enjoying her Sunday morning coffee on the porch

of her boathouse, her stomach pleasantly full of oatmeal and bananas.

She reflected back to her encounter with Bay yesterday at lunch and

regretted leaving in such a rush. It wasn't like her to be

inconsiderate, but something about Bay and how she asked those

questions about a husband had just set her off. It also brought home

the point that in the past month since the fall equinox, she hadn't

done much to process Steven's death and her feelings about their

relationship. Obviously if she had, she could have dealt with Bay's

question much more magnanimously.

Maya stared out at the water waiting for divine inspiration to

hit. It was an overcast morning which made it hard to define exactly

where the gray clouds ended and the water began. Suddenly a new shade of gray emerged from the water, a shiny head, a fin and then the back. Dolphins had come up the creek. This was only the second time Maya had seen dolphins since living here. The other time was out on the Pamlico Sound off Town Beach. She'd never seen them back up the creek but remembered hearing Dr. Allen at work saying this time of the year the fish were more plentiful back in the creeks.

Maya jumped up, screeching her rocking chair as she pushed it back and woke Doodle Bug from her morning nap. "Stay here, girl. I'll be right back." Doodle Bug obediently stood on the porch and watched Maya run down to her kayak pulled up on the shore. Luckily she'd left it there yesterday afternoon with her paddle and PFD ready to go. She got into the kayak, almost capsizing in her haste to catch the dolphins. Her eyes remained fixed in the direction where she saw the fin.

"Phew," she heard a dolphin exhale as it continued the search for breakfast. She quickly paddled to the middle of the creek and headed south towards the Neuse. Just in front of her, a dolphin crested and exhaled. Her heart raced in excitement at only being twenty feet from this magical animal. It was at least as long as her kayak and weighed hundreds of pounds more but she felt no fear. They seemed so loving and playful with no intention of harm, unless of course you were the speckled trout they had their sights on.

Maya paddled slowly, keeping her kayak somewhat in the middle of at least three dolphins. As she watched them feed and absorbed their presence, she wondered if they had appeared as a sign of some sort. The other day she'd had lunch with Lilith who'd shared that she was always on the lookout for unusual sightings of animals, birds, insects because sometimes they held messages meant for us. Maya had never heard of animal totems but evidently through the years, many cultures felt different animals symbolized different emotions, characteristics or events.

Maya thought that just for fun she'd Google the dolphin totem and see what they symbolize. She stayed with the dolphins for about twenty minutes and then turned back to her boathouse as they continued to head out to deeper water on the Neuse.

As Maya approached Hazel's pier, she saw the familiar Carolina Skiff anchored just off the end. Buster was casting towards the shoreline and his back was towards her. He must be looking for speckled trout and for her. Since their first encounter six weeks ago, Buster seemed to show up on Sunday mornings. He would fish and she would sit at the end of the pier with her coffee. They would talk about the weather, their weeks, politics, whatever came up. Maya had learned that Buster was 62 and mostly retired as a fisherman. He would go out on a fishing boat for a short trip but at his age found it hard to maintain his strength if out for more than a week. Maya also knew that Buster's wife had died of breast cancer eight years ago and he had three adult children busy with their lives in Kinston, North Carolina, Norfolk, Virginia and Atlanta, Georgia. Buster heard her paddle strokes and turned around.

"Good morning there, Maya Lou!" Maya wasn't sure where the Lou came from but with Buster it felt like a term of endearment.

"Morning, Buster. I was just paddling with some dolphins. It was amazing. They were between ten to twenty feet away from my kayak and so close I could hear them exhale out their blowhole. I think they even put me in a better mood," she said remembering back to her contemplation of Bay and her questions.

"Good for you, Maya. I know what you're saying. I've grown up seeing them off and on my whole life and I still treat it as a blessing when they cross my path."

"Buster, do you think seeing them has any special meaning? One of my friends said we should pay attention to unusual sightings of birds, insects and animals because they hold special messages for us."

"Maya, I don't know much about that. Seems to me you should be paying more attention to what your heart is saying then looking for signs from the animals. I mean, what would that mean for me? Been around fish all my life so I guess that should mean I'm cold-blooded if you followed that line of thought."

"You're anything but that," Maya said, thinking of how incredibly comfortable she felt with Buster. "It's just that I was thinking about something that's bothering me and then they showed up. I guess I'd like an answer for my predicament and hoped the dolphins would provide an easy one."

"So, if you can trust an old man, would you share this predicament?"

Maya had talked with Buster before about Steven. He knew he was dead and that she still hadn't disposed of his ashes but that was about it. Maybe a man's opinion would be helpful after all, he had also dealt with the death of a spouse.

"I've told you about my husband's death because of Katrina."

"Yes."

"I left out many of the details. My husband had a drinking problem and maybe was even doing drugs too. He took a lot of cash out of our joint account. The weekend Katrina was predicted to hit, he had already planned to be in New Orleans for a guy's weekend with some friends. He refused to change his plans because of the storm. I even left work early to get home before he left and asked him to stay, but he refused. I can't say that surprised me. Our relationship hadn't been healthy or happy for several years and he had made it clear many times before that his social life and partying took precedence over me."

"Maya, excuse me for interrupting, but did you say you weren't happy for two years and you weren't the most important thing to him?" Maya nodded, her throat tightening and tears welling in her eyes. Buster continued, "Why in the world did you stay? Surely you knew you deserved better?" Maya reached up and brushed away a few tears from her cheeks. "I'm so sorry. I didn't mean to make you cry. I just think so much of you and can't imagine your being in a relationship like that."

"That's OK, Buster. That's the issue I'm trying to work on. Not just that I stayed in such an unhealthy relationship but also because part of me felt a sense of relief at his death. His death gave me an easy way out and the chance to build a new life." It was a little easier sharing this with Buster since she had already told the women in the circle. "Sometimes when I'm having a good day and feeling happy about my new life here, I suddenly feel guilty because I have all this as a result of Steven's death."

"And you were thinking about this, saw the dolphins and hoped they carried some special message?"

"I guess so. Sounds kind of stupid now."

"No. Not really. What would you like the encounter with the dolphins to mean?"

Maya though for a moment and said, "I think I would like it to mean forgiveness and that it's okay to have joy in this moment no matter what circumstances got me here."

"Do you mean forgiveness of Steven?"

"Well, a little, but mostly forgiving myself, both for allowing someone to treat me so poorly and for feeling free because of Steven's death." As Maya spoke these words she realized it was the first time she had verbalized what needed to happen. She needed to forgive herself for what happened in the past and focus on the joy that was available right here in the present. Sounded like something she had read in a book before, but it didn't matter, that was exactly what she needed to do.

Buster smiled. "Sounds like those dolphins did help you find some solutions."

Maya took her paddle and splashed some water up onto his skiff. "Oh, so now are you going to send me a bill for counseling?"

"No. But another glimpse of you in the window should cover my charges," he said with a mischievous twinkle in his eye.

"That tab may go unpaid, but how about I fix us a fresh cup of coffee?"

"Sounds perfect."

Maya slid her kayak up on the bank and unfolded herself from the seat. Doodle Bug stood on the bank, wagging her tail.

Maya rubbed her head and hurried to the boathouse to make some fresh coffee. She felt better. Everything she needed to do to move forward was in her power. Just for fun though, she would Google dolphins and see what significance they held as an animal totem.

***

Maya, following the directions Ella gave her, pulled into the parking lot of The Pub and Grub in New Bern. She immediately saw Ella waving at her as she got out of her car. Maya laughed to herself when she saw Ella who was all decked out in a Chicago Bears jersey with matching earrings. As she got closer she could see Ella even had a Bears headband holding back her blond hair.

"Wow, Ella. You look like the official spokesperson for the Chicago Bears."

Ella smiled as they walked towards the entrance of the sports bar. "I know I go a little overboard, but growing up in the suburbs of Chicago, pulling for the Bears was expected and especially in my family. We love football season and when I was a child, Sunday afternoons were a fun, family time when we would gather around the TV and watch the game. Sometimes, if we were really lucky my Dad would find some cheap tickets and we would actually go to the game."

"That sounds like fun but this is a new experience for me Ella. Growing up in Virginia, we didn't have a professional football team to root for, besides I lived in a college town so our focus was on the ACC and college sports."

"I appreciate you coming with me today Maya, since it's not what you would usually do on a Sunday afternoon. Since I'm trying to connect with new people, and those meet-up groups didn't work, I thought finding some fellow Bear fans might be a good way. I was happy to see that The Pub and Grub was the official Bears place to watch the game."

Maya said, "Sure thing. But since I saw some dolphins this morning, I may have to pull for Miami instead of Chicago this afternoon."

Ella laughed as they walked in, "You may want to reconsider that once you see how passionate the Bears fans are."

Maya's eyes widened as she looked around the bar. Most everyone was dressed similarly to Ella and had their eyes transfixed on the multiple TVs on the walls and in the corners above the bar. Maya knew she would never be here if it hadn't been for Ella inviting her.

Shortly after she and Buster finished their coffee this morning, Ella called and asked if Maya could go with her to watch the game. She said she would feel more comfortable going the first time if she had a buddy. Even thought she didn't care much for football, she did care for Ella and was happy Ella felt comfortable reaching out to her. Maya still felt badly about leaving Bay so abruptly yesterday so was happy for the chance to redeem herself somewhat by helping Ella.

Maya and Ella walked towards the bar, looking for a place to sit. Maya was aware that Ella's beauty was not lost on the men in the bar. As they walked through, she could see men pausing to look at her, even men who appeared to be with other women. Maya wondered if Ella was aware of this attention or if she had gotten used to it. They found two seats at the end of a long table filled with navy and orange pom poms. As soon as they sat down, a man about Ella's age who'd been watching them from the bar, walked over, slid a chair up to Ella and asked if he could buy her a drink. Suddenly Maya felt invisible.

As Ella talked with him, Maya could feel the other women at the table watching and thought she saw a couple roll their eyes at each other and then turn their full attention on their dates. What was there problem? Ella was sweet, kind and unassuming. Why would they react to her like that? And then Maya understood why Ella had trouble making friends with other women.

Ella politely refused the drink offer and the man retreated back to the bar. Ella turned to Maya, "Lord, we can barely get in the door when some weirdo is trying to pick me up. That drives me crazy. I just want to make friends, not hook up with anyone."

Maya smiled to herself, knowing she'd never been driven crazy by men throwing themselves at her. "You sure were adept at getting rid of him though. Now, let's order some potato skins before kick-off."

At half time Maya told Ella she was going to head out since she needed to slowly build up her football watching tolerance. Ella laughed and said she was ready anyway so they gathered their purses and headed for the parking lot.

Maya said, "Sorry I wasn't up for staying the whole game. It's almost 5:30 though and I want to get a few things done at home before the week starts."

"That's OK. I didn't expect we'd stay they whole game anyway. I'm just gonna go over to my parents' house and watch the second half with them."

Maya could tell things hadn't worked out the way Ella had hoped. "I'm sorry you didn't meet anyone today. Maybe if you go back again without me it will be easier."

Ella looked away from Maya and her eyes filled with tears. "I don't know Maya. The women were stand offish and didn't seem to want to know me and the men who did talk to me were just trying to pick me up." Ella wiped away a tear that had slid down her cheek.

Maya just stood there for a second, her heart aching for Ella, understanding more deeply the isolation Ella felt. She stepped forward and gave Ella a hug. As they stepped apart she said, "Well, maybe football people just aren't your type. After all, we're friends and I really can't stand football."

Ella laughed, "Maybe you're right and now I see what a good friend you are since you let it slip how much you dislike football."

"Opps, I did just say that didn't I."

"No worries Maya. It makes me feel good you came all the way to New Bern to support me."

They hugged again and got in their cars. Maya had always thought that being gorgeous was a gift, but as she drove back to Oriental, she realized that perhaps it could be a burden as well.

Chapter 7

Wednesday November 7, 2007   Early Morning

Maya stepped out in the brisk morning air. God, how she loved running this time of year. She felt chilled in her shorts and T-shirt in the 50 degree air but knew she'd warm up quickly. As she and Doodle Bug walked to the end of the driveway, she could see Venus, the morning star, glittering in the east. It was 6:00 a.m. and a little later than usual for her run, but today was Wednesday, her mid week day off from Dr. Allen's office.

She loved only working four days a week and Wednesday was a jewel set in the middle of her work week. She used it mostly for fun and to get a few chores done. Usually she and Travis spent some part of the afternoon together, kayaking if weather permitted or taking a day trip to New Bern, Beaufort, or Bath. Today Travis was taking her to a small winery near Aurora for a private tour. She wasn't sure she would like the wine made from muscadine grapes, but if she was with Travis the trip would be worth it.

Maya and Doodle Bug began a slow jog to warm up and headed south towards town. Doodle Bug was prancing beside her, full of zest for life with the cooler temperatures. Maya picked up the pace and let her mind wander over the past few days. Nothing out of the ordinary, just work and then home. Now the days were shorter, she wasn't able to get out in her kayak after work but less daylight gave her more time for introspection and quiet. She definitely was more tuned into the cycles of nature living here in Oriental.

As she turned right onto Highway 55, Maya turned her focus to forgiveness. Ever since her talk with Buster a few weeks ago, she'd been making a conscious effort to think about how she could forgive herself. She wondered how that worked. Do you think about it long enough that one day you wake up and it's done? Are there some magic words you can say that will suddenly lift the burden off your heart?

The day was getting brighter as she and Doodle Bug closed in on town. Only a couple of cars had passed them so far. They must be heading to work in New Bern. Maya laughed to herself as she passed the Dollar General. This was the first business you come to in town which seemed funny for a town that started as a fishing village. Doodle Bug jerked her arm, pulling the leash taunt as she lunged for a squirrel scampering up a tree.

"Come on, girl. Just a little farther and we'll turn around. There'll be squirrels to chase when we get home."

When Maya turned her attention back to the road ahead, she saw another runner fast approaching. She usually didn't see anyone but since she started later than usual, she may be catching a runner who starts her run at six too. As the distance closed between them, Maya could see a bouncy, blonde ponytail backlit from the early morning glow of sunrise. She knew in an instant it was Bay. She hadn't seen her since the afternoon at Toucans a few weeks ago. Though she felt badly about how she left lunch so abruptly, she really wasn't in the mood for any sing song chit chat with Bay at 6:30 in the morning. Well, too late for that now. They were only twenty yards from each other. Maya, having dressed in the dark wasn't even sure if her shirt matched her shorts, but here came Bay with her pink and black Nike short and top set that matched the pink swoop in her Nike shoes. This woman sure knew how to put together an outfit, Maya thought. Before she could speak, Bay called out, "Maya, is that you? I've never seen you on one of my runs before. I'm glad we bumped into one another."

Bay and Maya were now face to face and had stopped running. Maya couldn't say she was glad to see her so instead said, "Today I started a little later than usual so that must be why our paths crossed."

"How far are you running? Maybe I could run with you for a while?"

"I was about to turn around and head back home if you'd like to go in that direction."

"That would be perfect. I just left the health club about five minutes ago to start my run so could run about twenty minutes or so with you."

Great, Maya thought. My deep morning musings cut short by Barbie. Maya was surprised by her own reaction. What was it about Bay that got under her skin? They both moved to the left side of the road and began heading back up 55 away from town. They were almost the same height and their footfalls fell into unison. Maya was disappointed to see that Bay easily kept her pace. So she could look cute and run at a decent clip.

"Maya, I'm glad to see you. I was worried about you after you left lunch so quickly a few weeks ago. I hope I didn't say something to make you mad."

It was easier talking to Bay sideways, than looking directly at her. "No. It wasn't you. I just wasn't in the mood to answer questions about my life. I shouldn't have left so abruptly and I apologize."

"No need for that. I understand. Believe me, I get enough of my own questions when people see me with Holden." Bay seemed to read Maya's mind and quickly changed the subject. "So, Maya, do you run often?"

"Yes, about five or six days a week and kayak when I can. Of course, you've seen me in the gym where I go as a last resort if the weather is bad. How about you?"

"I run about five days a week too and swim and lift weights at the gym. I've never tried kayaking."

"Do you ever run any races?" Maya asked, wondering if they were in the same age group and if she could beat her.

"No. I mainly run to keep myself sane." This answer surprised Maya who thought running would have everything to do with how she looked.

"Me, too. Running helps clear my head and get things into perspective. I haven't raced for a while, but used to run a couple of marathons a year."

"Wow, that's incredible. You must have been really sane, running that much," Bay said with a smile.

Maya thought back to the training for her last marathon, heading out for long runs just a few hours after Steven had gotten home from the bars. The heaviness of her disappointment with life made the first few miles tough but the load would begin to lighten after five or six miles. By ten miles she was totally in the moment, feeling her body work, smelling the salty air on her route by the Gulf.

By the time she returned home, she felt at peace and that she could tolerate another weekend with Steven and his erratic moods.

"Actually, Bay, it was more like my life was so stressful that it took all that running just to keep myself functioning normally." Oops. She'd opened the door to talk about Steven. She hadn't meant to. It felt like they were talking about running but it had morphed into something more. Bay must have learned her lesson at Toucans and didn't press for more about this.

"Well, isn't it great we have a positive outlet for our angst in life?"

"Yes. I'm always grateful for my runs."

"Hey and this morning I'm grateful for the chance to run with you. Sometimes I get a little lonely and this made a great start to my day."

"Thanks, Bay."

"Maybe we could meet again next Wednesday to run? I could run the second half of your run, like I did today."

They were nearing the left turn to Beards Creek Road where Maya guessed Bay would turn back. She wasn't sure how to answer. Running was her time for solitude but she didn't want to hurt Bay's feelings again. She seemed hungry for friendship. Bay had been much more tolerable then when she had more of an audience. Maya, who'd been trying to pay more attention to synchronicity in her life, thought maybe there was a reason they'd run into each other and perhaps something good might come from running together. "Sure, Bay. That would be nice. Let's plan on the same time as today. OK?"

"No problem. I'm going to turn back to town now but will look forward to seeing you next Wednesday, if we don't bump into each other before then. Have a great day."

Bay turned and began heading back, her blond ponytail swinging in time with her steps, not a hair out of place. Maya stopped a minute to watch her before turning down Beards Creek Rd. Lord, what have I gotten myself into? A regular running date with Bay, Miss Perfect? Maya and Doodle Bug picked up the pace for the last mile and a half home and Maya reluctantly admitted to herself that she did enjoy her time with Bay just a little. As they neared Hazel's driveway, Maya let Doodle Bug off her leash and they both sprinted the last 50 yards, Doodle Bug heading after a squirrel and Maya heading to her first cup of coffee.

Maya walked down the last part of Hazel's driveway, basking in the afterglow of her run, the cool morning air a refreshing contrast to the heat she had generated. It was 7:15 and the sun was just peeking above the trees in the east. She and Doodle Bug began walking down the path to the boathouse when she heard Hazel call her name.

"Maya! Good morning." Maya turned and walked back towards Hazel's back porch where she was sitting in a wicker rocking chair with a steaming mug of coffee.

"Hey, Hazel. You're up early today."

"I have some visitors later this morning and wanted to get an early start. Do you have time for a cup of coffee with me?"

"I'd love to. Let me get out of this sweaty shirt and throw on something warmer and I'll be right back."

Maya smiled to herself as she trotted to the boathouse. Only 7:15 and she'd already talked with two people, and had a date with Travis later this afternoon. Her life was certainly different from the life she had in Mississippi when she would go days without talking to anyone but Doodle Bug and her sister on the phone. She thought about how she refrained from making friends down there. This was partly due to being ashamed of what people would think of her if they found out about her marriage and partly because of her reluctance of getting close to others. The relationships with her parents and Steven disappointed her on a regular basis and she had come to expect the same from others, everyone except Kate, of course. Something had shifted since she left Mississippi though and especially since she'd come to Oriental. She definitely felt herself becoming more open.

As she walked back up the hill to Hazel's in her warm fleece
pullover, Maya thought that some of the change since leaving
Mississippi was because she was depending more on herself than ever
before. She had stopped focusing on what was missing in her life and
was more focused on making choices that made her happy. Maya
looked up and saw Hazel coming out the back door with a second
mug of coffee.

"Here you go, dear. You take it black, right?"

"Yup." Maya responded as she took the mug from Hazel.

Hazel and Maya settled into wicker rocking chairs and slowly
rocked as they gazed out at the water. Hazel's house sat up on a hill
so they looked over the boathouse, out to the creek. From this
vantage point they could almost see where Beards Creek emptied into
the Neuse River. The only sounds were the creaking of the chairs
and the crunch of the leaves as Doodle Bug chased the squirrels that
were busy gathering acorns for their winter store.

They spent several minutes just rocking and watching the
morning unfold. The silence between them was comfortable.
Though unspoken, their relationship had deepened since the fall
equinox women's circle. Maya felt that they had both shared their
shame and sadness and now had a common bond and understanding.

"Maya, we haven't talked about our women's circle recently. I can't tell you how happy I am that you're a part of that group. It has been meaningful to me over the years and you will add so much."

"I'm honored to have been included. I've never been in a group like that so it was a new experience, sharing something so personal with people I've just met. I didn't realize it would be so powerful to talk about the thing that I usually try to avoid. I felt a weight was lifted. You all supported and accepted me in spite of my past choices. Feeling that acceptance has made me less judgmental of myself."

As Maya spoke the words, she realized she had just described what had been so helpful about the equinox ritual. Instead of avoiding thoughts of how Steven treated her and his death, now she was able to work constructively with them as they arose. But, she still struggled with the guilt of surviving the hurricane and being happier than she was when Steven was alive.

"Beautifully said, Maya. I'm glad you're learning this lesson now and not waiting till 79 like I did. I actually knew in the back of my mind that sharing my story would help, but I was too paralyzed by my emotions to do anything. I tried to figure out what helped me finally open up and I think it has to do with you."

"How in the world could I have helped? I've only known you a few months."

Doodle Bug had come up on the porch and lay down beside

Maya pleasantly exhausted from her morning activity. Maya

scratched Doodle Bug's tummy as she looked to Hazel for a response.

Hazel looked directly into Maya's eyes. "It was the night of

the tropical storm. You were the first person to be in that part of my

house in over ten years. I usually only let people in my office area off

the driveway but when I saw you and Doodle Bug at this door, I

knew you needed to be with someone and I could help. I have

missed feeling needed since my mother died and was happy you

reached out to me, but was also filled with shame at what you saw in

my house. I was so appreciative that you didn't mention all the

clutter and mess. I wasn't ready to talk about it then but once you

saw it, it made me look at things from your perspective and helped

push me to take action to make things different."

Maya leaned back in the wicker chair and drained the last of

the coffee from her mug and thought about what Hazel had just said.

"So Hazel, how does all the clutter relate to what you shared in the

women's circle?"

"I'm not really sure, but I do know buying all that stuff makes

me feel better when I'm overwhelmed by my sense of loss."

Maya thought of her conversation with Bay this morning

about how she used running to manage her emotions. "Don't feel

badly, Hazel. I use running the same way. I know it's healthy to run, but I don't think it was a coincidence that I ran five marathons the year before Steven died."

Hazel smiled, "At least you ended up with strong legs and a small waist. All I ended up with was a bunch of stuff I'll never use."

Maya laughed, "I also got tendonitis in my knee and too many blisters to count. Hazel, what time are your guests coming? It's almost eight now."

"Not till nine, but I better head to my office to prepare."

On cue, Maya's stomach grumbled. "Yeah. I guess I better get my oatmeal cooking. I want to get some laundry done too before Travis and I head out this afternoon."

"So," Hazel said, "how are things going with Travis? You two seem to be spending a lot of time together. He's such a good kid. I knew his grandparents very well."

Maya laughed. "I'll tell you if you promise not to go spreading rumors. We're having a great time together. We usually see each other a couple times of week, on Wednesdays for kayaking or a day trip and then Saturday night for dinner at one of our houses. It feels good to be with someone who's so kind and makes me feel special." Maya purposely left out the strong physical attraction she had for Travis and their steamy make-out sessions on creek banks, their couches, or in the back seat of Travis' jeep. Hazel didn't need those visuals to attach to her handyman and family friend, but Maya did wonder about this aspect of their relationship. Travis had never asked to spend the night or even tried to progress their physical relationship beyond passionate kisses and embraces. Was there something about her that made him hesitate? Did he feel strange making love to her when she still had her husband's ashes in her house? Maya knew this was something better discussed with Lilith then Hazel.

"I have to say it makes me happy to see you two together. I think the world of both of you. Guess that love potion I put in the tuna casserole must have worked!"

Maya laughed, remembering how Hazel had seemed to orchestrate that evening so she and Travis would end up having dinner together.

As they stood to go, Hazel took both her arms and wrapped them around Maya's waist and lower back, pulling her in for a hug. Maya initially tensed, still unused to this much affection from anyone but her sister. She then relaxed, returned the hug and was amazed at how strong Hazel was for someone her age.

Chapter 8

Wednesday November 7, 2007 After Maya and Bay's Run

Bay parked her BMW in the empty space of their three car garage. The convertible Miata was on one side and Holden's black Cadillac Escalade on the other. She was surprised to see his car. It was only 8:00, but he had an 8:47 tee time over at Minnesott golf club and should have left at least 30 minutes ago. Well, maybe his daughter Laura called with another crisis that needed Holden's input. Bay was happy they remained close after his divorce from his first wife, but sometimes she just wished Laura could call her mother or have her husband help instead of always calling Holden. She would call with car issues, financial questions and sometimes just to vent about her husband, Luke. Holden would drop everything to spend 45 minutes on the phone with her calming her down or doling out advice. Well, it was his choice and if he was late for his golf game, that was his own doing, Bay thought, as she took off her running shoes in the mud room just off the garage.

Bay threw the morning paper she'd retrieved from the driveway on the kitchen table and headed to the coffee pot to get that started, so her coffee would be ready after her shower. As she headed up the winding staircase to their master bedroom, she reflected on her run with Maya. She hoped she hadn't said anything to offend Maya and looked forward to becoming better friends.

She was always self conscious about her behavior because she never felt like she fit anywhere. Growing up in Sanford in the trailer park with her mom, she'd always felt she deserved a better life than the one she had and never connected with the other kids who lived there. They used to call her stuck up and said she was acting above her raising. Once she graduated from paralegal school and began work at Holden's law firm, she didn't feel like she fit in there either. All the attorneys and other paralegals seemed to come from more affluent backgrounds, had traveled more, knew about the theater and music and knew which fork to use at an elegant meal. She never told anyone about her upbringing and by paying close attention was able to mimic their behavior and sort of fit in, but it took a lot of energy and effort. She had to analyze everything she said so as to use correct grammar and not to reveal the truth about her past. She never outright lied to her colleagues, but her omissions and insinuations nonetheless painted an untrue picture of who she was.

At one point she felt her masquerade had paid off when Holden became interested in her. It felt like a dream come true to have a dependable and financially secure man in her life. Now she was paying the price for this security. Holden had fallen in love with her when she was pretending to be someone she wasn't and now she ran the risk of losing him if she stopped being the beautiful and malleable Bay. She did love Holden but lately had begun to feel a growing resentment that their marriage was keeping her from having a more meaningful life.

Bay turned right at the top of the staircase and headed to the master bedroom at the end of the hall. As she neared the bedroom door, she could hear some moaning. Her heart lurched when she heard this and she sprinted the last few yards to their bedroom. The moaning had stopped and she couldn't see Holden. The king-size bed was still unmade but the draperies had been opened. Through the bathroom door she saw a wet towel left in a heap on the floor. So he had taken a shower but where was he? As if to answer her question, she heard another moan and ran through the bathroom to his walk-in closet.

The first thing she saw were his bare feet sticking out the closet doorway. Bay bounded into the closet and saw Holden lying face up on the floor. He had on his khaki golf pants and his chest was bare. His face was ashen but he seemed to be breathing fine and his brown eyes were definitely looking at her so he was alive. For an instant, as she bent to get close, she noticed how old he looked. Of course she'd aged in the fifteen years they'd been together but Holden was now sixty-five. At this moment, he looked too old to be her husband. That thought quickly passed as she took his hand. His eyes had followed her since she got to the closet but he hadn't said a word and his hand felt heavy and lifeless.

"Holden, what in the world happened? Are your hurt? How did you fall?" Holden didn't say anything and just looked at her. She noticed some drool in the corner of his mouth and then it hit her. He's had a stroke. "Holden, hang on, sweetheart. I think you've had a stroke. I'm going to run downstairs, get my phone and call 911." As she ran back down the staircase, she cursed herself leaving her cell phone in the kitchen. She felt she was wasting precious time. Finally, she reached her phone on the counter by the coffee pot. She called 911, gave them the basic information and their address, opened the front door widely and ran back upstairs to sit with Holden.

"Holden, they're on the way. We'll get you to the hospital and I'm sure you'll be doing better soon." Bay's breath came in short and quick bursts, partly from the dash up the steps and partly from her rising emotions. Holden had not moved an inch since she'd left, his right hand still lying in the exact position she'd left it when she ran to the phone. She picked his hand up again and moved some shoes out of the way so she could sit more comfortably in the closet. She waited for the sound of the ambulance. It would probably take at least ten minutes to get down to them. Bay looked at her watch, 8:27 a.m. Just two hours ago she'd been heading out for a run on a gorgeous morning and now she had no clue what the future held. She prayed Holden would be okay and only have to stay in the hospital a couple days. She heard the siren approaching and let out a sigh of relief. A few seconds later there were voices and footsteps in the main hallway.

Bay stood and ran to the bedroom door. "We're up here. Hurry, he's in the walk-in closet."

The paramedics ran past Bay with bags and a stretcher. She stood at the closet door watching them checking Holden's pulse and blood pressure and giving him oxygen through a mask over his nose and mouth. "I think you were right, Mrs. Witherspoon. Your husband most likely has had a stroke. We're going to transport him immediately to Craven Community Hospital in New Bern. We're calling in right now so they'll be ready for him."

Bay took a couple of steps back from the closet to absorb this news and caught her reflection in the bathroom mirror. Good Lord, she couldn't go to the hospital looking like this. She'd have to take a quick shower before she met them there.

***

Bay put on her lipstick and walked to her jewelry box. She grabbed her pearl necklace and bracelet that would go well with the black cashmere turtleneck sweater. She didn't want to be too flashy to go to the hospital. As she studied her reflection in the mirror, she felt tears well in her eyes. What was she thinking? Her husband was probably arriving right now at the hospital and here she was worrying about how she looked. Well, Holden always wanted her to look her best and dress well, so he'd be pleased she hadn't just hopped in the car in a baseball cap and sweaty running clothes. She should be there in 40 minutes and could do whatever they needed her to do then. Probably sign lots of paperwork.

She wasn't sure what to expect as she had little experience with hospitals and certainly had never been in one as a patient. The last time she was in a hospital was when her father died twenty years ago. She didn't remember much about that except her conflicting emotions of sadness and anger towards a man who loved her but could never put his family ahead of his addiction. He died from complications of cirrhosis of the liver.

Bay paid careful attention to her driving and didn't let the speedometer get above 60 mph. She knew it would be easy to drive carelessly. She thought about what else she needed to do. Before getting in the shower, she had called Holden's daughter, Laura, who was leaving work immediately and would probably be in New Bern in a couple of hours. Laura would call her brother in Tennessee. Holden's golf partners. They were probably wondering what happened. Luckily she had thought to bring his cell phone and when she took a look at it she saw a voicemail left by Fred. She hit re-dial and gave an update to his friends who were now on the eleventh hole. As she would have expected, they were upset and wanting to help in any way. Bay, not wanting to deal with more people than she had to right now, told them to wait a few days to visit and she would update Fred tomorrow so he could let the others know.

New Bern, 12 miles. Well, she was almost there, but part of her felt like driving right past New Bern and continuing until she was somewhere she'd never been before, maybe Austin, Texas or Albuquerque, New Mexico. Bay wasn't sure what to expect at the hospital but knew from hearing about her mother's friends who had had strokes that sometimes it can take a year to get back to normal. She was only 41 and spending a year helping her husband recuperate from a stroke was not something she had planned on. Of course, her mother had warned her of this when she married Holden, but somehow when she was 26 and he was 50, it seemed so unlikely. She didn't feel like calling her mother now to hear "I told you so" and decided to wait until she had more information. Maybe it was just a

small stroke, like a TIA and he would be back to himself in a couple
days.

Bay was trying to be positive but deep down felt scared. With
no movement that she could see and only moans for communication,
his stroke could be severe. What if there is permanent damage?
What if in a year or so he isn't able to be fully independent? What if
he requires her constant care the rest of his life?

Bay's hands gripped the steering wheel tightly as she turned
into the parking lot by the ER at Craven Community Hospital.
Once again, her eyes filled with tears as she realized that the whole
way here she had been focusing on how this would affect her and not
on what Holden was going through. What was wrong with her? She
took a deep breath and sat in her car now parked between a blue
minivan and a red Ford F150 pickup. She watched the people
walking into the emergency room entrance and wondered what
brought them here on a Wednesday morning, a child's high fever, a
broken bone from falling down the steps after tripping over a
bathrobe that was too long or maybe food poisoning. Would their
lives be changed forever or would they need just a few weeks of
recovery?

The sun was warm as it shone through the windows onto her
black sweater. Bay felt a bead of sweat trickle down between her
shoulder blades. Suddenly that bead of sweat was all she could focus

on and she felt it slide down to her lower back and then below the waistband of her camel hair pants and then she couldn't feel it anymore as it absorbed into the top of her Victoria's Secret thong. When she could no longer focus on that bead of sweat, Bay realized her hands were still gripping the steering wheel and she hadn't moved in the past five minutes.

Bay knew the façade of her marriage was held up by the roles she and Holden had played. She knew going inside the hospital to deal with what lay ahead would not conform to those roles. So what did that mean for their marriage and for her? Could she take on the role of dutiful wife and be by Holden's side to support him in recovery? Would she, for a second time, play a role and sacrifice herself to keep the approval of others and who were these others? Right now, she was feeling very alone.

Finally she opened the car door and began the walk to the ER entrance. It was only 100 feet but the weight of her emotions made it feel much longer. Despite the brisk autumn air, another bead of sweat began the descent down her back.

***

"OK, Mrs. Witherspoon, just one more signature right here." The nurse smiled as Bay signed Bay Witherspoon to the last form. The nurse neatened the pile and put them in a folder. She reached for a plastic, oblong box hanging from Holden's bed.

"Here's Mr. Witherspoon's call bell so if you need anything, just push the red button and either the aide or I will be right in. Are you staying with him tonight?"

Bay looked back at her with a blank stare. Stay the night, she thought. That hadn't crossed her mind. She didn't have her things. Where would she sleep? Quickly regaining her composure, Bay asked, "Would you like for me to stay tonight? Would that be the best for Holden?"

"Ma'am, you can do whatever you'd like but most wives like to stay and especially in your husband's case. Since he can't talk, it will be hard for us to know what he needs."

Wow, just 30 minutes ago this nurse thought she was his daughter and now it's 'ma'am' and she's copping a bit of an attitude. Hopefully Holden won't have to be here long. "Of course I'll stay. Please have them send up a rollaway bed later this afternoon."

Bay caught the nurse rolling her eyes as she turned to walk out the door. "That's a nice thought, but there isn't room in here for another bed, so we'll just bring you some extra bed linens so you can make up the recliner later."

Bay watched her leave and then turned back to Holden. The ER doctors confirmed that he had had a stroke and now they had been admitted to the neurological floor. He would have more evaluations tomorrow for physical, occupational and speech therapy, but right now, Holden was sound asleep. His right arm had slid off the bed and was dangling in mid air. She reached over and put his arm on the bed and under the covers so they would hold it in place. She stared at him and remembered the self-confident 50 year old man with his sexy brown eyes and salt and pepper hair. When he walked into a room, he commanded attention and usually took charge of the situation at hand. His money, good looks, and power was what had attracted her to him, but right now all that was gone, except, of course, his money. She wiped some drool from the corner of his mouth and as she sat back in her chair, she noticed a growing circle of moisture on the blanket covering him. She jumped up and grabbed the call bell from the bed, making certain she didn't touch the wet bed clothes. She frantically pressed the red call button and then went out in the hall to wait for the nurse.

Bay stood awkwardly in the hall, feeling very much alone. She wasn't ready to talk with her mother yet. Holden's daughter would be here any minute, but she and Bay had never been close so she wouldn't be supportive. In fact, Laura openly disliked Bay, so they were civil to one another for Holden's sake but rarely exchanged more than pleasantries. Bay understood that some of Laura's contempt came from the fact she was actually a year younger than Laura.

Bay turned to walk to the nurse's station to see what was

taking them so long, and saw Laura racing down the hall towards her.

Her eyes were swollen from crying and she was visibly distraught.

Bay raised her hand to wave her over to the right room. Not yet

ready to face a conversation with Laura, Bay flipped open her cell

phone to make a call, although she wasn't sure who exactly she

needed to talk to. She looked down at her phone and the last

number called was Maya's. Bay had her phone with her on her run

and before they separated, Bay had called Maya's phone so they

would both have each other's numbers. Laura was just steps away

and Bay hit call, not sure exactly what she was planning to say to

Maya but thankful for a few more minutes to gather herself before

she went back to Holden's room. As the phone rang, Laura and the

nurse's aide went in to clean up Holden and Bay turned to walk

down to the atrium near the elevator.

***

Maya was sorting some laundry to take up to Hazel's. The

boathouse had everything she needed except a washer and dryer.

After Maya's first visit to Hazel's in the storm, Hazel had given Maya

a key to her office door and shown her the laundry room that was just

the next room over, right across from the kitchen.

Maya hadn't noticed it that night in the storm but wondered

if Hazel had cleaned out the laundry room for her because it was relatively clutter free. That is to say, there was a walkway into the room and nothing on top of the washer and dryer but there was still a row of boxes lining the wall and stacked to Maya's shoulder height. She figured that was as high as Hazel was able to stack them. She tried not to be nosy or disrespectful since Hazel was sharing her laundry room, but each time she used it she would peek into one of the boxes on the top just to see what could be in there. Mostly she saw children's toys and clothes but sometimes came across tools and household items.

Maya put the lights at the bottom of her laundry basket, the darks on the top, grabbed some spring breeze scented Tide and was heading to the door when her cell phone rang. It was on the kitchen counter, so she dropped her load on the couch and ran back to the kitchen. Before she answered she saw on the caller ID that it was Bay.

Good Lord! Why was she calling already? They had just seen each other this morning. She stared at the caller ID as the phone rang two more times. What could she want? I enjoyed our run, Maya thought, but certainly don't want to get together again today. She thought about letting it go to voicemail but didn't want to be mean. Maya grabbed the phone and flipped it open. "Hello," she said, totally unsure of what may follow.

"Maya? It's Bay." Her voice sounded tense.

"Hi, Bay. I recognized your number. Are you okay? I can barely hear you."

"Maya, I need to speak with you for just a minute." Oh, there she goes, Maya thought, just expecting me to have time to talk.

"OK, but I just have a minute and then need to finish doing things around the house."

"Oh, that can wait a minute. Please just hear me out." With that, Bay's voice cracked and Maya could tell she was crying and trying to hold back the sobs. Maybe it was a mistake, giving Bay her number. She's probably one of those needy people who will be calling daily with a new drama.

Maya tried not to let her frustration seep into her voice and asked, "Bay, what is it? How can I help you?" Maya heard Bay take a deep breath at the other end of the phone.

"I know we aren't good friends yet, but I didn't know who else to call." Bay started to cry again but then continued, "When I got home from our run, I saw Holden's car still in the garage even though he should have already left for his golfing date. Well, long story short, I found him upstairs and he had had a stroke. I'm at the hospital now and he's been admitted to the neurological floor. Maya, he can't walk or speak right now and I don't know what to do."

***

Maya snapped her cell phone shut and sat down on the couch beside her laundry basket. She leaned back and closed her eyes, mindlessly squeezing one of her running socks that was on the top of the basket. What had just happened? Bay, whom she'd thought she had nothing in common with, just this morning had shown her a deeper side than the self-conscious woman with the flawless fashion sense, and now had just called her in tears about her husband. Bay had rambled on about the details of the morning's events and then just kept throwing out questions neither could answer. Will he get better? How long is the recovery? Will I have to provide help to him the rest of his life? Maya could only listen and try to reassure Bay that time would make things clearer. Bay was clearly thrown totally off balance by this turn of events. Hadn't she suspected she'd end up being a caregiver by marrying someone so much older, Maya wondered? Though she had certainly never been in Bay's position, Maya could identify with being fearful of the unknown. She had felt this way when she found out Steven was dead. It took a while for the shock to wear off and in that stage there are just questions with no answers.

Maya felt for Bay and hoped their conversation had helped her feel a little less alone. Maya felt a sense of satisfaction at being there for someone else. Since Steven's death, she'd been turning to others for support, her sister, brother-in-law, Hazel, Lilith and Travis and it felt good to be able to support someone else. Maybe, since she had the energy to help another, she was closer to being healed herself. She hoped this was the case and made a mental note to call Bay and check on her tomorrow. Maya stood, grabbed her laundry basket and headed up to Hazel's to finish her Wednesday chores so she'd be ready by three o'clock when Travis was picking her up.

***

Maya watched the scenery go by the jeep window and sang along with the Jimmy Buffet CD Travis was playing when she felt his hand on her left knee. She looked over at him, smiled and then covered his hand with her own. Their silence was comfortable as they drove down Hwy 306 towards Bennett Vineyards. Maya was learning to practice mindfulness when it came to her relationship with Travis and tried her best not to analyze it to death. She actually found she had much more fun enjoying her time with him and not trying to predict what the future would hold.

"Travis, have you ever gone to this vineyard before?"

"No. This is my first time. I've driven by the sign for it hundreds of times and always say I should stop but never had. It should be interesting. I've heard the owner is very entertaining and has lots of good stories. I'm keeping low expectations about the wine, though. I've never had muscadine wine but am thinking it may be too sweet for my liking. Have you ever visited a winery before?"

"Not in a long time. There are quite a few near Charlottesville, where I grew up and sometimes on Sunday afternoons my father would drag me and Kate on a tour. Guess that was his idea of family time but it wasn't so fun for ten and twelve year old girls." Maya left out how scared she and Kate had been as they rode home with their father after these visits. After the tasting, he would buy a bottle of wine to have with their picnic lunch. She and Kate had been old enough to know he was drunk and shouldn't be driving but were too scared to say anything to him. They just tightened their seat belts, held hands in the back seat and silently prayed to get home safely.

"So you haven't been since you were old enough to actually taste the wine?" Travis asked.

"No. This will be my first official experience."

Travis moved his hand from her knee to downshift as he turned right, following the purple grape sign directing them to the vineyard. He immediately slowed to make the left turn into the vineyard. Maya noticed a Pentecostal Holiness church on the right. She wondered what they thought about having a vineyard right across the street. She smiled thinking of the wine tasters drinking spirits across from the church goers who were catching the spirit.

Travis drove slowly to navigate his jeep around the pot holes in the dirt road leading to the tasting room. Fields full of grape

arbors lined the road. Maya had read on the website that the grapes
had been harvested about a month ago so all that remained were the
leaves, now yellowing and dropping to the ground. They pulled into
a worn dirt parking area in front of an old tobacco barn that had been
converted into the tasting room.

Before getting out Travis turned to Maya and said, "I'm not
sure how this wine will taste, but if I'm gonna drink bad wine, I'm
glad it's with you."

He leaned over and gave Maya a kiss on her lips, lingering for
just a moment. Suddenly Maya forgot about wine and was totally
focused on the warm, moist sensation of his lips. She reached her
right hand behind his head to bring him closer and then parted her
lips for a deep, long kiss that Travis readily returned.

Maya stepped out of the jeep, now feeling embarrassed at
how she initiated such a passionate kiss. This relationship was so
different from her marriage. She was relaxed around Travis and more
able to be herself without the constant worry that the wrong
comment would send him in a rage.

Travis and Maya spent about 45 minutes in the tasting room
and tried seven different wines. The owner told them the history of
the vineyard and about everything that went into making them.
Maya was interested to learn that the land the vineyard was on had
been granted to the owner's family by King Charles II in the 1800s.

Who would have imagined she'd find a bit of history so far out in the country?

Maya was pleasantly surprised that she liked almost all of the wines. She discovered that the complex taste came from using the techniques that the early colonists had used to make wine from the muscadine. She and Travis settled on a muscadine red wine called Blackbeard's Choice and the owner gave them two complimentary wine glasses to go with it. They went outside and sat at the wicker table that overlooked one of the fields filled with grape arbors. Travis began opening the wine as Maya ran back to the jeep.

"Where are you going?"

"Just a minute. I need something."

"Don't tell me," Travis said, "the woman who's never without food brought something to go with our wine."

Maya had grabbed her purse and when she got back to the table pulled out a small Tupperware container.

"Yes. I did bring something." Maya pried off the Tupperware lid to reveal a wedge of Brie cheese and some water crackers. "So, aren't you the lucky one to be with me and never go hungry."

Maya sat down beside Travis and he raised his glass. "I am the lucky one," he said and clinked his glass with hers.

Maya smiled and settled back in to the wicker chair. She was glad she had on her fleece jacket because it was almost 4:30 and the November sun was getting low. She and Travis sipped their wine and enjoyed the moment, again, in comfortable silence. Maya's mind began churning and she wondered if she should tell him more about Steven and their marriage. They seemed to be in the habit of not talking too much about their pasts and staying focused on what they were doing in the moment. This kept things easy and fun and Maya didn't want to complicate things now, so she kept quiet and spread some Brie on a cracker.

Travis pointed, "Look over there. Never seen that at a vineyard before."

Maya looked to where Travis was pointing and saw four small goats grazing under the arbors. As if they knew they had an audience, they began bleating.

"Glad I didn't bring goat cheese," Maya said. "They may have been offended."

She and Travis laughed and continued to enjoy their wine as the late afternoon sun dipped below the tree line.

Chapter 9

Sunday November 25, 2007

Doodle Bug watched the clothes tossed across the room, a sky blue argyle sweater on the floor under the creekside window, a plaid skirt across the bed, a black and white checkered scarf bending the prayer lily in the corner into unintended prayer. Maya stood in front of her small closet in her bra and panties, hands on her hips and eyebrows knitted together in thought. This is why I never go to church, she thought. I don't have the right clothes to blend in with the congregation and why the heck dress for church anyway. God doesn't care. Maya ran a hand through her hair still wet from the shower.

On Wednesday, before she headed out to her sister's for Thanksgiving, Hazel had stopped by and invited her to go to church today. Hazel had said others would have family members there for the holiday weekend and she'd be so happy if Maya would come as her guest. Because of her growing fondness for Hazel she accepted the invitation. She also had hoped for the chance to ask Hazel about how she reconciled the sacred circle with her Baptist beliefs. Now she was kicking herself and wishing she could have stayed at her sister's all weekend, but Kate, Worth and Rob had headed to the mountains on Saturday to spend time with Rob's brother. Maya glanced over at her clock and saw she had fifteen minutes till she met Hazel in the driveway. Nothing helps a decision like a deadline and Maya pulled a gray wrap dress off the hanger.

Fifteen minutes later, she was standing beside Hazel's ten-year-old Cadillac De Ville feeling mildly pleased with her church-going look. The gray wrap dress created an open V neckline which she accented with the pearl necklace her mother had given her last Christmas, a gift Maya had never used till today. She added the matching pearl earrings which were visible because her shoulder length hair was pulled back into a low ponytail. She felt very refined and cultured compared to her usual dress of jeans and a T-shirt.

Hazel hurried down her back steps, keys in hand, heading towards Maya. Hazel was usually the one in pearls but today her turtleneck sweater was adorned with a beautiful antique pin shaped like a sunburst, an amber stone set in the middle.

"Maya, you look gorgeous," Hazel said as she grabbed Maya's right hand and gave it a squeeze. "Let's get going so we're not late."

Maya slid into the leather seat and fastened her seatbelt as Hazel pealed out of the driveway, snapping Maya's head back onto the headrest. For an instant, she wondered at the safety of riding with a 79-year-old woman, but then relaxed knowing there would be almost no traffic on the five mile ride into town.

Maya gazed out the car window. The trees by the road were only half dressed, piles of red, yellow and gold at their feet. As the scenery passed, she tried to remember the last time she had been to church. She hadn't been since Katrina and certainly had never gone while married to Steven.

In an instant, Maya's brain accessed her last time even near a church. She was in the churchyard of the Bay St. Louis Baptist Church. It was only five days after Katrina and Maya was walking Doodle Bug around the neighborhood for the second time that day, just to pass the time and to try to let the reality of the destruction sink in. She had walked past the church yard many times in the last few days and never paid much attention, but today she heard a woman sobbing. It had a primal quality that Maya had never heard before, having grown up in a stoic family. Maya had turned towards the sound and walked to the site where the small wooden church once stood. She stepped over tree branches, half of a white plastic chair, shredded pieces of clothing and a water logged cookbook opened to a strawberry shortcake recipe. The randomness of the rubble left by Katrina was heart breaking. Nothing she saw strewn in

the church yard had come from the church but had been dragged
there by the storm surge and wind.

The seat belt began to feel tight across her chest and her
breath quickened. She wanted to stop the memory, but it played on.

Maya walked up the white marble steps, the only remaining
piece of the structure and then stopped cold. There was one other
thing. Directly in front of Maya was a wooden cross, fully intact and
standing solidly in what would have been the front of the church. It
must have fallen from the wall and somehow didn't get swept away in
the storm. Prostrate at the bottom of the cross was the sobbing
woman. She was on her knees, her hands clenched around the
bottom of the cross. She rocked side to side in rhythm with her sobs.
Every so often she would cry out, "Why, God?"

At this point Maya hadn't known what to do. Her sister was
one of the only people she had ever comforted in the past and she
didn't believe she could offer much to this woman. Despite her
doubts, Maya walked to the front of the church, knelt beside the
woman and wrapped one arm around her waist. The woman was
thin, her blond stringy hair pulled back into a ponytail and like Maya
she wore dirty shorts, an old T-shirt and smelled of sweat, mildew
and despair. Feeling Maya's touch she stopped her rocking, turned
and grabbed Maya in a tight hug. Maya tensed initially, not used to
this level of intimacy, especially with a stranger. She slowly relaxed,

returned the hug and felt the hot tears of this woman on her neck. She wondered what they must have looked like. Two dirty women kneeling in a hug before a cross in an otherwise destroyed church. The woman's sobs began to slow and Maya could hear her catch her breath. The woman leaned back and took Maya's hands.

"Thank you!"

Maya didn't know what to say. Her mouth felt dry and her throat tight. All she could choke out was, "You're welcome."

The woman released Maya's hands and now sat in the rubble beside the cross. "I lost my seventeen-year-old son in Katrina."

"My God," Maya said. "Have you listed him with the Red Cross missing persons yet?" She asked, remembering her own wait in that line to report Steven missing.

The woman's eyes moistened and tears fell again. She looked over Maya's shoulder towards the Gulf as she spoke. "My husband, my son, David, and I decided to wait out Katrina. We'd been through hurricanes before and didn't see the need to spend the money on gas and hotel rooms when most likely nothing would happen. Early Monday morning though, the water began rising in our house. The water kept coming and coming and we had nowhere else to go except out the second floor window and up to the roof. We were there several hours in the wind and rain praying for help. None came. Suddenly a wave came out of no where and swept across the roof. I held my breath and clung to a piece of antenna that was beside the chimney. When the wave receded, my husband was huddled on the other side of the chimney but my son was gone."

Hazel applied the brakes jerking Maya's neck again as she turned left into the parking lot across from the Oriental Baptist Church. Maya realized her breath was coming in short quick bursts and her right hand was clenched into a fist. Hazel was focused on parking and didn't notice Maya closing her eyes and consciously taking deep breaths. Her heart ached again for that woman. She never saw her after that and always wondered if she had ever found her son. Now that Maya was an Aunt and felt an overpowering love for her nephew, she couldn't imagine the pain of losing your child. Why would God let something like that happen?

Maya realized Hazel had been chatting away and she hadn't heard a word. She released her seatbelt and got out of the car, saying, "Uh huh," to cover for her lack of attention.

As Hazel and Maya walked across Broad Street to the church, Hazel said, "This church was built in 1902 and my grandparents were among the founding members. My family has always come here but since Mom died, I've mainly come alone. It's been a while since anyone has come to church with me." They walked into the church and Hazel grabbed Maya's hand and gave it a squeeze.

Maya took a program from the usher in the vestibule. She looked down the aisle and saw a wooden cross at the front of the church. Her eyes filled with tears as she followed Hazel to the middle of the fourth row and sat down. Hazel examined the prayer list in the program and Maya wiped her eyes and took in her surroundings. The church was small, holding maybe a maximum of a hundred or so in the plain wooden benches lined neatly in the small sanctuary. There was a stained glass window behind the pulpit that glowed purple, red and green. The church smelled of mothballs and dust and every so often Maya got a whiff of the intense sweetness from the calla lilies in this week's flower arrangement.

The choir began filing in and following Hazel's lead Maya rose and took a hymn book. She turned to "How Great Thou Art" and pretended to sing as she looked around the congregation. She recognized a few faces from the fitness center and coffee shop. Everyone looked clean, shining and peaceful as they sang, their faces turned upward. The hymn ended and Maya turned her attention to the front of the church where the minister stood ready to give the call to worship.

As Maya looked up at the minister, there was something familiar about the way he held himself under the robe. He turned his head from the choir and looked straight out at the congregation.

Maya's face immediately flushed. Her hands began to shake. The minister was Travis!

Travis, whose touch sent electricity through her. Travis, whom she'd spent so much time with, kayaking the creeks around Oriental, taking day trips to local attractions and romantic dinners at their homes. Travis, who she thought was a kayak guide and handyman, was actually a Baptist minister. Why hadn't he mentioned this? Why couldn't he tell her? Maya's mind raced, searching for clues she may have missed. This would explain why they never did things on Sundays, why they took day trips out of town and after that lunch at Toucans, never ate out in Oriental, just at one of their homes. Was he ashamed of their relationship? Was this why he never tried to have sex with her? How could she be with someone whose faith was so strong when hers was something on the back shelf, only to be brought out in emergencies?

Maya thought again of the woman by the cross asking "Why, God?" She wondered if Travis would be able to answer this.

Travis proceeded to give a beautiful sermon on gratitude for God's blessings, very appropriate for the Sunday after Thanksgiving. If he saw Maya in the congregation, he didn't acknowledge it in any way. Maya was focused on him more than his words. She was waiting for him to catch her eye, which he never did. She never even noticed a blush creeping up his neck. He must have been oblivious to her. Meanwhile, she could feel the sweat dripping from her arm pits down to a pool in the crevice of her elbows. She just hoped none of this sweat soaked through her dress. Maya could feel Hazel's eyes on her off and on throughout the service. Poor Hazel must have thought she knew Travis was the minister and was unprepared for Maya's reaction. But Hazel could have told her, too! Maybe she figured Maya already knew.

Maya shifted in the pew, uncomfortable with her rising emotion. She felt angry at Travis for not sharing this part of his life with her, angry at him for having a strong relationship with a god that she had never understood and finally, angry with God for the seemingly pointless death and destruction Katrina caused when supposedly God was loving and answered prayers. Being in church brought this anger to the surface and from its intensity Maya realized this was the first time she had allowed herself to feel angry after Katrina. Sadness and guilt came easily but anger was an emotion she was not comfortable with. It felt powerful and she wasn't quite sure what to do with this power.

The service ended with Travis giving the benediction. Hazel and Maya stood, waiting their turn to file out of the pews, out the door and right past Travis who was shaking hands with his parishioners at the front door of the church. Hazel looked back at her and must have read her mind. She took Maya's hand. "Come on

dear. Let's head to the front of the church and through that door on
the left. It will take us out a side door to the street so we don't have
to talk with Travis right now."

"Oh, Hazel. Thank you so much. I just can't deal with
talking to him right now."

"I know. I would feel the same way." Hazel led Maya out
the side door into the bright November sun. The cool, dry air helped
placate Maya's anger somewhat. Her mind was blank as she let Hazel
lead her back to the car.

They drove in silence for a few minutes before Hazel spoke.
"I'm so sorry this happened. I just assumed you knew Travis was my
minister since you two have spent so much time together. Somehow
I thought you'd already heard him preach. Anyway, I apologize that
I was the one that caused this to happen. I know you must be
confused and frankly I am too. I know Travis well, have known him
for years, since I was friends with his grandmother, and this type of
behavior doesn't seem like him. My experience is that he's always
upfront and honest. Surely he must have known how hurt you
would be when you found this out. This is too small of a town for it
to have stayed a secret for much longer."

"There's no need for you to apologize. You had no way of
knowing that Travis hadn't told me he was a minister; it had to come

out sooner or later. Thank goodness you were with me when it happened."

As Hazel turned into her driveway, she asked, "What are you going to do? Do you think this will change your relationship with Travis?"

"I don't know. Those are the same questions running through my mind. I'm just so angry right now I don't want to make any decisions until I take more time to think it through. I know being in a church should make you feel inspired and close to God but it has never worked that way for me and today is just another example. I feel further away from God than ever. Hazel, one day I want to understand your relationship with God and how you blend the church with your time at the Mother Tree. It feels so different to me. I felt so much more peace and acceptance when I was in the circle compared to today. Right now, though, I just need some time alone. I'll stop in to see you tomorrow."

As soon as Hazel parked her car in the driveway, Maya jumped out and began running towards the boathouse. Her shoes weren't cooperating so she took them off and held them in her right hand. In her stocking feet, she ran across the leaves, stepping on pecans that were hidden beneath them. At times she felt like she was sliding on ice. Her heart began to slow her pace. It was heavy and full and she felt with each step it was pulling her closer to the ground.

When she opened her door, there was Doodle Bug with wagging tail and big brown eyes full of love. As she stepped over her threshold, Maya slumped to the floor, burying her head in Doodle Bug's golden fur. The tears and sobs came uncontrollably. Doodle Bug stood quietly, absorbing the sorrow and then releasing it through her paws back to the earth. That was one of her roles with Maya, to provide a conduit for her emotions. When she was done crying, Maya lay back on the floor by the front door. She watched the mid-day sun coming through the window, making shadows on the wall and ceiling. Doodle Bug lay beside her, her head on her paws, watching Maya.

Why am I crying, she thought. Was all that emotion for Travis, or for the woman whose son died in Katrina, or for how Steven treated me? She didn't know, but it felt good to have gotten it out. Maya slowly pulled herself up to a sitting position with her back against the front door. She must look a sight. Her pantyhose were torn and a few stray leaves had attached themselves to her feet. Her mascara must be all down her face and her wrap dress was almost unwrapped. She sighed, looked at Doodle Bug and said, "Come on, girl. I know it's our day off, but the only way to shake this mood is to go for a run."

***

Maya stepped into comfy sweat pants and pulled a fleece sweater over her wet head. As she pulled her hair back into a

ponytail, she realized that she was famished. Since she'd gotten home
from church she'd had her little breakdown, ran four miles with
Doodle Bug and then showered. It was almost two and her stomach
was protesting the absence of food. Maya walked towards the kitchen
and sent up a prayer of thanks for the restorative powers of running.
She was still upset and hurt by Travis, but at least she felt more
centered and able to think things through rationally. Before she went
any further though, she needed a peanut butter and banana sandwich.
Doodle Bug sat behind Maya and watched intently as she made the
sandwich, hopeful a small crumb would fall or better yet, Maya
would step away from the counter and she could grab one of the
slices of bread. Suddenly Doodle Bug growled. That's strange, Maya
thought. I don't hear anything. Maya leaned over to look out the
small window over her kitchen sink. Doodle Bug had heard
something and it was Travis' jeep pulling in the driveway. Doodle
Bug recognized his door slam and ran to the door, her tail wagging in
anticipation of Travis' arrival.

Maya left the half-made sandwich on the counter and
watched Travis make his way down to her boathouse. He was still
dressed in the suit he must have had on under his robe. Each step he
took appeared to take effort and it was in contrast to the usual
bounce he had when he walked. Maya looked over to Doodle Bug at
the door. Her hind end and tail were wagging furiously. Once again,

Maya wished she could live life more like Doodle Bug, always in the moment, accepting people for exactly who they were.

Maya walked over to the door and opened it just as Travis stepped onto the front porch. Their eyes locked for a second and before Travis could say anything, Maya stepped back from the door and motioned him in. "Well, Travis, this is the first time you've been here on a Sunday. Are you here for personal reasons or do you stop by to see all your church visitors?" Maya surprised herself with her sarcasm and it must have had the same effect on Travis because he stopped short in her hallway.

"Maya, you have every right to be angry, but please hear my explanation before you go any further." His voiced was strained and tight with emotion. He sat down on her coach without an invitation.

Maya tensed immediately. No one had used that tone of voice with her since the day Steven left for New Orleans. Standing at the end of the couch by the creek windows, Maya looked directly at Travis at the other end of the couch. "Travis, I'm tired of people always explaining themselves to me after I've been hurt. Why couldn't you be truthful with me? The fact that you are a minister is way less of an obstacle to me then the fact that you lied. I thought our relationship was going to be different but this incessant lying has shown me otherwise." As Maya was talking, she could feel the emotion rising from her chest into her throat and now the tears streamed down her face. A sob escaped her lips despite her best efforts.

Maya backed into the corner of the coach and Steven leaned down over her, his left hand gripping the armrest. "What is your problem, you fucking control freak. I took out $500 to get new brakes for my car. Do you not have anything better to do with your time then constantly check the balance on our checking account? I bring home more money than you so why do you think you have the right to tell me how to spend it!"

Doodle Bug jumped on the coach beside her, watching Steven intently. Maya took a moment to weigh her words. She didn't want to escalate his rage and knew that pointing out he'd used the new brakes for the car excuse, just a couple of months ago when $300 was unexpectedly gone from their account, would do just that.

Steven was so close that the weight of his anger pressed into her chest, making it difficult to speak. Finally she said, "But, Steven, that's all the money we have until I get paid next week. We need groceries and I need gas for my car."

"That's your freakin' problem. If you didn't spend so much on that dog and all your running stuff maybe we'd have some money for groceries. I'm done with this conversation. I'm sick of your accusations. Sometimes I wonder why I'm still married to you. I'm going out for a beer. Don't wait up for me."

The front door slammed and Doodle Bug leaned her warm body into Maya. Maya stared straight ahead at the cover of the *Time* magazine on the coffee table, her humiliation so deep she couldn't even look Doodle Bug in the eyes.

Travis sat stiffly at the end of the couch, waiting for Maya to compose herself. For a few minutes Maya could do nothing but cry and berate herself for having her second breakdown of the day. Luckily Travis hadn't said anything yet and was watching her warily. She'd wondered if he noticed her reference to his lying as incessant. Of course, to her knowledge this was the only time he'd lied but she felt as if she had automatically begun to replay the many fights she and Steven had had about this. Maya grabbed a Kleenex from the box on the end table and blew her nose.

"Travis, I'm so sorry. I am angry with you, but I shouldn't have gotten so upset. I want to hear what you have to say." Maya sat back on the couch and took several deep breaths and focused on how her body felt right now, sitting on this couch in her boathouse in Oriental. She knew she had to stay focused so she could be fully present to Travis and not overlay his story with her past experiences with Steven.

Travis, sitting at the edge of the couch was nervously pulling at his pants as if to align the seam exactly down the center of his knee. He too was breathing deeply and now turned his attention away from his pants and back to Maya. "Maya, this is very difficult for me to put words to. I really didn't figure it out until my drive over here. Somehow for the past few months, I've just blocked out my role as a minister when I was with you. I just enjoyed being in the moment with you, talking about our families, nature, kayaking. Since Sarah and I divorced, I haven't met anyone I was attracted to until you, putting my focus on divinity school and then finding a job. I enjoyed the feelings I had when we were together. My work with the church is very meaningful and important to me and I knew I was keeping our relationship from growing closer by not sharing this with you. I was having trouble blending the man who's dating you to the man who stands in front of the congregation to supposedly deliver a message inspired by God. The way I ended up dealing with this, was not thinking about being a minister when I was with you. I was just Travis."

As Maya listened, she could feel her body relax and she scooted around on the couch so her back was against the arm rest and she was facing Travis directly. Travis continued, "The conundrum for me was I hadn't come to terms with the relationship between my sexuality and my new role as a 'man of God.' When we were together, I focused on just being Travis, not Reverend Starling and that made our time together much simpler for me. The other factor was the fact that several of the older women in the church have taken it upon themselves to find me a good Baptist wife. At least once a month, I'm invited over for Sunday lunch and some single daughter, cousin or friend of the family in my age range just happens to be in town. I guess part of me felt self-conscious about dating someone who was not affiliated with the church and worried how my congregation would react to that. I know you deserved the truth Maya, but I hope this helps you understand just a little. As you can see, I've got quite a bit of personal growth to do as I adjust to my new life as a single Baptist minister."

Maya sat quietly and let this sink in. "Travis, what you said makes sense to me and it certainly doesn't seem that you were lying to me in a malicious way, but what about Hazel, she could have slipped and told me many times or how about the times we were out together at The Bean or Toucans? What if we had seen someone from your church?"

"Well, all I can say is that none of this was premeditated. I didn't plot and plan how to deceive you. It just sort of happened. I really didn't think about how to avoid the truth coming out, but I have to say, I never expected to see you out in the congregation. It took everything I had to keep myself composed and not run right out there to explain myself to you."

They both sat silently on the couch. It wasn't an uncomfortable silence, just quiet. "So, Maya, where do we go from here? I don't want to lose you but from my actions, I don't think it's fair to you to be in a relationship right now. What do you think?"

Maya remembered the weight of his body pressing her deeper into the sandy creek bank, his lips moist and hungry for her. She thought about the easy way they cooked dinner together and shared the events of their day. She would miss that but also knew her relationship with Travis was a distraction that kept her from dealing with her past.

"I guess you're right. I think my reaction to you this afternoon shows I'm not ready for a serious relationship either. I haven't shared a lot with you about my marriage, but lying was something Steven did on a regular basis and this situation with you made me realize I still haven't made peace with that relationship."

Travis stood, "Sounds like we need to slow things down for both of us. Let's take some time and maybe meet for a coffee at The Bean at the end of the week after we've both had time to think about this."

"Sounds good to me," Maya said as she stood and walked with Travis to the door. They stood there awkwardly for a moment. The past few times they'd been together, their time had ended with a kiss that sometimes left Maya ready for a cold shower, but this afternoon had certainly changed that. They stood looking at one another. Maybe a brief hug would have worked but neither moved and finally Travis turned and said, "Take care, Maya, I'll call you in a few days." Maya closed the door behind him feeling better than she had immediately after church, but still unsettled. She went to the kitchen, grabbed her uneaten sandwich, her water bottle and a jacket and headed out the front door with Doodle Bug at her heels.

She sat on Hazel's dock in the sun and ate her sandwich as Doodle Bug frolicked in the chilly water. She felt the warm sun across her face. A gentle breeze released a few more leaves from their branches and they fluttered into the water. Maya stared at them floating in the water, moving with the current towards the middle of the creek, collecting water on their surface, and then sinking to the bottom. She slowly and deliberately ate her sandwich as she contemplated the leaves. Her mind was clear and so focused on watching the leaves nothing else entered her thoughts. At this very moment, Maya felt a sense of peace, despite the emotional day. As she finished the last of her sandwich, Maya smiled, realizing she had just practiced mindfulness. Totally being in this moment and quieting all the thoughts that usually ran through her head. It felt like a nice break after all she'd been through that day. She impressed herself. Maybe all those self-help books were starting to pay off.

Doodle Bug came out on the dock and lay down next to Maya to dry off in the sun. Maya took off her jacket, rolled it in a ball and used it as a pillow so she could lie down and rest her head on it. The sky was a brilliant blue with a few puffy white clouds floating across her line of vision. She became as mesmerized watching the clouds as she had been with the leaves. Suddenly the word forgiveness popped into her head. Yes, she would need to forgive Travis, which wouldn't be too hard after his explanation, but this word certainly seemed to be something that kept coming up. Today was a reminder that she hadn't totally dealt with her feelings about Steven. Nor had she yet forgiven herself for staying in that relationship. Maya continued to watch the clouds with one hand on Doodle Bug's back.

She knew. It was time. She was ready to move on with her life and not continue to put energy into dealing with emotions related to her relationship with Steven. Two years was long enough. Maya felt ready but not sure what to do next. Actually she didn't feel like doing anything this afternoon except lie right here on the dock. Later she would call her sister and perhaps Lilith too. Lilith usually had good advice to share. Maya closed her eyes and in a few minutes, both she and Doodle Bug were sleeping comfortably in the warm sun and cool breeze.

***

Maya had made it through the day without obsessing about Travis too much. Thankfully it had been busy. Maybe everyone was knotted up after spending too much time with family they didn't get along with. Maya may have been in need of an adjustment too if her parents had come to her sister's for Thanksgiving, but they had stayed in Charlottesville to be at the bookstore for Black Friday. Last year she, Kate and Rob drove up to Charlottesville for Thanksgiving, but it hadn't gone well. They arrived around ten on Wednesday night because of traffic, and their father was well into his second bottle of wine and their mother already in bed. The best part of Thanksgiving Day had been Maya's long run along routes she'd run in college, but the rest of the day was tense. On the way up, she and Kate had told themselves to keep their expectations low and to try to accept their parents for who they were, but somewhere inside both of them there were ten year old girls still wanting to be the center of their parents' lives. When Maya had returned from her run, Kate was sitting on a rocker on their front porch, drinking coffee from an UVa mug.

"How was your run?"

"It was great. It was fun running through the grounds and passing by all the dorms and apartments I'd lived in. I ran past the football stadium, down Rugby Road to see all the frat houses and did somewhat of a sprint up Observation Hill. Is everyone up? It's almost nine and time for the Macy's Day Parade."

"Well, Dad must be sleeping off his second bottle of Merlot and Mom did get up to make some coffee. She talked to me for a minute and then went into her study to read the paper."

As Kate finished her sentence, Maya could see her sister's eyes
filling with tears. "Kate, did you get to tell her you were pregnant?"

"No." Kate said as the tears spilled from her eyes. "Mom
seemed preoccupied and distant. I felt like it took all her effort to ask
me how school was going, so it didn't feel like the right time. I
wonder if she's taking her medications. There was a heaviness about
her this morning that makes me think she's back in a depression."

Maya sat on the step just below Kate and reached up to hold
her sister's hand. They sat in silence for a while and watched Doodle
Bug chase squirrels in their parents' yard. Neither spoke, but both
knew they were feeling the disappointment that came when they were
let down by their parents. Thank God they had each other.

Maya locked the door of Dr. Allen's office and headed to her
car. She reminded herself to drive over to Lilith's for dinner. She
had called Lilith last night to talk about what had happened with
Travis. Lilith had been in the midst of trying a new recipe for
pumpkin bread and couldn't talk long so instead, invited Maya over
for dinner since her husband would be at the Rotary Club's weekly
meeting tonight. Maya was looking forward to spending time with
Lilith, who felt like an older sister to her. They occasionally talked
on the phone and had met for coffee several times since the fall
equinox but this was her first visit to Lilith's home. Lilith lived in

Merritt, which was about halfway between Dr. Allen's office in Alliance and Oriental.

Maya followed Lilith's directions and soon was driving down a dirt road that paralleled Raccoon Creek. The road was dark already, even at 5:30. Maya turned on her headlights and could see she was driving through a thickly wooded forest. She had to go slowly to protect her Saturn form the pot holes and she kept a wary eye on the woods as it looked like Freddie Kruger could jump out at any moment. Finally, Maya saw the glow of lights ahead and could make out a small square cabin with smoke billowing from the chimney. The simple porch had flower boxes on the railings and two rocking chairs on either side of the front door. There were pansies planted in the flower beds on either side of the steps and a pot of mums at the top of the steps. Maya smiled as she got out of her car, appreciating all the touches Lilith had added to make her cabin so inviting. The smell of fresh bread made Maya hurry to the front door.

Before Maya could knock, the front door flew open and Lilith was silhouetted in the door frame. "Come in here, you wild woman. I'm so glad you're here." Lilith enveloped Maya in a hug and Maya hugged her back, with less hesitation than in the past. Thankfully, she was getting more used to being hugged.

"My God, Lilith! It smells incredible in here. What are you cooking?" Maya asked as she walked towards the stove, sniffing the air.

"Peasant bread and homemade vegetable soup. If you're like me, you ate plenty over the Thanksgiving holiday so I thought this would hit the spot without filling us up."

Maya lifted the lid on the soup pot and the smell of rosemary, garlic, potatoes and onions filled her nose. What a treat to have someone making her dinner, she thought.

"The bread will be ready soon and then needs a few minutes to cool so let's go sit by the fire while we wait. Can I get you a glass of wine? I have a bottle of Cabernet opened if you like red."

"That sounds perfect. Thank you so much." As Maya sank into the oversized chair by the fireplace, she looked around the modest cabin. It reminded her of the house Laura Ingles lived in on The Little House on the Prairie. The kitchen and living room were pretty much one in the same, with the kitchen and small dining room table at one end of the couch; the chair she was in and a coffee table made from the stump of a large tree sat at the end closest to the front door. There was a closed door between the fireplace and the stove that Maya imagined went into the master bedroom. When she walked in, she had noticed a loft over the kitchen but couldn't tell what was in there, perhaps a study for Lilith or Paul, her husband.

The furniture was shabby chic and had that stressed look without looking old. What really struck Maya were the beautiful pieces of art. There was a Native American dream catcher on the wall by the front door, some sort of goddess stature beside the fireplace and a beautiful painting of a woman and a wolf standing by a mountain stream over the mantle of the fireplace.

"Here you go," Lilith said, handing Maya a goblet of red wine and then settling herself into the couch with her own glass.

"Lilith, your home is beautiful. It feels so cozy, yet elegant at the same time with all the beautiful art work." Maya thought of how she had decorated her cottage, which now felt so plebian compared to Lilith's home. Well, Lilith was fifteen years older than her and had some time to collect things. Maya reminded herself that she had only had a few years on her own before she met Steven and then just the past few months. With time, she too could collect treasures from her different life experiences.

"Oh, thank you. Over the years I've just picked up things that caught my eye and have ended up with pieces that are meaningful to me. Luckily, Paul appreciates art with a Native American and feminine theme so had no problem with my doing most of the decorating. His passion is music so he's in charge of our auditory pleasures. In fact, the loft upstairs has all his records, CDs and an old stereo system. Well, enough about me. I want to hear your story, so tell me the scoop on Travis. How are you doing with all that?" Lilith took a sip of wine and looked directly at Maya, waiting for her to speak.

Maya looked back into Lilith's blue eyes and was suddenly overwhelmed with gratitude for this woman who was cooking her dinner and sitting there waiting to hear about something going on in her life. Like the hugs, she was beginning to feel more comfortable with accepting support. She took a deep breath and began her story.

First, Maya filled Lilith in on how her relationship had been progressing with Travis and then gave her all the details about seeing him yesterday at church, then his visit afterward. She was honest about her reaction to Travis and how that situation made her feel like she did when she and Steven were arguing. Lilith listened intently, only speaking when she asked probing questions about Maya's feelings.

"So that's the story, Lilith. Thanks for listening. Hearing it out loud has helped to confirm my thoughts about our relationship."

"And?" Lilith asked.

"I don't think Travis or I are ready for a serious relationship. He needs to come to terms with his new role as a minister and I need to figure out how to finally put closure on my relationship with Steven."

The timer on the stove went off and Lilith jumped up to take the bread out of the oven and stir the soup. "Hold that thought. Can you help me set the table and then we can finish this conversation."

"Sure," Maya said as she stood and walked into the kitchen. She took in a deep breath. "Lilith, that bread smells wonderful. I can't wait to slather a piece with some butter."

"Well, quit your talking and get the table set," Lilith said playfully as she handed Maya some napkins and silverware. Lilith ladled the soup into beautiful pottery bowls the color of mud and trees and then sliced the steaming bread and put it on a matching plate. She and Maya sat down at the dining room table, the sumptuous meal before them. Following Lilith's lead, Maya lowered her eyes and took a moment of silence to fully appreciate the simple feast before her. She picked up a piece of the warm peasant bread and used her knife to retrieve some of the real butter Lilith must have let soften for several hours. Maya slowly spread the butter across the hunk of bread, watched it melt and salivated at the expectation of what was to come.

"Ah hem, Maya. It looks like you and that bread need a room of your own, so go ahead and eat it already," Lilith said, her eyes sparkling.

Maya laughed. "Can you tell I'm starving and bread is one thing I adore, especially when someone has made it just for me." Maya took a bite and closed her eyes to put all her focus on the taste.

"Well, while your mouth is full, I have something to say. You know I always say what is on my mind so here I go. You said earlier that you needed to put closure on your relationship with Steven. Well, darling, I do believe keeping his urn of ashes with you for two years is not helping with that. You have got to do something with them. They are just a big fat symbol of the past. You've got to come to terms with the fact that your husband has been dead for two years and that it's time to move on! You said in the circle that you were ashamed you couldn't leave your relationship with Steven but now it seems you can't leave his ashes either."

Maya had never thought of it like that. She appreciated Lilith's frankness and hearing it so bluntly felt like a call to action. Maya lifted her eyes from the soup and met Lilith's eyes staring at her across the table. She held Lilith's gaze as she swallowed a spoonful of soup. Lilith had not eaten yet and kept her eyes on Maya. "So, did I scare you into silence? What are your thoughts?"

"You do have a way with words, Lilith. I've known since the equinox that I need to get rid of his ashes. I think I mentioned back in September that I realized forgiveness was one of the main things I needed to focus on. So, any suggestions? How will I know I've done the work I need to? How will I know for sure I've dealt with my

'issues'?" Maya used both hands to put quotes around the word

issues and then took another bite out of her hunk of bread, waiting

for some guidance from Lilith.

"I can only share how I know I've dealt with 'issues,'" Lilith

used the same air quotes "and you can use that guidance but the most

important factor is that you pay attention to your intuition and it will

always lead you where you need to go."

Lilith spent the rest of dinner sharing her story of dealing

with the infidelity of her first husband whom she married in her

twenties and then divorced at 32. Maya listened intently, grateful for

the opportunity to learn from this wise woman who had more life

experience than she. Again, this felt so new and precious to Maya

whose mother never talked about her struggles and never once

provided Maya with guidance on dealing with the aftermath of

Katrina and Steven's death. She couldn't even provide much comfort

and her only gesture to Maya had been to give her a copy of Elizabeth

Kubler Ross's book, *Death and Dying*.

After coffee and some leftover pecan pie from Lilith's

Thanksgiving dinner, Maya looked at her watch. "Wow! It's getting

close to eight. I'd better get home to feed Doodle Bug. Hazel was

stopping by this afternoon to let her run and play outside for a while,

but I know she's hungry." Maya and Lilith stood and took the dishes to the kitchen sink. "Thank you so much, Lilith. This has been a wonderful evening and exactly what I needed. I just don't know how I can return the favor." Maya's voice caught in her throat and her eyes filled. Lilith was much wiser than she, how could she ever repay her?

"You don't need to return the favor. This is not a business transaction. It's a friendship and you just being you is all I need." Maya hugged Lilith tightly realizing some of her healing had just taken place.

Maya drove home with a sense of urgency because she knew Doodle Bug was waiting for her. She pulled in her parking spot in Hazel's driveway and trotted down the hill to her boathouse. Luckily, she'd remembered to leave the front porch light on or else it would have been pitch black. As she got closer to the front door, she noticed something on her door. It looked like a note taped there. She pulled it down and opened it. "Maya," it began. "I let Doodle Bug out to run and potty at 4:30 and we were having so much fun that I took her back with me for a treat. Come to my office door when you get home," signed Hazel. Maya smiled as she imagined Doodle Bug and 79-year-old Hazel playing in the yard. Most likely she was throwing sticks for her. It made her happy that Hazel was fond of Doodle Bug and that she could bring happiness to Hazel as well. Maya stuffed the note into her pocket and walked back up the hill to Hazel's.

Hazel opened the door to her office before she had a chance to knock. Before they could even greet one another, Doodle Bug bounded out the door to do a happy dance all around Maya. Maya rubbed Doodle Bug's head. "Hey, girl. Did you and Miss Hazel have fun? Did ya? Did ya, girl?" Doodle Bug kept doing her happy dance.

"Maya, we did have fun. I hope you don't mind that I brought Doodle Bug up here, but I just found her to be such good company." As Hazel finished her sentence, she began coughing. It went on for a while and Maya could hear a rattle deep in Hazel's chest.

"Hazel, are you okay? Here sit down. I'll get you some water." Hazel shook her head no but did sit down in one of her office chairs and finally caught her breath. Doodle Bug went to sit right beside Hazel and looked up at her with concerned eyes before licking her hand resting on the arm of her chair. Hazel rubbed Doodle Bug's head, "I'm fine, Maya. Just choked on my own saliva. How was your dinner with Lilith? Are you feeling better about the situation with Travis?"

Maya made a mental note to probe Hazel about her cough at a later date. "It was a wonderful dinner. The combination of Lilith's food and good advice was great medicine. In fact, I almost feel thankful for the situation with Travis because it made it clear I still have work to do before the solstice gathering. Lilith has given me the jump start I needed."

"Yes, Lilith can deliver a harsh truth with kind words, can't she?" Hazel said.

Maya sat down across from Hazel in the chair she sat in the night she was here in the tropical storm. She looked at Hazel's desk. It was closed this time but she did notice a file cabinet beside it that was slightly ajar and bursting with papers. Maya knew it was nosy, but she was dying to know exactly what it was that Hazel did in this office. She couldn't make out any of the titles on the file folders, and when Hazel caught her gaze, she reached over, pushed down the files that were sticking out and closed the drawer. Maya was embarrassed Hazel had caught her trying to see her files but didn't have the courage to just ask Hazel what the visitors, the office and the files were all about.

"So, how are you? How is your time 'in the dark' going? Are you feeling better about what you talked about in the circle, Hazel?"

Hazel looked over at Maya and her eyes shined with the tears that seemed to come so easily lately. "You know, I think I'm making some progress. I believe the biggest healing came when I shared my story in the group and it was received with love and acceptance. Like we've talked about, I'm not sure exactly when I'll know I'm done with the work, but I definitely feel better."

"It's funny you say that, because I said almost the exact same thing to Lilith tonight and her response was to pay attention to my intuition and it will lead me to where I need to go."

Hazel was nodding as Maya spoke. "That Lilith, she is wise beyond her 55 years. She has much to teach me who's twenty four years her senior."

"Lilith is going to help me come up with some sort of ritual to do at our solstice celebration. My goal is to spread Steven's ashes, but I want to make it more meaningful then just dumping out some ashes. Do you know what you're going to do?"

"No. Not yet. Part of our tradition is that each woman does something at the solstice celebration to symbolize what she has sat with in the dark. Usually I just talk or maybe bring something to lie at the base of the Mother Tree, but this time I want to do something more significant. I'll follow Lilith's advice and pay attention to my intuition and see what I come up with, which reminds me of a photo I need to find again."

Maya looked at her watch and stood to go. "Getting close to my bedtime, Hazel. I better head back to the boathouse. Thanks so much for watching Doodle Bug this afternoon."

"No problem, Maya. I enjoyed it. Maybe Doodle Bug can come here on the days she doesn't go to work with you?"

"As long as it isn't an inconvenience for you. I know Doodle Bug would love it and it would make me feel better that she wasn't left alone."

Hazel stood, and in her bare feet, Maya was again struck at her small frame. She gave Maya a tight hug and said, "OK. Mondays and Fridays, Doodle Bug and I will hang out together."

"Sounds great, Hazel. Have a good night." As Maya walked down to her boathouse, she decided she would call Travis tomorrow and hopefully they could have coffee on Wednesday, her day off.

***

Maya parked in front of The Bean and looked at her watch. 8:50 a.m. Ten minutes until she was meeting Travis. Since Sunday, Maya felt better about her relationship with Travis and the fact that he hadn't been totally truthful with her, but she still felt a little nervous. How would he react to her? Would he be cold and withdrawn as Steven often was after a fight or would he be open to discussing things? Based on her impression of him, Maya felt sure the latter would be true but this didn't stop a wave of butterflies from going through her stomach. It was 8:55 and Maya got out of her car and walked over to The Bean. As she entered, she was surprised to see Travis already there since she hadn't noticed his jeep outside. He

smiled and waved her over to his table. He had already bought her a
cup of coffee. "Medium half caf, black. Isn't that what you usually
get?" Travis asked as she sat down in the chair across from him.

"Perfect. Thanks, Travis."

"Well, this is awkward, Maya, so let's start talking and figure
things out. I've done a lot of thinking since I saw you Sunday
afternoon and again apologize for not being truthful with you. As I
said, I wasn't even being truthful with myself, denying the conflicted
feelings I was having. I've realized that right now I need to focus my
attention on my relationship with God and my church since I'm just
at the beginning of my work as a minister. I hate to give up time
with you though and hope we can still be friends."

Maya smiled as Travis finished and said, "We're thinking
along the same lines. I respect your decision to focus on being a
minister. That must be challenging since it's a 24/7 kind of job that
takes all of you. When I leave my office, I just leave work there but
can't imagine the pressure of having to be on the job most of the
time. It must be especially hard in a small town when you could run
into someone from your congregation any time. Part of me wishes
you had figured this out before we met and we had kept our
relationship purely as friends and could have skipped the emotional
turmoil of Sunday. I also realize that I was a willing participant and
should have been aware that I wasn't ready for a relationship either.

Maybe that's why we attracted one another. Two people who weren't ready for a real relationship."

Travis laughed. "Well, speak for yourself but those great legs may have had something to do with it too!"

Maya blushed, "Travis, I thought we were keeping this as just friends?"

"We are, but I want to stay truthful with you and that's the truth. Friends can admire each other can't they?" Travis said with a twinkle in his eye.

Maya smiled as she felt the tension disappear and their comfortable easy way of being together return. She felt a pang in her heart though, knowing the hand holding, snuggling on her couch and passionate kisses were over. She liked that intimacy but how intimate had it truly been since they both were holding back from the other. Maya wondered if perhaps her body and heart were in different places right now, her body ready for some intense intimacy, but her heart was still mending.

"So, Travis, where does this leave us? How exactly do we continue as friends?"

"I'm not sure. Usually when a dating relationship ends, that's it and I don't see the woman any more, but this feels different. I still would like to spend some time together."

"I got some good advice recently to follow my intuition and it will lead me down the right path. How about we call the other when we want to talk or do something together? No set rules. We'll just see how it unfolds."

"I can live with that.   I have to say I must be maturing as we speak because this is the most dignified breakup I've ever had."

"I think that shows our emotions with each other weren't too deep to start with." Maya began laughing at herself.

"What's so funny?"

"I just heard myself talking and wonder if I've been watching too much Dr. Phil?"

"Well maybe you have Dr. Maya, but I think you're exactly right" It was good to hear Travis' laugh again.

Chapter 10

Saturday December 8, 2007

Bay stared out the door of Holden's room and watched some of the secretaries and aides putting together an artificial Christmas tree. They were playing Christmas music over the intercom system and even singing along with some of the songs. Several of the long time residents pulled their wheelchairs up to watch the tree taking shape, some moving their heads in time with the music and others staring off into space.

What a crock, Bay thought. It's nice they're trying to make it festive, but only about half the people here even know it's Christmas time. The other half, probably don't care in light of what they are dealing with. Bay was in the second group of people. The last few weeks blurred together. Holden was moved from the neurological floor to an inpatient rehab unit after only a couple of days. Here he received intense therapy for three hours a day. He was holding himself up better in the wheelchair, could answer yes/no questions some of the time but still needed two people to transfer him from his wheelchair to the bed or toilet. Even though he'd made small gains, it wasn't enough for Medicare to continue paying so they told her he must transfer to a skilled nursing facility, aka, nursing home. Bay had balked initially, not wanting him in such a depressing place. She even said she would pay out of pocket for him to stay in the more intensive rehab, but it wasn't allowed—her two options were either home or the nursing home. She wasn't ready to be a full time caregiver yet so opted for Craven Rehab and Nursing Center in New Bern where he would have twenty four-hour care and therapy five days a week. His Medicare and other insurance would cover three months and surely by then he would be well enough to come home without much assistance.

Bay and Laura had had words over this plan. Laura thought he should go home and have round the clock care. Bay used the excuse that he would get more rehab in the nursing home rather than telling the truth that she just wasn't ready to have him at home. She'd been able to overrule Laura since she was the wife and health care power of attorney.

Bay looked away from the Christmas tree that was now fully assembled and back to Holden who was asleep in his wheelchair. He had slid down in the chair and was slumped forward, his head hanging to the right side. A string of saliva hung from his mouth and formed a pool of moisture that darkened his light blue Ralph Lauren oxford shirt. Bay tried hard to put Holden in his usual clothes, but by the end of the day his shirt would be soiled with saliva and food and his pants with urine and sometimes stool if the aides weren't diligent about taking him to the bathroom and giving him a chance to try to go.

Bay sighed and walked behind Holden to pull him up in his chair and then took the hand towel from the bedside table and wiped his mouth. As she was blotting the wet spot on his shirt, he woke up and lifted his head.

"Did you have a good nap, Holden?" Bay asked. He just looked back at her with a vacant expression. She continued to talk as if he could understand. "Well, it's almost 5:00 so dinner will be here soon. I'll help you eat and then need to head home. Holden, look out in the hall. They're getting ready for Christmas. Can you believe that it is already December?"

Holden continued to stare at her with no expression on his face. He never looked out into the hall until Bay took her hand, caught his attention and pointed out the door. His eyes followed her hand and it looked to Bay as though he was looking at the tree, but his expression didn't change. He stared in a new direction.

Later, Bay walked into their kitchen, threw her keys on the table and flipped on an overhead light. She noticed the coffeepot and the breakfast dishes she had left in the sink had been washed and put

away, so it must be Saturday, the day Stella the cleaning lady came.

Bay glanced at her watch and saw it was 6:30, but she wasn't hungry

yet. Her clothes smelled of the nursing home and she would need to

change before she could think about eating. She grabbed a wine glass

and a new bottle of Merlot from their wine refrigerator and headed

upstairs to her study. The only room she really felt comfortable in.

Before she collapsed in her reading chair, Bay grabbed the

mail Stella had put on her desk. She threw the junk mail in the trash,

the electric and cable bill on her desk to pay later and then sat and

stared at the papers left in her hand. She must have picked these up

from her desk when she grabbed the stack of mail. I might as well

throw these away, Bay thought as she looked at the requirements for

entrance into North Carolina State's fashion design program. She'd

been looking at their website a few weeks before Holden's stroke and

printed these out, wanting to compare some of the pre-reqs with

courses offered at Pamlico Community College. Her idea was to take

as many college level classes as she could at PCC and then transfer to

NCSU to get a degree in fashion design. At least that had been her

plan.

What's the point of thinking about this? Right now her

purpose was to take care of Holden and help him heal. She didn't

have time for following her dreams. Holden had provided for her for many years and now she needed to take care of him. She drained half

a glass of merlot and looked around her beautifully appointed study,

the window treatments, artwork and furniture, all of the highest

quality. For many years she thought having beautiful things, plenty

of money and a man to care for her were all she needed, but how

wrong she was. She was already halfway through her life but only

halfway knew who she was. Looking into school had felt scary but

also exciting to pursue something she truly enjoyed. Now with

Holden's stroke, she might have to sacrifice school to care for him.

Bay finished off what would only be her first glass of wine as she

asked herself if that was truly what she wanted. She knew

immediately the answer as the guilt washed over her. Which would

be worse living with this guilt or not living her own life? That's why

Holden had to fully recover so she didn't have to make that choice.

She poured another glass of Merlot as her cell phone rang.

She saw it was Laura who wanted her daily update but Bay let it ring.

What was there to say anyway? Nothing had changed since

yesterday.

***

Maya laughed as Doodle Bug chased her tail, causing the bells

on her new Christmas collar to jingle. Maya had gone a little crazy at

the Dollar General, buying a collar for Doodle Bug, lights for the

bush by her front door and for the railing around her back porch, a small wreath to hang on her pantry door and several glitter encrusted

Christmas trees and angels to place on her tables. She was even

thinking of buying a small tree which she hadn't done for years. Of

course, last year her sister and Rob had put up a tree but she hadn't

had one in her own home for a while.

The first couple of Christmases she and Steven were married,

they put up a tree and he begrudgingly helped her get it in the stand

and put on the lights, but at least he had participated. After a few

years, he didn't even offer to help and her pride wouldn't let her ask

him. Sometimes after he'd had too much to drink, he would call her

childish for even bothering with the Christmas decorations. "All that

work," he chided, "for what? I don't give a damn about a tree and a

bunch of extra Christmas knickknacks sitting around." Finally Maya

lost her joy in Christmas and didn't bother with a tree but would still

set out a few decorations and put lights outside.

This year felt different. Maya could feel some of her spirit

returning for Christmas and life in general. Maybe it was having her

own place for the first time in ten years, maybe it was two years

having passed since Katrina and Steven's death or maybe it was a

combination of both along with her strong intention to move on

with her life. Because of the women's circle, she was also aware of the

upcoming solstice marking the longest night of the year followed by increasing light and longer days, another reason to celebrate this season.

She was admiring how the lights around her back porch reflected in the water when she heard a knock at the door. She wondered who was coming over at six on a Saturday night. Doodle Bug jingled over to the door doing her happy dance so it must be someone they knew or she would probably be growling. It still amazed her how Doodle Bug could sense things without actually seeing them. A quality she would like to replicate.

Maya opened the door to a pile of boxes and strands of artificial garland. "Hazel, are you under there? Here let me grab some of those boxes and please come in."

Hazel's face appeared after Maya removed a couple of boxes and she stepped into Maya's living room. "Maya, I saw your Christmas lights on the camellia bush and thought you might need some more decorations since you probably lost yours in the hurricane. As you can imagine, I have piles of decorations in there," pointing up the hill to her house, "that have never been used. I am beginning to clean things out and it feels good to share these with you." Hazel was smiling and moved farther into the room and placed two more boxes on Maya's couch.

Hazel opened each box and seemed to take great delight in describing the contents. "Here are some green and red Christmas balls you could put on a tree or in a glass bowl. This box has a nativity scene and this one, opening a large box, has several Christmas candles. I also brought some garland and a few red bows. Maybe you could string it around the picture window looking out onto the creek."

"Well, Hazel, you're my Christmas elf. In fact, with that garland around your neck and red bow around your wrist, you'd almost pass for an elf. Just need some bigger ears. Thank you so much. I will definitely enjoy using these things. Here, have a seat," Maya said as she moved a couple of boxes to the coffee table, "and I'll fix you a cup of tea if you can stay."

"I'd love to and you have to update me on how things worked out with you and Travis."

Maya walked around the couch to the kitchen and put the tea kettle on the burner. As she got the mugs and tea bags she said, "Hazel, it went quite well. We're in agreement that neither of us needs to be in a serious relationship right now but we do want to try to stay friends." Maya thought about sharing more but since Travis was her minister, didn't want to go into all the details. "Travis realizes he needs to focus on his role as a minister and I, as you know, need to focus on closure with my marriage to Steven. We're going to keep in touch and call and see one another whenever the spirit moves us."

"That sounds very mature of you both. I'm glad you'll be staying friends. Travis is such a sweet man. I try to stay out of it but lots of the old busy bodies in the church are constantly trying to set him up with women. I've tried to tell a couple to leave him alone, he's a grown man, but somehow they just can't stand to see a minister without a wife and the potential to be fruitful and multiply."

The tea kettle whistled as Maya said, "I think Travis will be able to handle them. I forgot, how do you like your tea?"

"Just two lumps of sugar, dear."

"I don't have any lump sugar, would two teaspoons work?"

"That's perfect."

Maya set a steaming mug of tea on the coffee table in front of Hazel and took hers to the straight back chair under the picture window, across from Hazel. She followed Hazel's gaze to the urn to Maya's left. Before Maya could say anything, Hazel said, "Maya, I've been thinking about our solstice gathering in a couple of weeks." Hazel took a sip of her tea and then fell into a coughing fit. She set the mug down, put a hand on her chest and coughed and rattled until tears came into her eyes. Maya jumped up and took a few steps towards her.

"Hazel, are you okay? What can I do? I'll get some water." Maya rushed to the kitchen and grabbed a bottle of water from the fridge. By the time she got back to Hazel, she had stopped coughing and had taken another sip of tea.

"Thanks for the water, sweetie, but I'm fine now. The tea just went down the wrong pipe. That's all."

Maya sat down in her chair. "Hazel, you've had one of those coughing spells almost every time I've seen you the last month or so. I think you should get it checked out," Maya said with genuine concern in her voice.

"Don't worry about me. I'll be fine. It could just be allergies or a touch of a virus of some sort. If it doesn't leave by Christmas, I'll go to the doctor. Anyway, getting back to the solstice ritual, I think I know what I want to do. Just figuring out my ritual has felt powerful and I look forward to sharing it with our group. How about you, Maya? Do you know what your ritual will be yet? Oh, wait, you better not tell me. If we discussed our rituals ahead of time, we might influence the other and then our rituals wouldn't truly be a reflection of us."

Maya glanced at the urn and then back to Hazel. "I don't know exactly what I'll do yet but I'll figure it out. So what will your ritual be?"

"You'll find out on the twenty-first, Maya. And you'll be fine. There is no wrong way to do this as long as you do what is meaningful to you. Like Lilith said, just follow your intuition."

They sat in a comfortable silence for a moment. Maya was thinking up the details of her ritual and hoping it would come together by the twenty-first. Hazel broke the silence. "Maya, what are your family's Christmas traditions? Will you go to your parents for the holiday? I don't believe you've seen them since you moved here, have you?"

Maya shifted uncomfortably in her chair and then looked over at Hazel's green eyes watching her closely. "No. I haven't seen them. To tell you the truth, I'm just not that close with my parents. My father owns a bookstore in Charlottesville so stays busy with that and my mother suffers from depression. Growing up, my sister and I never knew this. We always thought if we could just be good enough it would make her happy. Of course that didn't work. In college, Kate and I realized what was going on and talked with her and my father about it. She got on some medication for a while but refused counseling. She is sporadic with taking her medicine and the last time I saw her I think she wasn't taking it at all. Anyway, because she was so withdrawn, we never felt like she was a big part of our lives." Before Maya could add any more, she stopped because Hazel had dropped her head and her shoulders began to shake. She was crying. Maya ran over to the couch and moved several boxes of decorations to sit beside Hazel.

She wrapped an arm around her and asked, "What is it Hazel? I'm sorry to have made you cry. I have my sister Kate and we've somewhat made peace with who my mother is. Please don't cry for me."

Hazel sat up and patted Maya's hand that was resting on Hazel's waist. Ever the Southern lady, she pulled a monogram handkerchief out of the pocket of her khaki pants and wiped her eyes. "I'm sorry, Maya. It's not you. It's just your relationship with your mother hit a chord with me. You see," she continued, disentangling herself form Maya's embrace and moving to one end of the couch to look Maya in the eye, "I was like your mother. After I had the abortion, I went into a deep depression. I hadn't told a soul about it so couldn't discuss my grief with anyone. I kept all that pain and sadness locked up inside. I would use all my energy to teach the girls at Meredith and then have nothing left for Bill and Wynn. I was in my own world, barely having enough energy to make conversation at dinner much less be an energetic and engaged mother. Looking back I see Wynn did the same thing you and Kate did. He was a super achiever, graduating with a 4.0, becoming an Eagle Scout and excelling in basketball but I barely noticed from the depths of my pain."

Hazel stopped for a moment and a new round of tears began to fall. "I'm ashamed to say that there were many times I didn't go watch him play basketball because I either forgot or just didn't have the energy. Before I knew it, he had graduated and was off to MIT to study computer engineering. Like you, ever since then, he performs an obligatory visit once or twice a year, but it always feels tense. Even though I'm not as depressed, having that secret I shared at the circle kept me from apologizing and telling him the truth. I missed out on the child I had, mourning the one that never was." Hazel began silently crying again, her shoulders shaking.

Maya's heart broke to see someone she cared about and respected in so much pain. She remembered the woman by the cross after Katrina when all she could do was offer a hug. Maya scooted over to Hazel and enveloped her in a hug. Hazel returned the hug, buried her head in Maya's fleece sweatshirt.

Maya's eyes looked over Hazel's head and watched the reflection of her Christmas lights dancing in the ripples of the creek. As she held Hazel, she thought of her own mother. For so many years she and Kate thought there was something they could do to earn the attention of their mother but finally understood it was the depression. Still, parts of them both would hold out hope their mother would change and suddenly shower them with attention, love and motherly advice. But now, holding Hazel, Maya for the first time considered things from her mother's perspective. How truly empty her mother must have been to have nothing substantial to give back. At least Hazel had recovered and was a positive influence in other lives. Maya's mother continued to isolate herself from her, Kate, their father and the outside world. Her books and garden continued to receive her attention. Maya felt tightness in her chest, followed by tears filling her eyes, blurring the Christmas lights outside. Her tears were not for her, but for her mother. She had the epiphany that for all the hurt and anger she and Kate had had towards their mother, it was not as great as the pain and isolation her mother had felt because of her depression.

Maya realized that Hazel had stopped crying so hard and lifted her head off her shoulder. She saw Maya's tears and said, "Lord, now, I've gone and made you cry. We're quite a pair, really getting into the spirit of Christmas, aren't we?" Hazel blew her nose into her handkerchief and managed a weak smile up at Maya who had slid down to the end of the couch with her back against the arm rest, hugging her knees.

"Hearing you talk about your depression made me think about things from my mother's perspective. I've never really tried to understand her side, till now. I was mainly feeling sorry for myself and focusing on what I didn't have. You just made me realize that it really didn't have anything directly to do with me or Kate. Thank you for sharing what you went through. Not having children of my own, I can't begin to identify with what you experienced, but at the time, you were doing the best you could with the skills you had, right? Maybe now that you are coming to terms with that time in your life, you can begin to work on the relationship with your son."

"That would be harder than it sounds given who my son has become as an adult, but I'll give it some thought. Not that I haven't thought about it a million times before. Maya, do you have anything stronger then tea around here? I'm feeling like a little pick me up."

"Sure," Maya said. "I have some Fat Tire beer and a bottle of Merlot."

"I was thinking of something stronger then that," Hazel said with a coy look, "but I guess a glass of wine will do."

"Wait a minute, Hazel. I have a bottle of Jim Beam at the back of my pantry. I keep it there for Buster. A couple of times he came by in his boat in the early fall when I was having a glass of wine at sunset. He too preferred a stronger drink, so I bought that for him. Would that work?"

"Perfect. Just pour a shot in a glass over some ice."

Maya smiled as she prepared the drinks. She couldn't remember the last time she'd drunk liquor and she knew she had never done so with a 79 year old. She took the glasses in and sat on the couch beside Hazel. Hazel raised her glass to Maya, "Here's to coming out of the darkness in a few weeks."

"I'll drink to that," Maya said, clinking glasses with Hazel and letting the whiskey slowly burn a path to her stomach.

***

Hazel slowly walked up the hill from the boathouse to her back porch. She wrapped her arms around herself to ward off the cold night air. She hadn't worn a coat down to Maya's because she was so laden with her decorations. She felt a little fuzzy from the whiskey and made sure she carefully placed her feet on the worn path under the live oaks. She breathed in the cold night air and her breath caught in her lungs. She bent forward with another coughing fit. She was so sick of this nagging cough. Her stomach muscles were sore from all the coughing and hacking. Finally she caught her breath and walked up the steps to the back porch.

Since she'd had the whiskey, Hazel knew she should eat something. Many nights she just made do with tea and cinnamon toast but felt a little more substantial meal was in order tonight. She rummaged through the refrigerator and pantry and ended up with a ham and cheese sandwich, a handful of peanuts and an apple which she took out to eat at her desk.

She ate slowly, appreciating the flavor of the ham, Swiss cheese and the whole wheat bread she had bought from Lilith this morning at the farmers' market. As she ate and stared out the window she processed what had just transpired at the boathouse.

But what had just happened? She had gone down there with some Christmas decorations, feeling excited to share them with Maya and then she and Maya both ended up in tears. She felt there was a reason Maya had moved into that boathouse. Maybe it was to help them each understand their lives better. She already knew her son carried some anger towards her, but she wondered if like Maya, he had felt her inattention had something to do with him. Great, something else to feel guilty about, she thought. Suddenly the sandwich was tasteless and sticking to the roof of her mouth. Hazel pushed it aside and opened the file cabinet. She pulled out the first two files and put them on her desk. She flipped mindlessly through the papers in the first file.

It wasn't helping. Her meeting wasn't until the end of next week and preparing for it didn't help distract her mind. She turned on the new laptop computer Travis had helped her set up back in October. She had mostly used it to get on the Internet and that was her intent now. She watched the computer warm up and then clicked on the blue E hoping she would find some relief to her discomfort out on the web. It worked a lot faster than the catalogs. Shortly, her mind had moved on from the guilt and was immersed in deciding on the perfect new running outfit for Maya. As she perused the website, her conscious mind told her she had promised not to do this anymore, but she quieted it by rationalizing that this was a gift to be given to an actual person and would not end up in a pile in the guest room. That is, as long as this was the only site she went to.

***

Bay began to feel the effects of the Merlot on her empty stomach halfway into her second glass. I should probably stop, she thought, but, hell, if anyone has the right to drink a little too much it's me. Forty one years old, sitting home on a Saturday night after a day at a nursing home visiting my husband. What a great life. I deserve a better life than this, she thought. She stopped and realized what she had just thought and suddenly felt ungrateful and selfish. She had come from a trailer park and now lived in a 4000-square foot home and belonged to a country club and still wanted more. What's wrong with her?

Bay slid down in the chair, grabbed the pillow that was behind her and clutched it to her chest as she began to cry. Her mind continued to race and suddenly she screamed out to the empty house, "I am sick of this shit! I was just beginning to feel hopeful, making friends with Maya, looking into school and now Holden has a stroke and I'm left to care for him, deal with all the bills and deal with his daughter." During her rant, Bay had stood and began pacing about her study, her arms punching the air for emphasis as the tears continued to flow.

"This plain sucks," Bay said. She grabbed her empty wine glass and threw it towards the door. It landed on the carpet leaving drops of red wine in a blood spatter pattern on the white carpet. Bay lunged to retrieve it, still in a rage. "Stupid ass wine glass," she yelled, "I can't even break you to feel better." She picked up the glass and stepped out in the hallway to the landing at the top of the circular staircase. She leaned over the rail and hurled the glass towards the floor. It shattered as it hit the hardwood floor in the foyer. Bay stood for a moment staring down at the broken glass and then sat on the top step, resting her back against the wall, her rage now spent. She stared straight ahead feeling numb and paralyzed not knowing what to do to make herself feel better.

***

Maya hung up with her sister and looked at her watch. It was already 7:45 p.m. No wonder her stomach was beginning to growl. The time since Hazel had knocked on her door had gone quickly but at the same time felt like a lifetime ago. Because of their talk, a paradigm had shifted for Maya that made her re-think how she viewed her mother and childhood.

As soon as Hazel left, she'd called Kate to share how Hazel had experienced her depression and how this had helped Maya picture things from their mother's perspective. She now felt her mother's emotional distance was not so much a choice but a

symptom of her depression. Kate listened and seemed happy that
Maya had found a new peace with this issue, however, she needed
more convincing. She told Maya she would think about what Maya
had shared but being a mother herself, found it difficult to imagine
anything could get in the way of loving Worth. Maya had at least
been able to convince her to visit their parents for a few days between
Christmas and New Year's. Neither of them had seen their parents
since they visited Raleigh a few weeks after Worth was born and just
before Maya moved to Oriental.

    Maya sat for a minute with the phone still in her hands. It
had been good to talk with Kate but now she felt lonely and a little
left out. Kate had to end the conversation because their lasagna
dinner was ready. Rob was in the background making baby talk with
Worth. Maya could tell Kate was ready to get back to her family.
She was happy Kate had created such a sweet life for herself. That
had always been her goal, but Maya couldn't help but feel a little
envious. Her house was quiet except for the hum of the refrigerator
and Doodle Bug's snores coming from behind the pile of garlands.

    Not wanting her mind to dwell here for long, Maya flipped
her phone open again to check in on Bay. Since Holden's stroke,
they had talked every two or three days and had coffee the day Maya
had gone to New Bern to pick up office supplies at Staples. Bay
definitely needed a friend and Maya was surprised at how much she

got out of supporting Bay. She was still quite dramatic and could be demanding at times when she had an audience, but when it was just the two of them, she was able to drop that and be more real. Maya hit Bay's name on her cell phone and waited for Bay to pick up. Usually she answered immediately. Just as Maya was preparing what to say in a message, Bay picked up on the last ring.

"Hello?" Bay's greeting was drawn out with a southern drawl she usually didn't have.

"Bay? Are you okay? Did I wake you? You don't sound like yourself?"

"Oh, Maya. I'm fine. Well, actually I'm not. I've already had two glasses of wine and then after a big pity party threw the glass off the second floor landing. So really, I guess I'm not doing too well." Bay's words were thick from the wine but not thick enough to hide the desperation in her voice. Bay was silent now except for her breath.

What should I do, Maya thought? When Steven was drunk, Maya would stay out of the way, often the object of his rage but this was different. Bay needed someone.

"Bay, have you eaten yet?"

"No. My clothes still stink from the nursing home food and I'm not really hungry."

"Well, you need to eat. Go take a shower and I'll pick up a pizza at The Silos and bring it over. I haven't eaten either and am starving. I'll get a half gallon of iced tea too. Don't think either of us needs more to drink."

"Oh, Maya, are you sure? You don't mind driving out here? It would be great to have some company."

"I'm happy to. It was my idea, wasn't it? Now get up and go shower and I'll be there in about 40 minutes."

"OK. See you shortly."

Maya hung up with Bay and immediately called The Silos to order pizza, happy to have a mission for the evening. "Come on, Doodle Bug. Let's go out to potty. I'm going to be out for a while." Doodle Bug understood potty and met Maya at the door, tail wagging and ready for action. Maya was always amazed at how Doodle Bug could go from a sound sleep to chasing her tail in less than a minute.

They headed outside and Maya admired her lights on the camellia bush while Doodle Bug did her business. Maybe I'll put some of that garland around the front door and buy a wreath, she thought. Once back inside, with the cold air having revived her whiskey-dulled mind, Maya remembered she knew the neighborhood Bay lived in but didn't know the exact street, so called Bay again,

catching her just before she stepped into the shower, and got
directions.

Before Maya put the phone down, she saw she had a
voicemail. Maybe it was Kate calling back but as the message began
she heard Ella's voice. "Hey Maya. Sorry to bother you. Was just
checking to see if you were free and wanted to come over to my place.
I'm trying to put up my Christmas tree, the first one of my very own,
and well, it's hard to do all by myself. Just a minute ago I was trying
to get it straight in the stand and it fell on top of me." Maya could
hear Ella's voice crack. She sounded so young and sad and it
reminded Maya that Ella was only 26 years old. Ella continued,
"Anyway, was just calling to see if you wanted to come over for some
hot chocolate and to help me decorate my tree but that's OK. It's
after seven already so I'll just talk with you sometime tomorrow."

Maya put the phone down and hesitated. It sounded like Ella
needed a friend too, but there was only one of her and she had
already committed to Bay. She wished she could go to Ella's too.
Maya recognized the loneliness in her voice and had felt that way
many times since Katrina and even before, when she was married.
There were times she and Steven would be home together but if he
was in one of his moods and drinking, it felt like a deep canyon
separated them; each of them on their own side looking across at the
other, neither having the energy or skill to navigate the divide

between them. Maya wondered why she didn't try harder? Why

hadn't she pushed Steven to talk more about his past so she could

understand him better?

Doodle Bug jumped on Maya, putting her paws on her

thighs. "Down Doodle Bug. You know better than to jump on me."

Maya knelt down and hugged Doodle Bug's neck,

"But thanks for interrupting my thoughts."

Why was she thinking about herself again? It was Ella who

was feeling lonely. Guess this was just another indicator she needed

to keep working on her solstice ritual. She would give Ella a call on

her way to Bay's. Maybe they could meet for brunch tomorrow and

then she could help Ella with her tree.

Maya stuck her hands deep in the pockets of her down vest to

keep them warm. She was glad for the glow of her Christmas lights

because otherwise it was pitch dark outside. She scanned the sky for

the moon but didn't see it. Maya had heard of the 'Dark Night of

the Soul' but wasn't exactly sure what that meant. Maybe tonight

was one of those nights. In the past two hours she, Hazel, Bay and

now Ella had all been confronted with the darker parts of their lives,

depression, past relationships, regret, loneliness. Hmm, Maya

thought. Maybe there was something about tonight. She glanced at

her watch and kept walking towards the car. No time for

philosophizing, there's a pizza waiting at the Silos and that's bound to help things a little.

Maya drove slowly down Outrigger Drive with her brights on looking for #1208 on the left. She saw the mail box with those numbers and turned down the driveway still unable to see the house, hidden by the trees. After about 100 feet she rounded a bend in the driveway and saw the house in front of her, the front porch light on. The house seemed massive compared to her little boathouse. She pulled her Saturn up beside a walkway to the front door, taking note of the three car garage immediately to her left. As she walked up to the front door, carrying the pizza and iced tea, she couldn't imagine what you would use a house this big for. Even with two children, her parents never had a house this big. Well, they probably couldn't afford it anyway, but still. When she got to the front door, she saw a note on the door knocker. "Maya, come on in. I'm upstairs drying my hair."

Maya pushed open the door and stepped into the foyer. After catching her breath at the beautiful chandelier overhead, she surveyed the floor for broken glass and not seeing any walked farther in and set the pizza and tea on a table at the bottom of the stairs.

"Bay!" she yelled walking up the stairs. "Bay, it's me. I'm here. Should I come on up?"

"Hey, Maya. Come on down to our bedroom. I'm almost ready."

Maya went up the staircase and followed the hallway to the end, led by the bedroom light and the sound of country music. Maya didn't listen to a lot of country music, but thought she recognized the voice as Reba McIntyre. Bay spied Maya and stuck her head out the bathroom door. "Hey. Thanks for coming. Have a seat on the bed. I'm just about ready. Here, let me turn down the radio so we can talk."

Bay walked past Maya to turn the volume down on the radio. "Sorry that was so loud. Listening to country music cheers me up. Right now my life feels sort of like a country song," she said managing a smile at Maya.

"You sound much better then you did when we talked. Guess that shower helped counteract the wine."

"Yeah. That and several bottles of these," she said holding up a bottle of Perrier water.

Maya smiled and watched Bay finish her mascara and then apply some lip gloss. Maya laughed to herself as she assessed Bay's pizza ensemble. She had on some soft pink velour pants, pink ballet flats and an off white turtleneck. She walked passed Maya, over to her dresser and got a pair of diamond studs to put in her ears. She turned to Maya, "Okay. I feel much better and now I'm starved too. Where's the pizza?"

"I left it on the table by the stairs. Should we go to the kitchen to eat?"

"Oh, no," Bay said. "That kitchen is so big. When I'm alone, I spend most of my time up here in my study," she said pointing down the hall to the room right at the top of the stairs. "Run down and bring the pizza and tea up here. I've already gotten some glasses, napkins and a couple of plates."

As Maya walked down the stairs, she rolled her eyes and wondered again why she and Bay were friends. Here she was all decked out in her lounging wear telling her what to do. Maya took a deep breath, reminded herself what Bay was dealing with and headed back upstairs.

"Oh, thanks, Maya. See, this is much cozier than the kitchen. We can just sit on the floor."

Maya laid the pizza box on the floor and poured iced tea into the two glasses that were sitting on Bay's desk. Bay sat down with her back against an oversized chair so Maya walked over and sat down with her back against the loveseat, directly across from the desk. They both sat there a couple of minutes, silently eating the pizza. Maya felt slightly uncomfortable at the intimacy of being in Bay's home and sitting on the floor to eat. It felt different from seeing each other in town, running down Hwy 55 or talking on the phone. The

silence was beginning to feel a little awkward, so Maya blurted out,

"Bay, I just have to ask you. Do you always look so put together with

beautifully coordinated outfits, matching jewelry and makeup? I fully

expected you to have a wet head and be wearing a bathrobe after our

initial phone conversation."

Bay blushed as she looked back at Maya. She seemed to be

weighing this comment as either a compliment or an insult. She

must have chosen the former because she smiled and answered, "I've

just always loved fashion and coordinating outfits and accessorizing.

Ever since I was young I've always wanted to look my best. Just like

tonight. I was feeling horrible when you called but the combination

of your visit and sprucing myself up has made me feel so much better.

I enjoy picking out the outfit that matches my mood and the

occasion."

Maya couldn't help it and started to laugh. "And so for

eating take-out pizza on the floor with me, that is what seemed most

appropriate?" Maya laughed harder and harder not at Bay but at the

contrast between them. Again Bay was watching her, not sure how to

take this bout of laughter. "I'm sorry," Maya said, wiping her eyes.

"I'm not laughing at you. I'm just laughing at how different we are. I

rarely even think about what I wear. In fact, sometimes it's extremely

stressful to me to pick out the right outfit so I guess that's why I usually stick with jeans and on top, whatever is appropriate for the weather."

Bay's eyes had softened as she listened to Maya. "Well, I have noticed a certain predictability about your clothes, Maya. If you ever need a fashion consultant, I'm your girl. In fact, wait right here. I'll be right back." Maya watched Bay run down the hall. She returned with deep purple cashmere turtleneck sweater. "Here, stand up and put this on. It will go well with the color and cut of your jeans."

Maya stood, once again following Bay's command. Used to locker rooms and growing up with a sister, she wasn't shy and stripped off her fleece pullover and t-shirt. Maya slipped the sweater over her head and her ponytail loosened as she pulled her head through the turtleneck. As soon as she had it on, Bay undid her pony tail, fluffed her hair and hung a silver necklace around her neck that matched the silver hoops she always wore. "Here," Bay said, handing Maya a pale pink lip gloss, "put this on." Maya did as she was told and then followed Bay to the guest bathroom just down the hall from the study. Bay flipped on the light and walked Maya in front of the mirror. "See. Beautiful and you're just as comfortable as that fleece top but look so much prettier."

Maya had to agree she did look pretty good. Just a few small touches and she had a whole different look. "Wow, Bay. You are good at this. I feel very pretty and much more appropriately dressed to eat pizza with you. Now, I'm starving. Let's get back to that pizza."

Maya and Bay laughed as they walked back to the study and Maya felt a little ashamed at how harshly she had initially judged Bay.

Chapter 11

Maya put the bow on the last of Worth's presents. He was barely six months old and wouldn't even remember what she'd gotten him, but she couldn't resist spoiling her nephew on his first Christmas. She was sure Kate and Rob were doing the same. Well, they'd all have fun and remember it even though Worth wouldn't. Dr. Allen closed the office early today and they were off all next week for Christmas. Tomorrow was the solstice ritual at the Mother Tree and then on Monday Maya would head to Raleigh for Christmas with Kate and her family.

Maya sat with her back against the couch and a pile of presents to her left and unused wrapping paper and bows in front of her. She admired the Christmas tree in front of her creek windows. It was filled with lots of colored lights, thanks to Hazel, and decorated sparsely with the few ornaments Maya had salvaged after Katrina. Of course, Hazel had several boxes of ornaments she would have shared willingly, but one of the special parts of decorating a tree to Maya was pulling out each ornament, remembering where she had bought it or who had given it to her. It wouldn't have been the same to all of a sudden have 50 ornaments that someone else had bought. Maya did let Hazel pick out one of her favorite ornaments and she put that on the tree. It was a cupcake in a white baking cup, chocolate frosting and a pink icing rosebud on the top. Maya thought it was a little unusual for a Christmas decoration, but Hazel said it reminded her of her grandmother, so one day when she had been missing her grandmother, she ordered 50 out of a catalog she had received in the mail.

Maya wasn't quite sure what to do with herself. She felt like having someone over to share her decorations and celebrate the holiday. Hazel hadn't been feeling well so Maya had only seen her briefly each morning when she went over to check on her. She continued with that hacking cough but told Maya not to worry; she would get over it. Hazel said she'd been to the doctor and several afternoons in the past week, Maya noticed Hazel's car was gone, so she hoped that in fact she had gone to the doctor's. Today Maya beat Hazel home since she'd gotten off work early. She noticed Hazel's car was there now and figured she must be tired from the day and wouldn't want to be disturbed.

It was 5:30 so Bay was probably with Holden, feeding him his dinner and Lilith was at a Rotary Christmas party with her husband. She thought of Travis and wondered if he could come over. They had spoken on the phone a couple of times since they had had coffee at The Bean but hadn't seen each other in person since then. It would be nice to catch up, Maya thought. She picked up her cell phone from the coffee table and selected Travis' name from her list of contacts. He answered on the second ring.

"Hey, Maya," he said having recognized her number, "How are you?"

"I'm doing great because today is the beginning of my Christmas vacation."

"Good for you. Can't say the same for me. The holidays are even busier for me with Sunday service and then Christmas Eve the following night this year." His voice sounded tired and Maya had forgotten that he would continue to have obligations over the holidays.

"Oh. I'm sorry. I was calling to invite you over for a drink, some hors d'oeuvres and to enjoy my Christmas decorations with me but understand if you need time to yourself."

"Not at all. In fact, it would be great to see you and would help get my mind off church stuff. How 'bout I stop by Toucans and pick up an order of their homemade chips and some ranch dressing to go with whatever else you had planned?"

"That sounds perfect. I really don't have anything in particular planned as I just had this inspiration to have you over, but you know me, I always have food on hand. So, I'll see you shortly?"

After he said he was on his way, Maya closed the phone and began picking up the extra bows and wrapping paper and then moved Worth's presents under the tree. Something was missing, she thought. Christmas music, but then she remembered she didn't have any. Maya's stomach tightened when she thought of her lost Christmas CD collection. She had a wide variety including Kenny G, Dolly Parton and Kenny Rogers, Harry Connick, Jr. and Bing Crosby.

The Christmas before Katrina, she'd been baking some Christmas cookies for her work party and put on Kenny G as she worked in the kitchen. It wasn't loud but had woken Steven, who had been out late the night before with his drinking buddies. Maya had known when she heard the bedroom door open that she was going to have to deal with his anger. He came stomping into the kitchen.

"What the hell are you doing in here? Don't you know I'm tired and trying to sleep?" He picked up the case beside the CD player she had in the kitchen and read the title with heavy sarcasm. "Have Yourself a Merry Little Christmas. Maya, this is so childish. Don't you know that all this Christmas shit is just to get everyone to buy more things? I don't know anyone who has happy Christmas memories anyway."

As Maya had watched him, she could tell his anger was coming from a deep place that he had never shared with her. She guessed it had something to do with his childhood. He never spoke of his parents and only occasionally mentioned his brother who lived in Oregon. She was scared to ask him about any of it.

"Steven, I have good memories of baking Christmas cookies with my sister and was in the mood for some Christmas music. I'll turn it down even lower so you can go back to sleep. I'm about done anyway." It took a lot of effort for Maya to say this as his rage had a way of muting her.

"I don't want this shit playing at all. I'm gonna make sure it doesn't happen again." Steven took her stack of Christmas CD's that were on the counter, crossed the kitchen in three huge steps and almost tore the back door off the hinges as he threw it open. She heard him out by the trash can breaking each of the CD's one by one. She sat silently at the kitchen table with tears streaming down her face. Doodle Bug whined and laid her head in Maya's lap.

Steven stormed back in and stopped directly in front of her. "You need to grow up and act like an adult. No one I know has time for making cookies and listening to sappy Christmas music. You're lucky I stay with you. Nobody else would put up with this childishness." He turned and went back to the bedroom, slamming the door.

Maya continued to sit there staring at the crack in their linoleum floor, one hand on her coffee cup and one had on Doodle Bug's back. The voice in her own head didn't even yell back at Steven anymore. Maybe he was right, maybe no one else would want her.

Maya sank into the chair beside her Christmas tree, shaking with emotion. She felt hurt, anger and resentment and then this was replaced by sadness and even pity for herself. Why had she stayed with him? What was wrong with her? Why hadn't she just packed her bags that minute and she and Doodle Bug moved up to Raleigh and filed for divorce? Maya's eyes traveled over to the urn on the end table that was now pushed way back in the corner to make room for the Christmas tree. She remembered her focus over the last few months, forgiveness. Some was for Steven but mostly for herself. Maya reminded herself that she had been doing the best she could during her marriage, and she could only assume Steven was too. Because of Katrina, she had new options and was making the most of them. She was beginning to look forward to tomorrow to symbolically put the past behind her. Not that she would forget, but her experiences would provide a foundation for her growth rather than an anchor to hold her back.

Maya took a deep breath and stood up. She looked at her watch and realized that Travis would probably be there in the next ten to fifteen minutes so she had better get a move on with her preparations. Maya set some wine glasses, Christmas napkins and a plate of carrot sticks and hummus on the coffee table. At least they'd have something healthy to balance out those delicious deep fried chips Travis was bringing. She tuned the kitchen radio to 103.3 because they were playing continuous Christmas music. "Walking in a Winter Wonderland" was on and she did a little dance across the room to turn on the front porch lights and then stepped outside to plug in the Christmas lights on her camellia bush, happy Travis had thought to put a plug on the front porch. She went in to open the wine and promised herself to buy some Christmas CD's tomorrow after the solstice ritual. She poured herself a glass of wine and sat to wait for Travis.

Doodle Bug jumped up beside her with a jingle from her belled Christmas collar and laid her head in Maya's lap. She smiled as she realized how well she had brought herself back to the present and didn't let herself dwell on that memory of Steven. After two years, she was finally getting the hang of this mindfulness thing. Doodle Bug's head lifted from Maya's lap, her ears at attention. She jumped off the couch and ran to the door, tail wagging. A millisecond later, Travis rang the doorbell.

***

Maya reached over and turned off her alarm. As usual she had awoken five minutes before it was to go off. She pulled back the curtains and looked outside, still pitch black at 6:00 a.m. The women were gathering at the Mother Tree at 7:00 a.m. and this time Maya was going to ride with Hazel in her skiff. It would be easier since it was cold and she had to carry the urn, her thermos of coffee and the loaves of egg nog bread she'd made for everyone. Maya felt a sense of nervous anticipation as she thought of the morning ahead. She was looking forward to completing the ritual but was worried she wouldn't do things correctly or that it wouldn't make sense to the others. Well, Lilith had said to follow your heart and intuition and that is what she had done so she supposed there was no way to get it wrong. Doodle Bug stood at her sleeping place beside Maya's bed and looked at her intently, signally she was ready to go outside.

Maya came in from letting Doodle Bug do her morning business, promising her a late morning run when she returned. She went to the sink and quickly washed the wine glasses and dishes from last night. Travis had stayed a couple hours and she had enjoyed herself. They shared some details of their day to day life and laughed at Doodle Bug running around with her jingle bell collar on. Although it was not awkward to be together and the conversation flowed, Maya felt just a bit uncomfortable. They didn't talk about

their relationship or the issues that had interfered with it. Maybe this
was the way to rebuild their relationship as just friends. Maya wasn't
sure, but it was good to see him and fun to have someone to share her
decorations with. As Travis was leaving, he hesitated, not sure of
how to say goodbye. Maya, with practice from her new women
friends, had initiated a friendly hug that Travis easily returned.

At 6:40 a.m. Maya left Doodle Bug snoozing by the
Christmas tree and headed to the dock to meet Hazel. She looked up
the hill to the house and saw the glow of a flashlight heading her way.
She wondered if Hazel was a little nervous too. Maya stopped and
waited for Hazel.

"Morning, Hazel. How are you feeling?"

"Hey, Maya. I'm feeling a little better this morning. Don't
we have a beautiful morning for our gathering?"

"Yes. It's gorgeous."

Hazel smiled at Maya but the look in her eyes made her seem
a million miles away. She was wearing a green wool pea coat
buttoned up to her neck to keep the cold out. Of course, she had on
her standard khaki pants that today were stuffed into rubber boots
that came almost to her knees. She was carrying an L.L. Bean bag
full of whatever supplies she needed for the ritual. Maya caught a
glimpse of the talking stick peeking out of the top of the bag.

Hazel continued walking and seemed focused on getting to the boat. Maya wanted to ask Hazel about her doctor visits but could tell from Hazel's demeanor that she didn't want to talk much. As they walked out onto the dock, Maya looked over to her boathouse and could see her Christmas tree lights in the window. Maya had left them on specifically so she could admire them from this angle.

"Hazel, thanks again for giving me all those Christmas lights. I'm enjoying my tree so much."

Hazel paused before getting in the skiff and followed Maya's gaze to her creek window.

"They do look lovely, dear. I'm so glad you could use them and I'm enjoying looking down at the lights on the bushes by your front door. In fact, you inspired me to get out my little table top tree. I put it on the table in my office and covered it with the cupcake ornaments. It's funny how something so small like that can lift your spirits, but it does. Looking at all those cupcakes makes me feel closer to my grandmother."

Hazel turned and boarded the skiff. Maya followed suit and began unwrapping the lines around the cleats on the dock as Hazel started the engine.

"So," Maya asked over the engine, "why do cupcakes remind you of your grandmother?"

Hazel backed the boat away from the dock and began heading up the creek before she answered. "My grandmother and I had a special birthday tradition we did that involved cupcakes. I know you're thinking that everyone has cupcakes for their birthday but our tradition was just the two of us and involved more than just eating them, though we certainly did that. I'd love to share that story sometime but right now I'm focused on our winter solstice ritual. This feels like one of the most important ones for me."

"I know. If you don't mind, Hazel, what are some of the issues you've taken in the dark before?"

"Till now, I've never been as brave as you to tackle an issue that affected me so deeply. I've usually stuck to more superficial things. Well, they weren't really that superficial, but because I was trying to avoid the pain of what I discussed at our last circle, I could never really deal with those other issues like my relationship with my son, my role in the church, my shopping compulsion. I did my best to grow and learn but without addressing this other thing," Hazel still had trouble saying the word abortion, "I never truly resolved those things. I'm hoping today will help me with that. I just hate it took me until I'm 79 to have the nerve to talk about this but hopefully it will make my life more peaceful from now until I die."

They were in deeper water and away from other houses so Hazel pushed down the throttle and the engine revived as they picked

up speed. Maya wanted to ask Hazel more about her relationship
with her son and if she thought that might change after today, but
the engine was so loud now it precluded any talking. Maya had the
impression Hazel had done that on purpose. She must be feeling
nervous because she had an edge to her this morning that she didn't
usually have. The only other time Maya had seen her act this way
was the night she and Doodle Bug arrived on her doorstep in the
tropical storm.

    The wind created by the speed of the boat intensified the
morning chill. Maya zipped up her fleece jacket wishing she had
brought along a windbreaker too. They were only about ten minutes
away now and on the way home she would have the benefit of the
morning sun. Maya stuffed her hands in her pockets and sat back in
her seat, rehearsing what she would say when the talking stick was
hers.

    Hazel slowed the boat as she began the right turn down
Hungry Mother Creek. They had passed Ella, in her kayak who told
them Violet and her husband were five minutes ahead of them.
Maya wondered if Lilith had camped again last night. It had gone
down into the mid 30s but that was easily tolerable with the right
camping equipment. Maya smiled, thinking of Lilith. She was a true
wild woman. As they approached the beach on Hungry Mother
Creek, Maya did see Lilith's gorgeous kayak pulled up on the shore.

Violet was gathering her things in her boat. Her husband helped her slip over the side of the boat into the shallow water that hit Violet just below her knees. She had on rubber boots similar to Hazel's but this time had forgone the wrap around skirt for a pair of blue jeans stuffed into her boots. She wore a turtleneck with a red wool sweater and for her outer layer wore an oversized, thick flannel shirt. Maya guessed it must be her husband's. He handed Violet her bag and she headed to shore calling out good morning greetings to Lilith who had appeared from the woods and was stowing her tent in her kayak. Violet's husband, Ben, slowly backed his boat away from shore and then threw up a wave to Hazel and Maya as they pulled into the spot he had just vacated. Maya thought it was so sweet that he brought Violet and then came back in a couple of hours to retrieve her. She wondered what he did while they were meeting.

"Maya, can you help me with the anchor?" Hazel called. Maya went to the front of the boat and helped Hazel throw out the anchor to secure the boat. With the splash of the anchor, Lilith and Violet turned towards them.

"Good morning and happy winter solstice," Hazel said.

"Hey," Maya said, "I've brought some coffee and egg nog bread to share if we have time to have a snack before our ritual."

"That sounds great, Maya. Let me help you get your stuff out of the boat," Lilith said.

Lilith, like Maya, had on kayaking boots and waded out to their boat. Hazel handed Lilith her L.L. Bean Bag and Lilith helped her down. Maya did the same and as they walked to the beach Ella's kayak slid up.

"Well, 7:00 a.m. on the button," Violet said.

"I know. I was worried I'd be late but when I turned down Hungry Mother Creek I had a tail wind which helped me get here on time."

"Come on up, Ella." Lilith said. "Maya brought us some coffee and egg nog bread to start off our morning."

Maya poured the coffee into Styrofoam cups and handed each woman a miniature loaf of bread she had tied with red and green curling ribbon. She told them to save their loaves and cut each a slice from a larger loaf she had made especially for this morning. Before eating, Lilith suggested a moment of silence. There they stood, five women of varying ages in varying winter water apparel, looking towards the east where the pinkish orange glow was intensifying. Maya looked around in appreciation for these women in her life. This led her to think of Bay and she wondered how she was holding up and felt a little sorry that Bay didn't have a group like this. She'd give Bay a call this afternoon. It must be difficult spending Christmas time in a nursing home.

The group chitchatted for a few minutes about the events in their lives and about 7:20 Hazel moved them back to the circle by the Mother Tree. The woods looked different than they had in the fall. There was a thick coating of leaves on the ground and as Maya looked at the bare branches pointing towards the sky she couldn't help but be reminded of the trees that had been stripped of their leaves after Katrina. At least this time the bareness was part of the cycle of nature and not a reminder of the destruction of Katrina.

Everyone sat in the same place as before, Maya between Lilith and Violet. She was glad she had brought her camping chair to protect her from the cold hard ground this time. Hazel began preparations and Maya wondered if things would be the same as at the fall equinox ceremony. Hazel pulled out five large pillar candles and placed them in front of the Mother Tree. There were two red, two green and one white. Around the candles Hazel placed some pine boughs she had picked up as they had walked back into the woods and then added some holly she must have cut from the bushes around her house. The other women sat quietly in their spots watching Hazel.

One more time she reached into her bag and this time brought out a bell. It looked like the kind a church handbell choir would use. Hazel looked up at them and smiled. "Yes. I swiped this from my hand bell choir practice on Friday but they'll never miss it.

Thought it would be a nice way to center our group and begin our ritual." Although she tried to joke about the bell, Maya could hear the tension in her voice. She seems more nervous than I do, Maya thought. Hazel had been carrying her burden for over 40 years and Maya only two, so she guessed her load was heavier.

Hazel sat quietly holding the bell upright with the open end towards the sky. She moved her gaze around the circle and made eye contact with each one before slowly ringing the bell. The bell was medium-sized so the tone was mid range, probably equivalent to the pitch of an alto singer. This morning was quieter than the morning of the fall equinox. No scurrying squirrels, only a few birds chirping their morning call, and no leaves to rustle in the light breeze.

Hazel moved her arm and the bell rang out through the woods and its sound was carried by the water. It created a sharp contrast to nature's near silence and to Maya, felt eerily out of place. She wondered if this was a normal part of the winter ritual or something Hazel just did this time. Maya glanced around the group but couldn't get a read on anyone else's expression. It felt that the ringing went on and on and when the vibrations from the last one died out, Maya had counted thirteen. That's weird, Maya thought. Why would Hazel choose an unlucky number? Why not a number that had more symbolic meaning like five, for each woman or even twenty-four for the number of hours in a day?

Hazel set the bell down and after some silence said, "For those of you who don't know the significance of thirteen to our circle," Maya realized she was about to get her answer, "I will explain it. The number thirteen is often considered unlucky, but is actually a powerful feminine number. There are thirteen full moons each year and menstruating women have thirteen cycles each year, so for people like us, in touch with the natural cycles, we can appreciate the significance of this number. I thought it was appropriate as we end the twelfth month to recognize the number thirteen. If women had been in charge of the calendar, maybe there would have been thirteen months," Hazel said with a smile.

"Now, let us begin our ritual. Maya, this is your first winter solstice with the group so I'll explain what we're going to do. It's pretty much the same as before. We'll pass the talking stick, share out insights about the issue we've focused on in the dark and then light the candle and place anything we brought as symbols of the work we've done at the base of the Mother Tree."

Maya looked down in her bag and saw the blue and yellow top to the urn with Steven's ashes. Her pulse quickened as she thought about what was to come. Part of her wanted to just disappear and not do this, but a larger part was ready to move forward. Maya looked around the circle and wondered who would go first. She laughed to herself when she remembered what Lilith was taking into the dark and thought that may be a good way to end the circle, with a good laugh. Well, that wasn't going to happen because Lilith was reaching for the talking stick now. She smiled as she picked it up. Her enthusiasm and zest for life were easy to discern as she almost seemed to glow against the backdrop of the dark woods.

"So, I imagine you all are waiting with bated breath to see how my sex life has progressed over the past couple of months." Everyone laughed and Maya felt herself blushing and suddenly very warm in the cold December air thinking of how she missed the passion she had shared with Travis.

"Well, I'll tell you. It has definitely improved. I think the most important part was just setting the intention of focusing on my sexuality. I did things for myself like bubble baths, massage and even broke out my vibrator. I had to buy new batteries because it hadn't been used in so long but it definitely still works," Lilith said with a smile.

Maya looked around wondering what the others were thinking. She was floored. She had never known a woman who used a vibrator or at least who talked about it. Lilith certainly seemed comfortable with it and Maya could understand how it might help your sex life. Of course she didn't have a sex life to be helped at this moment.

Lilith continued, "Paul and I set a date night every week that we knew would end in sex, or should I say we would initiate sex no matter what and then see what happened. Of course, for him, just knowing what was coming at the end of the evening was enough to get him going and I'm happy to say things always turned out well." Lilith laughed and lifted the talking stick towards the sky for emphasis.

"But on a more serious note," Lilith continued, "putting some focus and energy towards my sexuality created a better balance in my life. Just like I pay attention to my health, my social life and my spirituality, my sexuality is also something that needs attention. Relighting this fire, so to speak, has created more intimacy and connection between Paul and me. It also has given me more energy and creativity. I even broke out my easel and water colors which I haven't used for years."

Lilith laid the talking stick back in the center of the circle and took the lighter Hazel had brought. She lit the green candle at the far left end of the row and then pulled a Ziploc bag from her coat pocket. It took a minute for Maya to realize what was in there. It was a fresh fig. Maya wondered what that had to do with anything. Lilith gently took the fig from the bag, pulled it open and laid it in front of her candle. Maya knew immediately why she chose the fig. The folds, curves and color of the fig's hidden interior closely

resembled that of a woman's hidden folds. Maya would never look at
a fig the same way again.

The group sat in silence watching the flame on the green
candle pulse and jump in response to the gentle easterly breeze.
During the silence, Maya thought about what Lilith had shared. It
had been funny, but she also had some good points. Sex was not
something she really ever thought about. It was just something that
happened when she was in a long term relationship. Up until the last
two years with Steven, she'd always enjoyed it but it was not
something she usually initiated or sought out, but that had changed a
little with Travis. Hmm another area of growth, Maya thought. She
could probably find a book on that to add to her self-help collection.

She looked around the circle and wondered what the others
were thinking and what their experiences were. She would have liked
a time for the other women to comment after someone had shared.
She wasn't sure the protocol for changing the ritual but would talk
with Hazel about it later. She didn't think Ella was in a relationship
so was probably in the same boat as she as far as sex. She just guessed
that it had been many years since Hazel had had sex, unless she was
having a secret affair with Doug, the UPS man, since he came so
regularly. And Violet. She'd been married for 52 years to the same
man. She wondered how sex changed over that period of time or if it
even still had a place in their relationship. Violet just happened to

look over at Maya and their eyes met. Violet smiled and then reached to the center of the circle to get the talking stick. Maya quickly looked away, embarrassed that she had been contemplating Violet's sex life.

Violet sat back in her chair and was silent as she held the talking stick. She definitely looked the part of a loving grandmother. Maya could easily imagine her pulling chocolate chip cookies out of the oven and hugging a distraught grandchild to her chest. Maya remembered their lunch together just before Thanksgiving and how she had hugged her goodbye. There was something so soft and nurturing about her presence that was different from Hazel, Lilith and even her sister, but they all had something special to offer.

Maya brought her attention back to the circle as Violet began, "You may remember, my goal was to work on my fear of Ben dying and having to live without him. It had begun to interfere with my enjoyment of all the things happening right now and I didn't like that. My goal was to be more fully present in each moment Ben and I have together. I talked with him about this and he liked the idea of mindfulness and has been learning more about it too. We agree that it will be a useful skill to have when one of us dies. Thanks to Maya for lending me those books on mindfulness. Inspired by that reading, I decided to keep a rock in my pocket as a reminder to stay present. As soon as I became aware that I was worrying about something that might happen in the future, I would pull out that rock and roll it around in my hand. I would focus on how the rock felt against my skin and how my breath felt in my body. That was usually enough to bring me back to what I was actually doing in that moment. If I really felt the need to think about the future and how my life might be without Ben, I allowed time for this but did it mindfully and by choice. Sometimes I wrote in a journal and other times just talked with him or one of my daughters. I'm still a work in progress as we all are I guess, but have found this practice becoming more natural."

Violet reached in her pocket and brought out a white, black and gray speckled rock. Maya imagined she must have found it in the Neuse or a nearby creek. It was about the size of a plum but flat. Violet walked to the Mother Tree laid her rock in front of the red candle next to the one Lilith had lit, and then lit her red candle. Before sitting down she reached in her pocket and pulled out another rock. Maya could tell this one was store bought as it was oblong and perfectly smooth and white and had the word NOW etched into one side of it. "Ben just gave me this rock on the way over here today because he knew I was leaving the other. I will carry this one with me and it is even more special since it was a gift from him."

Violet still had the talking stick in one hand and her rock in the other so didn't have a free hand to wipe away a couple of tears that were sliding down her left cheek. "I've just realized," Violet said with a shaky voice, "that if Ben does die before me, I'll have this rock not just as a reminder of him and staying in the present, but it will remind me that he wants me to be happy in the here and now even if he isn't with me to share it."

Violet laid the talking stick back in the middle of the circle and took her seat, still holding the NOW rock in her left hand. Her right hand pulled a white handkerchief from her pant pocket and wiped her eyes.

Maya looked around and there wasn't a dry eye in the circle. What had resonated with Maya was one should continue living her life even in the face of the death of her spouse. Of course, there was no comparison between her marriage to Steven and Violet's to Ben, but it was just another reminder to not get lost in the past. Maya was also touched by the deep love between Violet and Ben. This relationship provided inspiration that she could find someone who loved her unconditionally.

Maya looked around the circle and wondered who would go next. She wasn't really ready but could go if she needed to. Hazel had already told her that she wanted to be last. Maya felt awkward as everyone sat in silence. She still wasn't totally comfortable being in a group like this. She was about the pick up the talking stick when Ella stood from her spot to retrieve it. Maya sighed with relief but knew that she had to be next.

Ella sat back down and looked thoughtfully around the circle. Maya watched her and was struck again by her beauty, high cheek bones, sapphire eyes and blond hair that fell to her shoulders. Today it was held back by a red head band that matched her red down jacket. She now understood how beauty could be a double edged sword and was interested in Ella's take on her social life since the equinox

Ella began, "I have to say I wasn't sure how this little project would work. I had originally set a goal of coming here today being able to say I had three or four new friends, but now I realize that wasn't a realistic goal so will share what has happened. A few weeks after we met for the fall equinox, I went on the Meetup.com determined to find several groups that looked interesting and in no time thought I would have a busy social life. I did find a couple of groups. One was a girl's night out group for women in their twenties and thirties and the other was a Meet up for transplants to North Carolina so everyone, like me, was originally from another state. I set a goal of going to each group at least twice and I did that but nothing really clicked with either group. It felt too forced. Like we were all auditioning for friends. After that, Maya went with me to watch a Chicago Bears football game at Half Time Pub and Grub. I'm a huge Bears fan since I grew up near Chicago and thought it would be fun to connect to others who have that in common with me. That didn't really work out either". Ella looked up and gave Maya a grateful smile. "A couple weeks after the football outing, I was taking my usual two mile morning walk around the neighborhood when I met Sara, who's about the same age as I am. She was coming down the steps of her townhouse to go for a walk just as I was passing by. We said good morning and started talking since we were both heading to the greenway trail in the neighborhood. So long story short, we hit it off, talked the whole two mile walk and now meet three mornings a week to walk and have gotten together for dinner and a movie a couple of times. She's just moved to my townhouse neighborhood after breaking up with her boyfriend of three years. Thanks to our chance meeting, I can tell you I have one new friend and a new outlook on friendships. First, they can't be forced so I will continue to stay open to new people in my life and follow up when I meet someone who interests me. Second, I realize I don't need 25 friends to be happy. I'm very satisfied with you guys, Sara, my parents and my sister and her family. I will enjoy everyone in my life now but not be afraid to pursue new friendships when they present themselves. On that note, I will include the intention to be on the lookout for a romantic relationship too." Ella smiled at this and then caught Lilith's eye and said mischievously, "And Lilith, after hearing what you said, I'm more inspired than ever to improve that aspect of my life."

Ella stood and took a small statue and placed it by the green pillar candle at the right end of the row of candles. The statue was of four figures in a circle with their arms wrapped around one another. She lit the candle, put the talking stick back in the middle and took her seat on the other side of Lilith. The women took a moment of silence in respect for what Ella had shared and Maya noticed Lilith squeezing Ella's left hand and giving her a smile. Then Maya realized it was her turn.

Only two candles were left and they were for her and Hazel. Maya looked across the circle and caught Hazel's eye. She nodded her head and Maya could see the tension written on her face. Hazel definitely seemed nervous and preoccupied today. Maya had looked her way while the other women were speaking and she had a faraway look in her eyes. She seemed to be looking through whoever was speaking and back into the woods. Maya hoped Hazel would feel better after her ritual.

Maya became aware that the silence was lasting longer than usual so that was her cue to retrieve the talking stick. Her heart was in her throat. As she sat back down, she could feel her hands trembling so moved the talking stick back and forth between them to keep them occupied. Where should she start? Maybe with how she's feeling right now.

"Even though this is my second time here, I'm feeling a little nervous. I hope I've correctly done the work I needed to do." Maya hesitated a moment to take a deep breath to slow her racing heart and then felt Lilith's hand on her right knee giving it a gentle squeeze. She could almost hear Lilith saying to her, "as long as you followed your intuition, you did the work you needed to."

"First, I want to thank you all for being so supportive when I shared my story in the fall. I think that was the biggest help. Not feeling judgment from you guys helped me see that perhaps I didn't need to be so harsh on myself. Over these three months, I've realized that forgiveness was what will help put this behind me, not so much for Steven, as for me. I spent many hours berating myself for staying in that unhealthy relationship. I also spent a lot of time feeling guilty every time I felt happy about a chance for a new life after he had died. I realized I'm my own worst enemy. I was angry with myself for staying in a bad relationship and then guilty when I was actually out of it with the chance for a happier life. I'll never forget what happened with Steven, our marriage and his death, and I can't change any of the decisions he or I made. All I can do is learn from that experience and make different choices in this phase of my life. From here on out, I will do my best to have compassion for myself and realize that I deserve to be happy in this moment. My being angry or guilty will not change the past. It just makes the present a lot less fun."

Maya smiled at the group and could feel each woman focusing on her. Each one exuded a different energy; Lilith's being the most exuberant, congratulating her for her new insights, Violet's was soft, enveloping and full of genuine happiness that she was moving forward, Ella's was quieter and respectful of the lessons Maya had learned and Hazel's energy was different from her usual. Maya mainly felt sadness coming from her, compassion too but mainly grief. Maybe Hazel was regretting she hadn't learned the lessons Maya had till so late in life. Anyway, it would be Hazel's turn to share in a minute and hopefully Maya would better understand her mood then.

Maya slid forward in her camp chair and said, "I would like you all to walk back to the creek with me so I can scatter Steven's ashes." She stood and picked up her bag. The others followed her out of the circle and down to the water's edge. It was about eight o'clock now and the sun was above the tree line. They sky was a brilliant blue, not a cloud in sight. Because the colder temperatures had killed off the algae, the water was clear and the bottom of the creek could easily be seen. A breeze stirred and Maya felt the crisp December air on her face. She stood in silence in about two feet of water staring down Hungry Mother creek in the direction of Beards

Creek. She remembered standing by the water of the Gulf with Steven the first time she had visited and the excitement she felt at this new love and being in a new place. Part of her wanted to grab her younger self and say hurry, run, don't stay but instead she sent her former self love, support and forgiveness for the mistakes she would make in the coming years.

Maya took the yellow and blue urn out of her bag and threw the bag back up on the beach. She turned the wide lid on the urn and when it was free, put this in her coat pocket. Maya was not sure exactly what human ashes looked like. At the request of Steven's brother, who finally returned her call, the man at the crematorium in New Bern had packaged half of the ashes to be sent to Oregon. She looked in the urn and saw it was lined in a thick plastic bag. After pulling out the bag, she took a few steps back to the beach and set the urn on the sand. Looking through the translucent haze of the bag, the contents looked like regular ashes. Just as if someone had cleaned out their fireplace.

She walked back into the water and found it surreal to be standing there, holding what had been Steven. As she leaned down to open the bag, she felt Ella, Violet, Lilith and Hazel walk out in the shallow water beside and behind her. Each one put a hand on her. She felt their touch on her arm, shoulders and lower back. She could do this. She was not alone. Slowly she turned the bag upside down and released her grip on the opening. The ashes began to slide into the water.

Because the water was so clear, she could watch them catch the current and then dissolve out of sight. Near the bottom there was a small chunk of bone mixed in with the ashes and this reinforced the fact this used to be a human body and a sob caught in Maya's throat. The last of the ashes were in the water and she turned and was immediately enveloped in a group hug by the other women.

She sobbed for Steven's death and his unhappy life; she sobbed for the sadness and shame she endured while with him and sobbed for the dreams she'd had about marriage that never came true. All the while she was held until her sobs subsided. The women remained silent and Maya realized it was because she still had the floor, even though the talking stick wasn't in her hand. Maya put the urn back in her bag and walked back to the sacred circle. She remained standing while everyone else sat. She looked at these four women with overflowing gratitude and couldn't help but notice their eyes were damp as well. Maya took several breaths to center herself and then in an instant of inspiration removed the urn from her bag and took it to Lilith. "Lilith, I hadn't planned this, but will you take the urn for me? Feel free to throw it away, donate it or sell it at the farmers' market. I just don't want to take it home with me."

Lilith smiled and nodded her head in agreement as she took the urn and set it by her feet. Maya faced the candles at the base of the Mother Tree and pulled a frameless picture and a shoe lace from her coat pocket. Now holding the talking stick again, Maya said, "I brought two things to leave with the Mother Tree. The first is a picture of me and Steven on our wedding day. I wanted to bring that to honor all that our marriage has given me. In the beginning, Steven was capable of love and affection and we had lots of fun together going to New Orleans, dancing, walking on the beach near our cottage. As you know, there were many, many hard times too but I'm just beginning to see how they have helped me grow and become the person I am today. I also brought a shoe lace from an old running shoe in thanks for my running which helped provide a positive outlet when things were tough. My self-esteem was pretty low because of all of Steven's degrading comments, but running allowed me to feel successful and in control of at least one area of my life."

Maya walked over and lit the red candle next to the green one Ella had lit and placed her picture and shoelace in front. She stood for a moment looking at the flickering flame and then the wedding picture. She remembered that day, May 16, 1998. The picture was taken just after the ceremony on her parents' property. The grass was lush and the mountains behind her glowed with the yellow green of spring. She was wearing a white satin strapless gown. It was floor length, and very simple. She had worn a pearl and diamond necklace that had been her grandmother's and luckily had found some matching earrings. She remembered feeling beautiful that day. Steven was handsome in his black tux. His green eyes were piercing, even looking at her now from the picture. Maya turned to put the talking stick back in the middle when a sudden gust of wind came up from the water and blew her wedding picture into the trees behind the Mother Tree. Ella rose to retrieve it, but Maya held up her hand to stop her. She put the talking stick down in the middle of the circle and sat down.

Now in front of her red candle there was just a shoelace and she could see the picture, face down in some leaves to the right of the Mother Tree. The group sat in silence in respect for Maya's ritual. Maya felt drained from being the center of attention for what seemed like a long time. She tried to determine if she felt any different after having completed her ritual but couldn't tell yet. She wasn't sure what to expect and she guessed part of her was hoping to feel immediate closure. Instead, she felt tired and neutral. She figured time would tell if this had been helpful. The group now turned their attention towards Hazel.

Maya could tell Hazel's breath was shallow and quick and as she reached for the talking stick, her hands were trembling. Maya's heart went out to her knowing how she must feel as she prepared to make herself vulnerable in front of the group. But this was the place to do it and not be judged. Hazel sat back in her chair and coughed several times into her monogrammed handkerchief that was always in her pocket.

Once her throat cleared, she began, "I've been in this circle for years and am thankful for all the love, support and growth that has transpired. The blessings of this circle are the result of the energy of the women who have sat here over the past 100 years combined with the wisdom of the universe and God as represented by our beautiful Mother Tree. Today I call on all the women who have ever sat here and you wild, wonderful women in front of me to support me through this ritual which is the product of 40 years of hidden grief."

As Maya listened she could hear Hazel's voice strengthening and with each sentence she was sitting taller in her chair, her shoulders back, head high looking at the candles and the Mother Tree. It was as if the energy from the women of the circle past and present were infusing her with strength. Maya looked around the circle, and Violet, Ella and Lilith all watched Hazel intently. The silence of the women seemed deeper somehow, maybe in reverence for Hazel, their elder and the one who had sat in this circle the longest. Hazel reached in her L.L. Bean bag and brought out a small

square photo that looked like it was taken a long time ago. She held
it up to the group.

"This is a picture of me and Hay having one of our picnic
lunches at Meredith. One of the yearbook photographers was out
wandering around, taking spring time photos of the campus and just
happened to find us. Luckily, she thought we were just two
colleagues having lunch on a beautiful day. In this picture, I was six
weeks pregnant, but, of course, Hay didn't know. It was only a week
after this picture was taken that I had the abortion."

Hazel stopped for a minute to compose herself. Her voice
had become very thick and tight with the last sentence as if her throat
was constricting around the word abortion and didn't want it to pass
her lips. Hazel stood and took a few steps to light the white candle in
the center of the others. She stuck one edge of the photograph in the
flame until a new flame leapt up and the left corner of the picture
began to melt in the heat. She dropped the picture onto the ground
and watched it quickly incinerate.

"I know burning this doesn't erase what happened, but it
symbolizes for me that it needs to be left in the past. I can't tell you
how much time and energy I've spent looking at that picture or
recalling that scene in my mind and thinking about all the what if's
instead of focusing on what is in my life. In preparing for this ritual,
I reviewed my life and found many positive things I could have

focused on. I spent so much time grieving the life that was missing, that I didn't acknowledge all the lives that I had touched in a meaningful way. To honor this neglected part of my life, I have composed a list of names to read. These are students, friends and co-workers whose lives I positively impacted in some way. I feel a little self-conscious acknowledging the good things I've done but then that is part of the issue I am trying to overcome. So, here goes."

Hazel had remained standing in the middle of the circle after burning her picture. To her left, was the Mother Tree and behind her the forest. The sun was higher now and sending rays of light streaming through the trees and illuminating the gray hair that framed Hazel's face. She began, "Crystal, Sara, Wendy, Ronda, Megan, Beth …"

It took Hazel several minutes to read through the list she had compiled. Maya could tell it was meaningful to her and she paused after each name as if to recollect a specific memory with that person. Hazel continued to stand holding her list and before she could say anything else, Maya heard Lilith to her left say, "LILITH!" Oh, Maya thought, she's adding her name to the list. Then Violet said, "VIOLET ADLER!" and Ella said, "ELLA JOHNSON!" Maya finished by saying "MAYA SOMMERS," happy that in such a short time she had been so positively impacted by Hazel. Hazel's eyes glistened again with tears but this time Maya knew they were of gratitude and not grief. She smiled broadly at them and said, "Thank you for that. It means so much to me."

Hazel took her list and placed it under the white pillar candle she had lit earlier. She went back to her chair but continued to hold the talking stick, so the group remained silent and waited. Maya wondered what else it was Hazel was going to say. Hazel coughed again into her handkerchief and then said, "I do have one more thing to share and that cough was a good transition because I need to tell you more about it. I know Maya has noticed, and maybe you others have too, that I've had a nagging cough over the last couple of months. Well, the first week of December, I went to my family doctor in New Bern. He listened to my lungs, took some X-rays and then sent me to Dr. Greenburg, a pulmonologist at Craven Regional Hospital. After more tests and a biopsy, they told me I had Stage IV lung cancer that had metastasized to my liver." As quickly as those words left her lips, all four women in the circle gasped.

Maya's heart lurched and began racing. She felt so many levels of sadness. Sadness that Hazel had gone through this process alone, sadness that now, just as she had made some peace with her life she had to deal with this and then sadness for Hazel's death which would most likely be sooner than expected.

Hazel remained calm and focused and continued. "I know you will need time to process this like I did. I've done nothing but think about the cancer for the last two weeks since I was diagnosed."

She'd known for two weeks and hadn't told anyone, Maya thought. I wish she'd have let me take her to the hospital for all those tests.

As if reading her mind, Hazel said, "I know I could have called on any one of you for help and support but I needed to do this alone and the past few weeks have allowed me to somewhat come to terms with this cancer before I told you all. As you probably know, Stage IV cancer with mets to the liver has a very poor prognosis. Even with aggressive treatment, I only have a small chance of living more than a couple of years. After several long discussions with my oncologist to understand my options, I have decided against any treatment. At 79, I don't see the need to put my body through the assault of radiation and chemotherapy. Their side effects would greatly impair my quality of life and there is no guarantee it would make that much of a difference. Dr. Greenburg said I could expect to live three to six months without treatment and I want to spend that time here, by the river, in the home I grew up in, not driving back and forth to New Bern for treatments and then perhaps having to be hospitalized for complications." Hazel paused again and Maya began to cry. She had only known Hazel for six months but could not even imagine life in Oriental without her. Maya looked around the circle and saw the other women crying as well but Hazel remained composed.

"I know this is a shock to everyone and to me too, especially because I never smoked or was around a smoker. But anyway, the idea of death is not so shocking. As Violet knows, once you pass 65, you realize everyday is a blessing and at any point your body could give out. I guess the blessing here is that I have some sort of a timetable. I can create a meaningful end to my life rather than just not waking up one day. I do want you all to be a big part of the next few months and am hoping we can gather more often as long as I'm feeling well. As we prepare to close our ritual, please remember that tonight is the longest night of the year, but beginning tomorrow, there will but just a bit more light and the days will begin to lengthen. Let's focus on the gift we have of being together right now. We'll join hands and have a few moments of silence and then blow out our candles to end our ritual."

The women all stood, stepped in towards the center of the circle and held hands. Maya had Lilith on her left and Violet on her right and was directly across from Hazel. With their hands now otherwise occupied, the tears continued to stream down all the women's faces except Hazel's, who looked amazingly peaceful considering what she had just disclosed.

Lilith and Violet were both holding Maya's hand tightly and she could feel the warmth of their hands moving into her own. They stood silently, their eyes cast downwards towards the center of the circle. Maya could feel their breath synchronizing. Her tears subsided and the power of their breaths and connection helped unknot her heart. In this silence, connected to these four other women and to the women who had stood here over the last 100 years, Maya felt a deep sense of peace and appreciation for the cycle of life. The world was as it should be and everything was connected, past, present and future. Maya raised her head and looked over Hazel's head to the creek beyond the trees.

The others had also lifted their gaze and were looking at one another, smiling. Lilith and Violet gave her hand a tight squeeze before they released it. One by one, in the order they performed the ritual, they each blew out their candles, Lilith, Violet, Ella, Maya and then Hazel knelt to blow out her candle. As Hazel stood, Maya couldn't hold back anymore and stepped across the circle to grasp Hazel in a tight hug. The others gathered around and enveloped Hazel as well. No words were spoken. Maya could feel Hazel shaking against her chest and when she looked down, saw Hazel had begun to cry. Lilith rubbed Hazel's back to comfort her. Who knows how long they stood there but the moment was broken with the hum of Ben's boat engine.

Chapter 12

Monday December 31, 2007

10, 9, 8, 7, 6, 5, 4, 3, 2, 1 "Happy New Year!" It was only eight o'clock in the evening but they were having an early celebration at the nursing home. Bay stood behind Holden who was wearing a plastic top hat with 2008 in silver writing on it. She wasn't sure if he knew it was New Year's Eve. He was able to count down from 10 but then was startled by the cheers and noisemakers and looked around in confusion. Bay walked around and knelt in front of him.

"Holden. It's okay. Everyone is celebrating the New Year. Tomorrow will be January first, 2008." He did focus his eyes on her but as usual she couldn't tell if he understood her. She pulled a chair around and sat in front of him as others were getting their fruit punch. She could hear the crackle of the plastic as people removed chocolate chip cookies from the plastic trays they came in. The cookies were accompanied by potato chips and French onion dip whose smell was making Bay sick. What a contrast to last year.

"Holden, remember New Year's Eve last year? We went to the club house at River Dunes? You looked so handsome in your tuxedo and I wore that gorgeous light blue sequined dress? We went with the Phillips and the Harrisons. Remember those are the men you play golf with. We ate baked Brie, shrimp, roast beef, scalloped potatoes, creamed spinach and crème brulée for dessert. Remember the band Holden? They played a lot of beach music and we shagged? You always were such a wonderful dancer."

Bay clasped both her hands over Holden's right hand that was in his lap. As she talked, his eyes left her and were watching the other residents eating their New Year's Eve snacks. She realized she had lost his attention so continued to reminisce in her own mind. She remembered how dashing Holden had looked that night in his tux. He was very charming with both the men and women and all night they were surrounded by people. She felt important to be his wife and she could tell he was proud of her. He kept a hand in the small of her back or around her waist most of the night. She had always loved it when they were out at social events because they seemed to connect better there than when they were at home, just the two of them. Maybe it was because they both felt comfortable with their public personas but privately weren't sure how to be together. They had never quite perfected those roles and with no audience, it didn't really matter anyway except that it did because most of the time they were outside the public eye.

Bay wiped the drool that was coming from the left corner of Holden's mouth and sat back in her chair trying to feel proud and important to be Holden's wife now, like she had last New Year's Eve, but couldn't. Now that he was different, her feelings had changed. She cared about him and desperately wanted him to recover, but more the way you care about your favorite uncle, not your husband.

One of the nurses' aides broke her train of thought when she walked up to Holden with some food. "Mr. Witherspoon, Happy New Year! I brought you some punch and cookies." She turned and handed Bay the cup and plate knowing he was unable to feed himself. Bay bit her tongue but desperately wanted to say, "Happy New Year. What is there to be so happy about? Holden hasn't shown any improvement in the past month and the doctors aren't hopeful anything will change. Potentially I am looking at a man I'll have to take care of for the rest of his life. Basically two lives have been sacrificed so excuse me if I don't feel so happy about a New Year." But she didn't say this and instead said, "Happy New Year to you too, Belinda, and thank you for bringing this over to Mr. Witherspoon."

Ever appearing to be the doting wife, she broke one of the Wal-Mart brand cookies into smaller pieces and fed it to Holden.

She glanced at her watch to see if she'd been there long enough and could go yet. It was 8:15 p.m. That was time enough.

Bay pulled out of the nursing home parking lot feeling restless. Here it was almost nine o'clock on New Year's Eve and she was heading back to an empty house. Maybe she would just stop somewhere for a glass of wine and feel a part of the real world. Not that make-believe world in the nursing home that glossed over the fact that for most of the residents, the best days of their lives were over.

Bay remembered a cute pub where she and Maya had had lunch one day when Holden was still in the hospital. She would drive right past it on her way home so might as well stop by for one drink. As she headed towards Morgan's Tavern and Grill, she was glad she had dressed for Holden's party and would feel comfortable going out. She had on a pair of fitted dark denim jeans, silver strappy heels and a silver scooped neck top. Her blond hair was down and fell just to her shoulders. She had makeup in her purse to freshen up before she went in. Suddenly her mood lifted just a bit and she turned the radio to her favorite country station as she neared the pub.

Bay pulled into the small parking lot and got the last space. When she opened her car door, she could hear the thump of music coming from inside the bar. They must have gotten a live band for tonight. With one last look at herself in the rear view mirror, she slammed the car door and headed in. Some Marines, who must have been from Cherry Point, held the door for her and let her enter first. As she walked towards the bar she could feel their eyes following her, and she smiled. It felt good to have men appreciate her. Holden hadn't even said her name since his stroke.

The next morning Bay woke up with a headache and dry mouth from too many glasses of Chardonnay the night before. She had a millisecond of amnesia, and then what she had done hit her full on. She rolled over in her bed and saw it was after ten already. She hadn't gotten home till two. Bay lay there under her 600 count cotton sheets and tried to decide exactly how she was feeling. She had to admit a part of her thoroughly enjoyed last night even if it was a one night stand. She hadn't had sex like that since before she married Holden, raw passion and pleasure. Her body had missed sex and the wild abandon of just being totally in the moment as you give and receive physical pleasure.

It had probably been six months since she and Holden had last had sex and it definitely didn't have the intensity of last night. Bay knew both she and that young Marine were just using each other for the immediate satisfaction, but she was OK with that because it had been a relatively clear choice on her part. She had to admit that her judgment may have been somewhat clouded by the Chardonnay and intoxication of all the focused attention Duncan had given her.

As she thought more about last night, the guilt began to set in. She was still married and had made a promise to be faithful. She'd always been, even when tempted in the past. She knew Holden had also upheld his vow and although they weren't totally connected at all times, she had never felt his attention straying towards another woman.

Her eyes moistened as she thought about Holden and how well he'd always treated her. Any material thing she wanted, he got her. Any place she wanted to travel, they went. The worst thing he ever did was to be indifferent towards her, especially when she talked of wanting to pursue her education and a possible career in fashion design.

Bay leaned over and grabbed the water bottle she'd left by her bed and drained about half of it. She flopped back on the pillow and looked at the ceiling. She did feel different. Last night had definitely put her back in touch with her sexual self but also last night she was just Bay and not the caregiver, not the younger, attractive wife, not trying to fit in, just Bay and she liked that feeling. This felt like too much to think about alone. She wondered if Maya was home and wanted to meet for New Year's brunch over at Toucans.

***

Maya walked up the staircase to Hazel's bedroom carefully balancing the tray with coffee, a scrambled egg and cinnamon toast on it. Thankfully Hazel had let Maya help her get rid of some of her things over the past few weeks and the steps were now mostly clear of boxes. The dining room and two guest rooms were still full, but the laundry room, kitchen and hallways were free of the precarious stacks of boxes that had lined the wall like paparazzi lining the red carpet.

The Sunday after the solstice ritual, they had even tackled the living room that looked out onto the creek and the grandfather clock that had been obscured was now waxed, ticking and chiming the hour. Many of the things from the top few layers were good enough to donate to charity but as they worked down towards the floor to the older things, they could salvage less. At times, it was quite disgusting and Hazel cried, realizing how much filth she'd been harboring in her family home that she loved so much. They found mice skeletons, cockroach droppings and even a snake skin. Most of the items near the floor were rotted, rusted, warped from the weight on top of them, or nibbled by the many creatures the piles must have sustained.

"Hazel, here's some breakfast," Maya said as she set the tray on top of the bed tray Hazel had put across her legs.

"Thank you so much. I could have gotten my own breakfast this morning, but when you called and offered to come over, I couldn't refuse being waited on. In the past couple of days, my energy has been low and going up and down those steps once a day is almost more than I can do now."

Maya sat in the white wicker rocking chair that was beside Hazel's bed and involuntarily began to rock. This was only the second time she'd been in Hazel's bedroom and it felt like going back in time. Hazel had told her the room was decorated almost exactly as it had been when her grandparents had used it as their master bedroom when Hazel was just a child. The wallpaper had small lavender flowers with the green leaves and stems creating a diamond pattern. White lace curtains framed the windows. Hazel's bed was in the far left corner. There was a window just to the left of her headboard that overlooked the roof of her office.

The headboard of the iron bed reminded Maya of a rising sun with a semi circle arch that was connected to the base of the bed by six iron posts. The bed faced the creek and that wall had a set of double windows and then French doors that opened up onto the upper porch. Maya appreciated the elevated view of the creek and being able to see where the mouth of Beards Creek met the Neuse.

Maya watched Hazel breaking off a small piece of cinnamon toast to eat. It was amazing how quickly the cancer was affecting her. It was almost as if once she told everyone, she relaxed and then gave into the symptoms. Her color was more gray than tan now. This morning, she was wearing an ivory satin bed jacket that she'd rolled up at the sleeves and tied with a purple ribbon at the waist to keep it from swallowing her. Her movements were slow and deliberate and

Maya was aware of each breath Hazel took. Hazel glanced up and caught Maya's gaze.

"Sorry I'm not a great conversationalist this morning. We haven't seen each other since you left Christmas Eve day. How was your Christmas? Weren't you and your sister going to visit your parents? How did that go?"

Maya looked away from Hazel and thought a minute about how she could best describe her Christmas, especially her time with her parents. She didn't want to say anything that would upset Hazel, like the night Hazel brought over the decorations, but knew she had to be truthful.

"I had a great time at Kate's, helping her and Rob celebrate their first Christmas with Worth. I'm lucky they let me be a part of their Christmas morning and it was just the four of us, and of course Doodle Bug. Worth could feel our excitement. He was laughing and very keyed up. Like most babies, he loved all the wrapping paper and bows more than the actual presents. Lord, he had plenty of presents. After his Santa presents, presents from Kate, Rob and me, he had more from Rob's parents, brother and sister- in- law who came over around two. Rob's brother has two children, a son who is four and a daughter who is two so with five adults and three children it was a full house. It did feel festive as we all prepared the Christmas meal together with the two and four year old running all around high on their buzz of new toys."

"Maya, that sounds lovely and just how Christmas should be."

"It was, Hazel, but I was exhausted by the time we went to bed. I'm so used to being alone that it was draining being around that many people and especially the children who are so high energy. What did you do for Christmas? Did your son drive down from New Bern?"

Maya knew Hazel had invited her son, daughter-in-law and grandson over for the day but wasn't sure if that had worked out. Hazel set her cup of coffee in the saucer and looked out the windows to the creek. What was it about staring at the water that helped get one's thoughts in order, Maya wondered. As she watched Hazel, she recalled the hundreds of times since moving here that she just stared at the water as she tried to make sense of her thoughts.

Hazel turned back to Maya, "He couldn't come Christmas day. He, his wife and my grandson were going to her family's in Clinton, about two hours from New Bern so he said it would be too much driving for one day. Ben came and picked me up about eleven and I had a lovely Christmas lunch with Violet's family. Like you, I enjoyed being with a large family with lots of children but it did exhaust me. Counting me, there were twelve of us at the table. By

2:30 I was ready to come home. I spent the rest of the day right here, napping and reading. Hey, where's Doodle Bug? I've been missing her too."

"I left her in a sunny spot on the couch napping. We did a longer run this morning and she was tired. I also wasn't sure if you were up for a 60 pound lab jumping in your bed and licking your face."

"That would have been good medicine for me so please bring her by later today if you have time. Do you have any plans for today since it is New Year's?"

"No. Not really. I went to bed early last night so I could do a long run at sunrise to welcome in the New Year and then made blueberry pancakes. I haven't planned much past that besides getting ready to return to work tomorrow. Did you ever get to see your son and does he know about your cancer?" Maya asked, realizing Hazel had never finished that story.

"I guess I did try to breeze past that topic. Yes, I saw Wynn the day after Christmas. He came alone. He said Luke was spending time with his high school friends while he was home from college and Emily was hitting the after Christmas sales. He brought us a take-out lunch from Brantley's. That was always his favorite restaurant here in Oriental. When he arrived, he was shocked and very pleased to see the cleaning you and I had done. We were able to sit at the kitchen table to eat rather than balancing plates on our laps out in my office like in the past. Anyway, I began coughing, as usual, and this gave me the chance to tell him about the cancer. It took me a while to convince him I was totally committed to my decision to forego any treatment. He wanted me to go to some oncologist he knew of at UNC Chapel Hill. He seemed to go into action mode wanting to do something and so I'm not sure how he really felt about my cancer. He seemed agitated with me that I wasn't fighting it and couldn't seem to accept that I was at peace with dying."

Hazel stopped and began to cry. She reached for a Kleenex in the box on her bed side table. "Maya, I'm sorry to get upset again. It just feels like Wynn and I are such different people and have trouble communicating and understanding one another. It always feels tense when we're together and this was no different. I thought knowing I was approaching death would change how he acts towards me, but so far it hasn't. Emily hasn't even called to check in on me and I'm sure he must have told her." Hazel stopped to blow her nose and Maya, her own heart swelling with hurt for Hazel, reached out and rubbed Hazel's back.

"So, I didn't have the courage to tell him about the past, why I was depressed and why I had all this stuff in the house. I don't know if I'll ever be able to tell him. It doesn't feel possible that our relationship can change after over 40 years, especially when there are only a few months left." Hazel began to cry harder and through her tears said, "Maya, sometimes I feel like I was the worst mother possible and I ruined both our lives."

Maya moved her hand from Hazel's back to hold her right hand. She felt awkward, not quite sure how to comfort Hazel, especially since she wasn't a mother herself. She worried she wouldn't have the right words to help but also knew she couldn't just sit there silent. So, once again following Lilith's advice, she followed her intuition and hoped it could give her the right words.

"I'm sorry things didn't work out like you wanted, but you can't stay focused on this. Remember your ritual and all the names that were spoken? You can't take total responsibility for your relationship with Wynn anyway. For the past 30 some years, he has been an adult and could have come to you. Remember at the ritual how you said you wanted the last months of your life to be meaningful? Well, if you spend most of your time on what you have regretted in life rather than what you are grateful for, I don't think the last few months will be what you want them to."

Maya finished, released Hazel's hand and sat back in the rocking chair. She was proud of herself for saying what she thought Hazel needed to hear. Hazel seemed to be letting this all sink in and Maya hoped her silence didn't mean her feelings were hurt or she was angry with her.

Hazel was smiling at Maya through the tears that still lingered in her eyes. "Thank you for that reality check and reminding me of the intention I had set at the solstice ceremony. I'm proud of you. You are becoming wiser and braver."

"I'm not so sure about that, Hazel. I didn't say anything to you that I haven't said to myself many times over the past few months."

Hazel finished her breakfast and Maya stood and removed the tray of dishes and the bed tray and set them all on the trunk at the foot of Hazel's bed. "Hazel, do you need any help getting dressed?"

"I can take care of that later, but thanks for the offer. Now Maya, I think you've also been avoiding a topic. How did the visit with your parents go?"

Maya sat back down in the rocking chair. "Like you, things didn't go as I would have liked. The long story short is that Kate just couldn't bring herself to go with me. Ever since she had Worth she's putting most of her energy towards her current family rather than trying to understand our childhood. She used to be the one who always had the high expectations every time we saw our parents and was let down when things didn't work out like she'd hoped. I was always more cynical and never really expected things to be different, except for this visit. After our talk before Christmas, I thought I understood my mother better. I had hoped that when I told her how you'd help me see things from her perspective she would open up and we would be able to begin forging a closer relationship."

Maya paused and Hazel interrupted, "Maya, I think I see the ending coming. You shared your new perspective with your mom and nothing changed."

"How did you know?"

"Like you just told me, it takes two people to make a relationship work and based on what you've told me, it doesn't sound like your mother wants to change."

"Yeah. She even implied that I was exaggerating about her depression and just said she was overwhelmed with her job and chronic headaches and needed a lot of time alone. I tried to explain how ignored and unimportant Kate and I had felt growing up but she just got defensive and focused on how hard she and Dad worked to provide for us. Then she abruptly changed the subject and asked me what books I'd read lately. That is always a comfortable subject in our family. I was there another twenty-four hours but our conversations were never deeper than literature, politics and her garden. She did seem interested in my life in Oriental and how I was adjusting, so that was positive."

Maya paused while Hazel coughed. This spell lasted at least a minute and had Maya worried but finally Hazel caught her breath. "Hazel, are you okay?"

"Yes. Yes. Please hand me that bottle of cough syrup that's in the bedside table drawer. The doctor said I could take it up to four times a day and I haven't had any yet today."

Maya got the bottle with the measuring cup on top and handed it to Hazel. Her emotion about her mother quelled as she focused on Hazel. Hazel took a capful of the purple liquid and then a sip of water.

"Ah, much better. Sorry I interrupted you. So how are you doing now, since your visit?"

"I just got home yesterday afternoon, but doing okay. Like Kate, I've realized I just have to accept the relationship for what it is because it won't change until my mother wants to make a change. Kate and I talked for at least an hour on my cell phone as I drove home and having her to share this with is a huge help. Thank God, we've always had each other."

"You haven't mentioned your father. Was he there? Could you talk with him about your mother?"

"He was gone most of the time with the after Christmas sale at his bookstore. I never saw him alone and anyway, they always seem to cover for each other, he for her depression and she for his drinking so I didn't bring anything up with him." It felt nice to be able to share this and then it hit Maya that her times like this with Hazel were limited.

Maya busied herself with picking up the tray of breakfast plates so Hazel couldn't see the tears in her eyes. Hazel rested her head on the pillows behind her and Maya could tell she was tired. "Maya, I think I'm going to take a mid morning nap before I get dressed. Thanks again for New Year's Day breakfast in bed. Maybe you and Doodle Bug can come by later this afternoon. I have some work to do at my desk so hopefully will be in my office. "

"We'd love to. I'll just wash up the dishes and head home." Still holding the tray in her hand, Maya bent down and gave Hazel a kiss on the cheek. Hazel squeezed her arm and then scooted down under the covers to nap.

Maya walked down the steps of Hazel's back porch and followed the well worn path under the grove of live oak, river birch and pine trees to her boathouse. The sun felt warm on the top of her head and shoulders. She looked up and appreciated the cloudless blue sky. With such low humidity, it was a brilliant blue and the brightness seemed to mock how she was feeling inside. As Maya stepped into her living room, Doodle Bug jumped up to greet her, her tail wagging with such unadulterated joy, you would have thought it had been ten days they'd been apart instead of a couple of hours. Maya smiled and knelt down to hug Doodle Bug, her greatest mentor when it came to mindfulness.

Maya stood, walked to her couch and lay down facing the creek windows. She lifted her legs up so Doodle Bug could jump up on the other end, do her ritual of three circles and then plop down, becoming a furry footstool for Maya. She glanced at her watch and saw it was only 10:30. She was also feeling a little sorry for herself since it was New Year's Day and she had absolutely no plans for the rest of the day.

She wondered what Travis was doing. She hadn't heard from him since he came over the night before the solstice. Her heart tugged a little when she thought of him and for a minute she fantasized about how it might feel to have woken up together this morning, sharing New Year's Day, drinking coffee, reading the newspaper, and maybe cooking together.

Maya rolled her eyes to herself. What was she thinking? It would never work with Travis. She was just feeling lonely. Maybe she would call Ella to see if she wanted to get together. She grabbed her phone off the coffee table and saw she had missed a call from Bay about twenty minutes ago. She just couldn't deal with her today. Bay needed a lot of support right now and today Maya wasn't up for it. She dropped the phone back on the table and stared out the windows.

The longer she lay on the couch, the deeper her funk became. Finally, she caught herself as she was imagining her life as a lonely old spinster 30 years from now, living in this same boathouse, trying to make ends meet on her social security income. Maya sat up and yelled, "STOP!" out loud, startling Doodle Bug whose head popped up from her napping position. She had let this pity party go too far and needed something to help her change her line of thought. Just then the glint of sun off the water caught her eye. Kayaking.

Without a second thought or wasted motion, Maya grabbed her cold weather kayaking gear, let Doodle Bug out for a quick run around and potty break and then headed for her blue kayak. Already her mood felt better as she anticipated gliding across the water, now so clear because of the cold temperatures. It had probably been a month since she'd been out. Today the wind was minimal, so Maya decided to paddle towards the mouth of Beards Creek. Maybe she'd just paddle on into town and get a bowl of chowder at M & M's cafe. With each paddle towards the Neuse, Maya could feel her perspective change. It was so much easier to be in the moment when you were exercising. She was aware of the tightening in her upper back as she paddled, the cold breeze on her face, the sun on her shoulders, the occasional call of a sea gull.

She paddled hard for fifteen minutes and reached the junction of Beards Creek and the Neuse River. Maya just floated for a minute, feeling full of gratitude for her surroundings and that this was her full time home. What a gift. She thought back to New

Year's Day last year and again was so thankful for how much better her life was overall despite feeling a little down today. She lived in a beautiful place, had met new friends, had made progress on dealing with Steven's death and was becoming better at giving and receiving affection. She smiled, turned her kayak towards town, already craving M & M's chowder. As she paddled, she saw a boat on the horizon heading her way. As it came closer she recognized it as Buster's Carolina Skiff and she began waving her paddle at him. He slowed his boat, waved back, and then slowly approached her so his wake wouldn't capsize her.

"Hey, good looking," Buster called out. "Happy New Year!"

"Happy New Year to you too. What are you doing out here? I thought you were in Florida?"

"I was but after Christmas I got antsy for home so got here a couple of days ago. I was actually heading over to see if you and Hazel were home. Thought I'd stop by for a New Year's visit. Glad I ran into you out here. How've ya been?"

"I'm good, Buster, but a lot has happened since you left at Thanksgiving. I was headed to M & M's for some chowder. I'd love it if you'd join me and we can catch up."

"Sounds perfect, Maya. I'll head on over, tie up at town dock and then meet you there in about fifteen minutes."

"Great. See you there."

"Oh, and Maya, hope there isn't a New Year's Day dress code cause those Gortex pants and neoprene boots may not make the cut!" Buster laughed and turned his boat towards town before Maya had a chance to respond. She laughed at his joke and wondered how he always seemed to show up at the right time.

***

Hazel woke up and it felt like it took all her energy just to lift her eyelids. The room was bright and sparkling with winter sun and she imagined it must be after lunch. Her watch was on her bureau across the room so she didn't know for sure. She lay there a minute letting the sleep roll back like a heavy morning fog. She slid herself up in the bed and moved her pillows behind her as a back rest.

Never had she felt such fatigue as this. It reminded her of the time she fell off her grandfather's boat one winter, probably when she was nine or ten. They were up towards New Bern fishing for stripers. She had been standing on the gunnels of the boat casting when the wake from another boat threw her off balance and into the river. She'd had on several layers of clothes and a heavy coat to stay warm. Once wet, their weight literally pulled her down towards the bottom of the river. It took all her efforts to fight to the surface and grab the life ring her grandfather had tossed. That's how her body felt now, like it was weighted down with heavy wet clothes.

Her full bladder wouldn't let her wait any longer so she pulled off the bed covers and slid her legs so they were hanging off the side of the bed. She sat there to catch her breath and eyed the bathroom down the hall. Since this was such an old home, there was no bathroom right in her bedroom and the one down the hall served the entire upstairs. Hazel stood, knowing she had no other option. She certainly wasn't going to pee in bed. She took a few steps and began the trek to the bathroom, her limbs loosening up a little now she was upright and moving. With steady progress, she made it to the bathroom at the top of the stairs. She stood in the doorway, catching her breath and regarding the goal of all her efforts, the toilet. Is this what my life is coming to, she thought? My only reason for getting up is to use the bathroom?

Hazel realized she had made some peace with death but hadn't given as much attention to the actual process of dying. She could feel the tears welling in her eyes but then remembered the open file on her desk downstairs which provided her with a higher purpose than the toilet. With renewed strength she finished in the bathroom and made her way back to the bedroom to get dressed.

Hazel set her cup of tea and mint Milano Pepperidge Farm cookies on her desk top next to the manila folder and then slowly let herself down into her chair. She took a sip of tea and then a small bite of cookie, comforted by the chocolate and mint combination.

These cookies had been a favorite of her mother's and a staple in the house ever since Hazel had moved back in twenty years ago. She knew she should be eating something more healthy and substantial, but just didn't have the energy to prepare anything else. Maybe if Maya came by later with Doodle Bug, she could heat up a can of soup for her. Hazel rejected that idea quickly, not wanting to take advantage of her relationship with Maya but for the first time felt scared about how she was going to make it through this and remain in her home. She didn't let herself dwell on those thoughts and opened the folder to review the budget sent to her by the organization she was meeting with on Tuesday. Immediately her focus was on the numbers, goals of the program, outcome measures and target population and her worries settled for the time being.

***

Maya pushed open the door of M & M's and looked for Buster. There was a crowd today for the New Years brunch and she finally saw Buster waving to her from the bar. She weaved her way through the people waiting for a table and took the seat Buster had saved for her.

"Buster, I think I fit in fine here in my red Gortex pants, but I do think my boots left a trail of puddles behind me. Ah well, at least it's so crowded that nobody will even notice what's on my feet."

"Maya, it's good to see you no matter what you have on. I missed you while I was in Florida, so tell me what excitement has been going on around here?"

Just then, Thomas the bartender came up to them. "What'll it be, Buster? Your regular?"

"Yup, Jack and Coke sounds good and Maya, what would you like?"

"Well, since it is New Year's Day, I'll have a glass of Merlot. Oh, and Thomas, can you also bring us two bowls of chowder and an order of crab dip to start with?"

"No problem. Be right back with your drinks and, Buster, it's good to see you back."

"Thanks. It was nice to have a change of scenery, but I'm glad to be home too." Buster turned back to Maya, "So, you were about to give me an update."

"Buster, I want to hear about your time in Florida too."

"I know. I'll get to that. Now give me the scoop on everything that's been going on."

"Okay. A quick update on me. You'll be happy to know I finally got rid of Steven's ashes. Thanks to you, Hazel and some other women I've met, I was able to move on. I'll never forget what happened of course, but will keep it in its rightful place, the past. After I did that I left for my sister's and then my parents' and only got home yesterday so haven't had much time in my normal routine yet to see how things may be different now that the urn is gone."

"Maya, that's great. I know it took a lot of soul searching and effort to get to this point, as well as some secret messages from the dolphins," Buster said playfully.

"Yeah. It probably was those dolphins who brought me to my senses. Anyway, it's Hazel." Maya paused and took her time to compose her thoughts.

Buster's smile left his face and he immediately looked concerned. "What's going on? Is she okay?"

"No, she's not," Maya hesitated not sure exactly the best way to tell Buster. "I just want you to be prepared. This is not good news. Hazel found out in the middle of December that she has Stage IV lung cancer that has metastasized to her liver." Maya hated to break this to Buster. She knew he had known Hazel for most of his life.

Buster was quiet and his face clouded over. Maya wondered if he was thinking of his wife who had died from cancer. After a moment, he said, "I know Hazel is almost 80 so I shouldn't be too shocked that she's sick, but she's always been so energetic and vibrant. I just never thought of her as ever dying. Is she getting treatment?"

Maya filled Buster in on the details of Hazel's diagnosis, decision to forego treatment and how she was doing this morning.

After hearing the synopsis of events, Buster said, "Unfortunately I have some experience with this since I cared for my wife until she died. Based on what you're telling me, I don't see how Hazel will be able to make it alone, even with hospice stopping in. If she wants to stay in her home, we need to figure out a plan to help her. Someone should be there with her most all of the time."

Maya was amazed how quickly Buster switched to action mode. She had been focusing on feeling sad and hadn't really thought about a plan to help Hazel yet. "You're right. After seeing Hazel this morning, it doesn't seem possible that she can take care of herself much longer." Maya's mind began to plan and was clicking along with ideas. "I can call our women's group and I know they would help and maybe I could talk with Travis too and he could coordinate people from the church."

Buster looked at her thoughtfully. "Those are great ideas, Maya, but I've known Hazel a long time and privacy is important to her. I don't know if she would feel comfortable with lots of different people traipsing in and out of her home. In fact, I'll be surprised if she lets Hospice come."

Maya and Buster both leaned back from the bar to let Thomas serve them their drinks and crab dip. Buster immediately spread some dip on a triangle of pita bread that came with it. "Oh, this is great. I'd been craving this while I was in Florida."

Maya made one for herself and then clinked her wine glass with Buster's highball as he said, "To Hazel."

"To Hazel."

They sat in silence a moment and enjoyed the crab dip. There was a buzz all around them. It looked like several large groups of people, probably families or groups of friends, Maya thought. She pondered what Buster had just said. He was right. She doubted Hazel would let lots of people have full access to her home to help care for her. She wasn't even sure if the women's circle had ever been there. But she had, and Hazel must feel comfortable with her around since she'd let Maya help clean out her house and make breakfast this morning. Maya took another sip of wine and realized there seemed to be only one logical answer.

"I can take care of Hazel. She definitely seems comfortable with me around so I could be the primary one in her house and all the others I mentioned could help me by bringing food, running errands for me, staying for short times to give me a break." As Maya verbalized her thoughts, the more resolute she became. This is what she needed to do. It felt like the right thing. She just hoped Hazel would agree.

"But, Maya, what about your job? This would require most of your time and once the cancer progresses, Hazel shouldn't be left alone at all so I don't see how you could work."

What was she thinking? Her concern for Hazel clouded her mind and she had totally forgotten that small issue of having a job. Maybe since she'd been off over a week, she'd lost track of that fact. "I totally didn't think about that. I can't get by without any income, but maybe I can talk with Dr. Allen and see if there is a way I could work from home. I mean, it probably wouldn't be for that long." As the words left her mouth Maya realized the meaning of what she was saying and her voice caught in her throat. In her excitement to make this plan work she had overlooked the final outcome. Her eyes filled with tears and Buster gently held her hand. She looked at him and he was almost in tears too.

"Maya, first I think we need to have a heart to heart with Hazel before you talk with Dr. Allen."

"You're right. I'm taking Doodle Bug over there in a couple of hours. Why don't you come too and we'll discuss it."

"That'll work. Now let's change the subject for a minute and I'll tell you about all the great fishing I did in Florida."

Thomas brought their steaming bowls of chowder and Buster kept her entertained with his stories, most of them probably embellished, but at least it kept her mind from dwelling on Hazel.

***

Bay looked at the clock and saw it was already past noon. She must have fallen back asleep. She felt a little better. Her headache was gone and she even felt a little hungry. She glanced at her cell phone and saw Maya hadn't called back. Well, she may still be out of town.

They hadn't talked since the week before Christmas and Bay couldn't remember her schedule. She was lonely and ready to talk with Maya. Over the holidays, she'd talked only with the staff at the nursing home, Laura and her mother. Well of course, that wasn't counting the Marines she'd met last night. She hadn't seen any of Holden's friends since his stroke. At least once or twice a week they used to meet other couples for dinner but none of them had called or contacted her except to check in on Holden. Well, she had to admit she wasn't too surprised. They were all Holden's friends first and it was hard to connect with those women who were almost her mother's age. She always felt they just tolerated her because of their feelings for Holden.

Bay threw off the sheets, swung her legs out and sat on the edge of the bed. Last night, so many things had felt good in the moment, the fourth glass of Chardonnay, the potato skins, the feel of a man's hands on her, but now in the daylight, all these things made her body feel contaminated. Bay stood and headed for the drawer in her bureau with all her running clothes. A hard run and hot shower would help cleanse her of last night.

Refreshed after her run and shower and now cozy in her black leggings and sweater, Bay started the coffee maker and promised herself she would never repeat last night. Immediately the voice in her head said, "But that would mean you may never have sex again until Holden dies." She hadn't thought of it like that before. But it was true. Barring a miraculous recovery, this was her life until Holden died unless she divorced him so she could move on with her life.

Bay began pacing the kitchen floor as she waited for the coffee to finish brewing. Of course, leaving him had crossed her mind but she would immediately dismiss this thought. Today though, she let herself begin weighing the pros and cons of this idea. Even though she was alone, it was as if she could feel the eyes of others on her whispering about how selfish and ungrateful she was. God, what was she thinking? She would be selfish and ungrateful if she divorced Holden. Their vows had been in sickness and in health and now she had to uphold her word.

To distract herself, Bay went into the family room and switched on the flat screen over the fireplace. Her father had watched a lot of football and this was one thing they had done together. Even though he was usually drunk by the third quarter, Bay had mostly good memories of watching games with him and as she got older, she could even banter with him about the bad call, player stats and offensive strategies. She switched channels until she found the Rose Bowl game. She settled on the couch with her coffee, a bowl of yogurt mixed with granola and water. She had a couple of hours before it was be time to go back to the nursing home to feed Holden his dinner. Laura had said she would be there most of the day so Bay didn't want to get there too early.

Bay tried to put her full attention on the game but ended up spending more time staring out the window behind the couch, wondering if next New Year's Day her life would be the same.

Chapter 13

Tuesday February 19, 2008

Maya gently pushed open Hazel's bedroom door and saw she was still asleep. The past week she'd been sleeping more then she'd been awake, but the hospice nurse said that was normal for someone in the late stages of cancer. Maya quietly walked in and laid the stack of Valentine's cards Wilma had brought over from Hazel's Sunday school class on the bedside table. She sat in the rocking chair by Hazel's bed and turned her face towards the window behind the bed so she could feel the warmth of the late afternoon sun.

Maya could hardly believe it was mid February and for the past five weeks she'd mainly been at Hazel's. Luckily on New Year's Day when Buster and Maya had spoken with her, Hazel readily agreed to Maya caring for her but only if she waived Maya's rent, took care of her food and paid her $500 a week. Maya had resisted this initially, but she could tell that was the only way Hazel would agree with the plan. This, of course, solved the problem of income and she was assured by Dr. Allen that she could take a leave of absence and come back whenever it was best for her. Maya knew there would be lots to catch up when she returned but was happy he was willing to hold her job.

Hazel must have sensed her presence because she opened her eyes and scooted up in bed. "Hey, Maya," she said sleepily. "How long have you being sitting there? What time is it?"

"I just sat down and it's almost 4:30. Here," she said reaching for the stack of cards, "Wilma just brought these over for you. They're for Valentine's Day which was last week."

"Valentine's Day? Is it February fourteenth already? I can't keep up with the days anymore. They're all starting to run together."

Maya could tell Hazel's connection with the present was loosening. She lost track of time, the day and had begun to refuse visitors on most days. She spoke often of the past, especially times with her mother and grandmother. Hazel still held the stack of Valentine's cards in her hand. "Hazel, do you want to open your cards?"

"Oh, OK." Hazel laid the stack beside her and opened the top one. All of them contained a heartfelt sentiment from a member of her Sunday school class, most of whom she'd known her entire life. As she pulled out the last one she exclaimed, "Oh, look, Maya, a pink cupcake. This reminds me of my grandmother. She loved cupcakes from Della's bake shop in town. They closed years ago but back then, they had the best cupcakes. Guess I got a little carried away when I had to get that case of cupcake tree ornaments."

"Don't worry about that. I bet by now Goodwill has sold all those decorations and half of Pamlico County will have a pink cupcake on their tree next year." Whenever Maya referenced time, she felt her heart clench, knowing Hazel would not be here next Christmas. "So, Hazel, tell me more about why those cupcakes from Della's were so special. I never heard the story about what you and your grandmother did with them for your birthday."

"My grandmother and I had the same birthday, June twenty-first. I remember my tenth birthday when Ma-Maw was turning sixty."

Maya sat back in the wicker chair, picked up her mug of tea and waited for Hazel to continue.

"Early in the morning of my tenth birthday someone was calling my name and gently shook me awake. It was Ma-Maw. I remembered that when I opened my eyes, I could make out the light pink glow of dawn in the east. I looked over at Ma-Maw and she put her fingers to her lips. 'SHH Honey,' she said. 'It's our birthday and I have a surprise for you. Come on, get up.' I loved surprises so quickly got up to follow my grandmother."

As Hazel told this story, she sat up taller in the bed and her voice was stronger. Maya could tell it brought her great joy to remember this time with her grandmother.

Hazel continued, "Ma-Maw said not to get dressed but just come with her. I knew it was our birthday but didn't know where she was taking me. She, my mother and I usually had a bon-fire the night of our birthdays, which was also the summer solstice. It was just us girls since my Daddy and Grandpa were usually out fishing, but we had never done anything at sunrise and never just Ma-Maw and me. I followed her down the back porch steps and across the wet grass towards the dock. Beards Creek was glowing in the pink pre-dawn light and the water was smooth and dark like the top of those perfect chocolate pies Momma would make on Sundays."

Hazel stopped to take a sip of the tea that Maya had brought her. "So that's how that path was made between your house and my boathouse," Maya asked.

"Yes. Probably about 100 years of footsteps from the back porch to the dock has worn that path. Anyway, that morning I can only imagine what we must have looked like, two apparitions in white cotton nightgowns floating down to the end of our dock. We passed our wooden row boat, Grandpa's old sail boat no one used anymore and the space where my daddy's fishing boat would tie up. Ma-Maw motioned me to sit down at the end of the dock, facing

east. As we walked down, I had seen our picnic basket sitting at the
end of the dock and Ma-Maw sat beside it resting her arm on top. I
remember my legs were too short to touch the water and they
dangled in the air just above the creek as we sat waiting for the
sunrise."

"Hazel, you remember so much about that day. It must have
been very special."

"It was, Maya. Just wait until you hear the end. It's funny
how it seems easier for me to remember details about my tenth
birthday than what I did three weeks ago. Ah well. I remember
leaning into Ma-Maw. She felt warm and soft and smelled of
lavender. I looked up into her face, tanned from years in the sun by
the water. She smiled and her blue eyes sparkled. She seemed
magical that morning. It seems like yesterday and hard to believe
that now I'm older than she was that day. She told me to close my
eyes. My heart was pounding with anticipation. I knew this would
be something good since it was Ma-Maw's doing. I felt her take my
hand and place a soft lump in it. It smelled of chocolate."

"Ah, we're getting to the cupcake part," Maya said.

"Yes. When I opened my eyes, I saw that in my hand was a
chocolate cupcake with chocolate frosting and lots of colored
sprinkles, my favorite from Della's Bake Shop. Exactly in the middle
was a candle all ready lit. I looked over at Ma-Maw and she had one

too, her favorite with white butter cream frosting. Then she said, 'I'm

going to tell you a secret my grandmother shared with me many

birthdays ago. If you make a wish at sunrise on your birthday, it will

surely come true. Since today you and I are beginning a new decade,

I wanted to share this family secret with you. Today you and I will

get to make a ten year wish.'"

Maya leaned forward in her chair mesmerized by Hazel's

story of her tenth birthday. Hazel seemed lost in the memory and

continued talking as she looked out the creek windows.

"I had never heard this tale before, but if Ma-Maw said it was

so, I knew it was true. I didn't have much time to think of my wish

but that was okay. I always wished for the same thing when given the

chance. We both held our cupcakes up to the sky. The glow of our

candles mingled with the glow of the orange sun, just rising above the

creek. A blue heron cried and rose up from the grasses beside us. We

closed our eyes, made a wish and blew out the candles."

Hazel leaned back against the pillows, tired from her long

story. But she smiled as she continued to look out the windows.

"Hazel, that's a wonderful story. Do you still do that on

your birthday?"

Hazel turned her head to Maya and said, "Yes. I try to.

There were some years when I was living in Raleigh that I couldn't do

it here, but I always found some body of water to be near at sunrise on my birthday. I can say that for all my decade birthdays though, I did come here and sit at the end of our dock. This June..." Hazel's voice trailed off and she didn't finish her thought.

Maya held back her tears as she finished the sentence in her mind. This June would be Hazel's 80th birthday and most likely she wouldn't be here to have her cupcake ritual. Maya looked over at Hazel and saw she had fallen asleep again, her breathing slow and steady.

***

Maya and Doodle Bug took a right on Highway 55 and headed towards town to meet Bay. It was a perfect morning for a run, 35 degrees, clear and Maya could just make out the beginnings of the sunrise in the east. During the winter months, she put a blinking orange light on Doodle Bug's collar so she could be easily seen. It was still pitch dark when she left at 6:00 a.m. but would be light by the time she got home. Thankfully, Buster had offered to come and sit with Hazel for several hours each morning so Maya could get her run in, shower at home and enjoy her breakfast. She usually got to Hazel's around 8:30 which was plenty of time because Hazel didn't wake up until at least 9:00 a.m.

A car passed Maya and its lights reflected off Bay's shirt as she headed their way. As they drew closer to one another, Maya and

Doodle Bug crossed over to the other side of the road and changed directions to run with Bay back to the boathouse.

For the past month they always started the conversation the same way. "How's Hazel?" Bay would ask and "How's Holden?" Maya would ask. They were running together twice a week on Mondays and Wednesdays now that Maya didn't have to drive to work. They called their running time a caregiver support group. These mornings had become a lifeline to them both. Maya wasn't sure what was worse, hearing that nothing had changed with Holden or sharing Hazel's steady decline. Maya ultimately knew she did have the better circumstances since she had willingly volunteered to care for Hazel and the truth of it was that it was time limited and she knew it wouldn't last forever. On the other hand, Bay had no timetable.

Doodle Bug ran happily between Bay and Maya and they took up most of the left lane, which was not an issue because there was so little traffic at this time of day.

"Maya, I think I need a vacation somewhere tropical. I'm really getting stir crazy. For almost three months my day has revolved around going to the hospital or the nursing home. It's cold and everything is brown here and I just need some warm sun and a tropical drink."

"Why don't you do that? You could go the Bahamas for a long weekend pretty easily if you fly out of Raleigh."

"I know. I've actually looked into it but on Friday we have a big meeting at the nursing home about Holden. Since he continues to make very little progress and three months are almost up, Medicare won't pay for him to be there anymore. We have to decide what to do from here. So, until that gets resolved, I can't go anywhere and if he comes home, I guess I won't be going anywhere for a long time."

Maya could hear the resignation in Bay's voice. She could tell Bay was getting depressed. She had lost her piss and vinegar as Maya's grandmother would say. Maya had even noticed that Bay had been putting less effort into her dress and makeup. When they saw each other for lunch occasionally, Bay was starting to look more like Maya with her hair in a ponytail, sparse makeup and less accessories.

"Bay, how could you have Holden at home? He can barely walk, your bedroom is upstairs and you're not strong enough to lift him in and out of bed."

"Well, the therapists have been trying to teach me how to help him but I really don't think I would be able to do it all alone."

"What about Laura, could she help you at all?"

"She lives all the way in Raleigh so I guess she could come on weekends. She and I barely speak right now so I'm not sure what she'd be willing to do. She doesn't think I care well enough for him now, so if the plan is for him to come home with me, I wouldn't be surprised if she puts up a fight. I think she would prefer to have him in Raleigh, close to her."

Maya and Bay turned left, off Highway 55. Their pace was steady, but not too fast so as to interfere with their conversation.

"Well, at least you'll know something by Friday and can begin to plan around that. What would you like to happen?"

"Oh, I don't know. I just never thought I would be dealing with something like this at only 41. Enough about me. How's Hazel doing?"

And so the conversation followed its usual flow. Maya updated Bay on Hazel and shared the cupcake ritual which had really stuck with her since Hazel had told her that story yesterday. When they got to Hazel's driveway, they hugged and promised to touch base by phone on Friday after Bay's meeting. Maya and Doodle Bug headed down to the boathouse as Bay reversed her course back to the health club.

***

Bay sat in her car in the parking lot of Craven Rehab and Nursing Home. It was 9:45 a.m. and she had fifteen minutes until the care meeting to discuss the next step with Holden. Why did she feel like she was next in line for an execution? Since her run with

Maya on Wednesday, she hadn't left the house at all. She called the nursing home and told them she was sick, but really she knew she was depressed. She felt like she was sinking in quicksand and slowly suffocating.

The thought of having Holden home, requiring twenty-four hours of care a day, that she would be responsible for was overwhelming. It would be for anyone, but Bay imagined it would feel different if you were bringing home your one true love to care for. Bay had known it for quite a while, but since Holden's stroke she had to be honest about the fact that she was not in love with him. Certainly she cared about him and was grateful for all he had done for her, but that was it. In fact, that was probably all it ever was. When they met she was more in love with the life he could create for her than she was with him.

The past two days she just watched movies on The Hallmark Chanel, stayed in her sweats and didn't even shower. It took all the energy she could muster to make herself presentable today. The glint of the sun off a car pulling into the parking lot caught Bay's attention. She saw it was Laura's car. She whipped into a spot near the front door and hurried inside. Bay looked at her watch and saw it was 9:56. Well, she might as well go in, find out what they were recommending and go from there. She watched the digital clock in her car change to 9:57, then 9:58, unable to motivate herself to go inside. She wondered what would happen if she didn't show up. Would Laura just take over and she would be free and clear? This sounded enticing but as the clock moved to 9:59, she knew she had to go in.

Bay walked down the hall towards Holden's room but was met by his social worker, Cassie before she got there. "Hi, Mrs. Witherspoon. I was just looking for you. Everyone is in the conference room waiting."

Without saying a word, Bay turned and followed Cassie to the conference room near the entrance. She was trying to remember who would be there besides her, Laura and Cassie. She followed Cassie into the conference room that contained a large oval table. She saw the medical director, Dr. Bainbridge at the head of the table. He was probably in his mid 50s and had salt and pepper hair. To his right was Margaret Caldwell, the director of nursing and to his left was Laura. Everyone was silent and Bay could tell Laura was purposely avoiding eye contact with her. Bay sat next to the nursing director, who had a stack of charts in front of her.

Dr. Bainbridge leaned back in his chair and began tapping a pen on his right thigh. He looked over at Cassie. "Is everyone here? Can we get started because I have to be at the hospital in 30 minutes?"

Thirty minutes, Bay thought. We are going to decide the course of my life for the next few years and you only have 30 minutes? Then you'll drive on to the hospital, carrying on with living your life while mine and Holden's are destroyed. Bay could feel her neck flushing with anger. Her rational mind knew getting angry at Dr. Bainbridge wouldn't help matters, so she busied herself with pulling out a small notebook and pen from her purse.

Cassie began, "Laura, Bay, thanks for being here. As you know, Holden has been here for almost three months. Medicare and his BCBS supplement will only cover for another week so we need to decide on the best plan for him when he leaves us."

Bay sat quietly. She, Cassie and the therapists had all talked about this informally before. She knew he needed twenty-four hour supervision and that despite the therapist's training she received, Bay was unable to move Holden alone. No one said it, but Bay could feel the real reason for this meeting was to have her and Laura in the same room. Legally Bay had the power to make the decisions, but as involved as Laura had been, she felt the staff wanted to ensure everyone was on the same page.

Bay wondered what Laura may have been saying about her as she listened to the nurse detail Holden's current condition. She couldn't help feeling like everyone at the table somehow knew she didn't love Holden and thought she was self-centered and callous.

Dr. Bainbridge interrupted Bay's thoughts, "Well, before I leave, do either of you have any questions for me?" he asked, directing the question to her and Laura.

Laura lifted her eyes and glanced over to Bay, her scorn and dislike very evident. Bay sat up and slid to the edge of her seat. "Dr. Bainbridge, do you think there is any hope that Holden will continue to make progress? At least to the point where I can move him or he and I can have a two way conversation?"

"Mrs. Witherspoon, if I had a crystal ball, I could tell you, but otherwise it's hard to predict. With intensive outpatient therapy, he may show some improvement but to be honest with you, that's not very likely since he hasn't improved much in the past month with our daily therapy here."

"So, for planning purposes, I should expect that he will not get any better and be at this level of care until..."

Before she could finish her sentence, Laura, unable to withhold her contempt anymore, exploded, "He dies. Isn't that what you're asking? Will he need this much care until he dies and I know you're trying to calculate that too. How much longer will he live? How much longer until you can move on and find another sugar daddy to take care of you!"

Bay's face flushed red with anger and shame. She tried to speak but Laura continued, fueled by years of pent up rage at Bay.

"Bay, I have despised you since you tricked Daddy into marrying you. I always knew you just used him for money and to escape the trailer park."

Bay's eyes widened. She didn't realize Laura knew where she'd grown up. At this, Dr. Bainbridge looked at his watch, rolled his eyes at Nurse Caldwell and walked out. Neither Laura nor Bay noticed.

"Yes. I know where you came from. I hired a detective to look into your past because I don't trust you. It breaks my heart to think you could end up with the responsibility of caring for my father and I'm glad I hired that detective because he's been keeping an eye on you for the past month or so."

Bay's mouth opened in disbelief. She'd been being followed? She was surprised by the intensity with which Laura hated her. Laura continued on her rampage, unfazed by Cassie's attempts to silence her. "Bay, all my instincts about you were right. You were being followed New Year's Eve. So, yes, I know all your dirty little secrets."

Now Bay's face drained of blood as she realized what Laura knew. She felt ashamed and just continued to sit there not sure how to come to her own defense, not sure even what her defense would be. Bay could feel all eyes on her. She imagined Laura had already told Cassie and the nursing director about what had happened and she could feel their judgment as they looked down the table towards her.

"So," Laura spat at her, "what do you have to say for yourself?" Before waiting for an answer, she continued, "I've already talked with Cassie and it appears I have enough information to give me a chance of getting guardianship of Daddy. Here," Laura said sliding some papers towards Bay, "the hearing is next Tuesday."

Bay continued to just sit there, trying to process what had just happened. Laura sat back in her chair, spent from the power of her emotion. Cassie, sitting across from Bay, cleared her throat.

"Bay, what this means is that Laura has filed for guardianship of Holden. At the hearing on Tuesday, the judge will decide whether to override your spousal rights and grant guardianship to Laura. Whoever the judge chooses will be responsible for Holden. Even given the information Laura has, I would be surprised if the judge takes away your rights as a spouse, but Laura has a right to have her side heard by the judge if she chooses."

Bay, finally thinking again, had for a brief second, seen a way out, almost hopeful the judge would award Laura guardianship. But now Cassie seemed to be saying that her legal role as a wife was strong and there was a good chance she would remain responsible for Holden.

Laura leaned forward in her seat, addressing Bay. "Still nothing to say? It's hard to argue with the truth isn't it, Bay?"

Bay looked over Cassie's head at the picture of a garden scene hanging on the wall. What was the truth for her? Of course, everyone at the table knew of her one night stand so the façade of a faithful wife was gone. She couldn't pretend with them or herself anymore. Bay had never felt so conflicted. She could end this right here and now since Laura was clear that she wanted to care for her father or she could continue to play the dutiful wife role and fight to care for Holden. What if doing the right thing wasn't the same as doing what would make you happy? Which do you choose, she asked herself.

She had played out the consequences of her caring for Holden but hadn't thought about what would happen if Laura was totally responsible for him. Would she get a divorce then? Probably so. But where would that leave her? Totally on her own and that felt scary too. She was used to feeling trapped by the life she and Holden had had, but at least it was predictable and safe. If she walked out of Holden's life right now, she couldn't predict anything, except of course being in control of her own life.

The nursing director began neatening up the papers in Holden's chart and then stood. "I guess we can't make any decisions until we know the outcome on Tuesday but at least you both understand the amount of care that Mr. Witherspoon requires."

Bay watched the nurse walk towards the door. "Wait. I do have something to say." This brought everyone to attention. Nurse Caldwell sat back down in the chair closest to the door and looked at her, waiting. Laura, still seething, begrudgingly looked at Bay.

Bay took a breath to muster some strength and clarity. Her heart was beating so fast it made it difficult to speak. She pushed the guardianship papers back towards Laura. "Laura, I don't need these and I won't be there on Tuesday. You win. I won't fight for guardianship of Holden. In fact, to make it easier I should probably file for divorce." Bay could hardly believe what she had just said, but somewhere inside her a voice stronger then her own took over.

Laura looked shocked and then smiled. "Thank you, Bay. And don't think you're getting any money out of this divorce. Daddy let me read your prenup and if you ever cheated on him, you get nothing except to keep the things he gave you as gifts. Why don't you stop at the courthouse on your way home so we can get this process started?"

Bay stood letting her anger rise, 'I'll get an attorney and get started, and don't worry, I don't want any money. Holden has been more then generous with me over the past fifteen years." As Bay said this, her anger left and she was overwhelmed with sadness. The tears

overflowed and wet her cheeks. The impact of what she was doing
hit her. She felt sad about leaving Holden. In their own ways they'd
loved each other and provided one another with something the other
needed.

Laura, unmoved by Bay's tears said, "Give it up, Bay. You
don't have to pretend you love my father anymore. You're soon to be
his ex-wife and I will be making the decisions now so why don't you
just leave?"

Bay turned and without another word, walked out of the
conference room, leaving Cassie and Margaret with their mouths
open. She walked blindly to her car and got in. She placed both
hands on the steering wheel and stared straight ahead without even
starting the engine. What had she done? She had just walked out on
Holden, her husband of fifteen years. The person she vowed to love
in sickness and in health. What kind of woman was she? But then
what kind of woman would she be if she continued to live a lie and
sacrifice her dreams to care for a man she wasn't in love with. He
would get better care from Laura and having his grandchildren close
by would surely be better medicine than just the two of them in their
house down at River Dunes.

Bay wondered if she was tricking herself, but she was actually
beginning to feel that she was doing what was best for Holden. He
would be well-cared for by a daughter that worshipped him and

unless something drastic changed, he may never realize she wasn't around anyway.

Bay started the car and headed to the exit. As she was about to turn left and head home, it suddenly hit her, Holden. She couldn't just drive off and leave him after fifteen years of marriage. She sat there for a moment trying to come up with a plan. If she went back now, Laura would be there and she couldn't handle being around her again. Holden had at least another week here so she'd come back and feed him lunch and say goodbye on Monday. She doubted Laura would be there then, since she would be in town on Tuesday for the guardianship hearing.

Bay's right foot moved from the brake to the accelerator and she turned left towards Oriental. She dug in her purse for her cell phone to call Maya. She prayed Maya could get away for lunch. She really needed to talk this through with her and was hopeful Maya would support her decision. Her mother would be another matter, but she'd deal with that later.

By the time she was heading out of New Bern, she'd made a date to meet Maya at Toucans at noon. She picked up speed on Highway 55 and her mind raced with questions. Where will she live? How will she support herself? Could she even afford to go to college? Will she ever find a man she truly loves?

No need to worry about all that yet, she told herself. First she needed to eat lunch and talk with Maya and then find an attorney to help with the divorce. Bay's eyes filled with tears again making it hard to focus on the road. One part of her was sad, thinking of Holden, slumped and drooling in his wheelchair, with little chance of regaining his independence and another part of her was filled with anticipation at the prospect of gaining hers.

***

Maya, wrapped in a fleece blanket, sat with her coffee on her creek side porch. It was about 45 degrees and the sun was warm on her face as she leaned back in her rocking chair. Although it was only February, she could feel spring, straining to burst onto the scene, full of life, a sharp contrast to watching the life drain from Hazel. Yesterday Angela, the hospice nurse, had sat her and Buster down and told them Hazel was close to death. She needed more and more morphine to keep her pain controlled and was sleeping most of the day. When she was awake, she would fluctuate between clarity and disorientation and sometimes would have conversations with her mother or grandmother. The nurse said this was normal as Hazel loosened the hold on her body in preparation for death. After she and Buster talked with the nurse, Buster said he would call Hazel's son and Maya had called Travis, since he was Hazel's friend and

minister, and then called Lilith so she could let the other women in
the circle know.

Maya looked at her watch and saw it was already 9:30. She
should head up to Hazel's since Buster had been there since six.
Doodle Bug was lying beside her and she rubbed her head. As
meaningful as it had been to care for Hazel, she did have to admit she
was getting tired and missed sleeping in her own bed in the
boathouse. She and Doodle Bug were sleeping in the guest room just
down the hall from Hazel's bedroom. At least her using that room
had provided a reason to clear it of Hazel's accumulated purchases.
Hazel hadn't even had the energy to supervise so Maya just threw
away what was unusable and the rest was picked up by the Baptist
Men's group at Hazel's church who would sell everything at their
spring yard sale.

Maya found Buster at Hazel's kitchen table, reading the
newspaper. Doodle Bug ran over to him doing her usual happy
dance.

"Hey, Doodle Bug," Buster said, "Did you have a good run
with your Mommy? Did you beat her this time?" Doodle Bug put
her head in Buster's lap and he gently rubbed her while she gazed up
at him with her big brown eyes.

Maya could tell Buster was tired too. He was here every day
from about 5:45 am until 9:00 or 9:30 and on many days would

come back in the late afternoon to check on her and Hazel. Buster hadn't said anything, but Maya knew watching Hazel die must make him think about his wife's death.

"You doing OK, Buster? You look a little tired. Why don't you take tomorrow off? I need a day off from running anyway and that would give you a chance to sleep in and have the whole day to yourself. Our women's circle is coming tomorrow morning anyway, so it's not like I'd be alone all day."

Buster folded the paper and said, "Thanks, but I need to be here so that's what I'm going to do. Especially now that we know time is waning for Hazel, I hate to take a day off. Oh, I spoke with Wynn yesterday and he plans to come by this afternoon. Thought I would come back then so I could see him."

"Thanks, Buster," Maya said, leaning down to hug him from behind and kissing the top of his head. "I don't know how I could have done this without your help."

Buster stood to leave and Maya could tell he was blushing, a little embarrassed by her gratitude. "Okay, then girl. I'll see you around four. Call me if you need me for anything." He hadn't specifically said it, but Maya knew he meant to call him if Hazel died.

"Sure thing. Enjoy your day."

Maya followed Buster to Hazel's office door and watched him drive off. She plopped down in one of the chairs. It felt surreal to be waiting for someone to die. She was living moment by moment just poised between what is and what will be. She felt badly to plan her life for after Hazel's death, so hadn't, but she had trouble keeping her worries at bay. What would happen to the house? Could she still live in the boathouse? Would her son want to sell everything? Hazel had not talked about what her wishes were regarding her property and Maya hadn't asked, respecting that that was between Hazel and her son.

Doodle Bug's ears perked as Hazel rang the small bell that was at her bedside. Maya stood to head upstairs when she noticed Hazel's file cabinet was partly opened, so she pushed it closed, wondering again what were in all those files and about those visitors to Hazel's office. The last visitor she knew of was the first week of January. In fact, that was the last time Hazel had been downstairs. Maya hated to be nosy, but she really wanted to know why those people were coming. Maybe she should just ask Hazel. She could always say no if she didn't want to share anything. The bell rang again and Maya followed Doodle Bug, who was already bounding upstairs. Doodle Bug beat Maya into the room by about 30 seconds and already had her front paws on the bed near Hazel's head and Hazel was gently petting her.

"Morning. How are you feeling?" As this question left her lips, Maya wished she could take it back. It seemed a silly question to ask someone who was dying.

"Hi, Maya." Hazel said with a weak voice, keeping one hand on Doodle bug's head.

"I'm just tired, dear. I can't imagine that I have much longer the way I'm feeling now." Her breath was shallow and raspy and it seemed to take all her effort just to engage her chest muscles and diaphragm to breath. Those were about the only muscles she had used in the last two days since she'd stayed in bed the entire time. The hospice nurse and home health aide had shown Maya how to change Hazel's adult diapers and keep her clean. Although her bodily processes were slowing down, they were still working and needed attending to. Maya did all this with compassion and respect and Hazel acquiesced, knowing there was no other option.

"Hazel, did Angela talk with you yesterday?"

"Maya, I'm sure she did but I don't remember anything she said."

"She talked with me and Buster yesterday before she left and she agrees with you. She said she doesn't think that you have much time left." Maya's heart clenched and her eyes filled with tears. Again, she felt like this was surreal, sitting here with Hazel whom she'd known less than a year, talking about her death which possibly was only a few days away.

Hazel moved her right hand from Doodle Bug's head and reached it towards Maya, who took it in her own hand. "I know, dear. It must be difficult to be talking about my last days here, but from my perspective it feels natural, just the continuation of the cycle. Remember, I've lived twice as long as you have so have had more time to think about my death. Feeling my body slowly giving out just reinforces that my time here is coming to a close. It's time for you and Buster to get back to living your lives too. I so appreciate your sacrifice and don't want to ask more of you then I need to."

Hazel dropped her hand and put her head back against the pillows, spent from her short soliloquy. Maya watched her, listening to her breathing, wondering how it must feel to know you would die in the next few days. Then it hit Maya that, although there was less probability, there were no promises that she wouldn't die in the next few days herself. Someone texting and driving could hit her while she was running tomorrow. She could have an aneurism in her brain she didn't know about that could burst in her sleep. OK, none of these things would probably happen, but going through this process with Hazel reinforced how precious life was and that there was no guarantee she would see tomorrow.

"Hazel, would you like a cup of tea and some cinnamon toast?"

Hazel turned her head towards Maya without lifting it off the pillow and without opening her eyes said, "Ma-Maw, can we go out on the boat? It feels like a long time since you've taken me on a ride." Hazel's voice lowered to a mumble and Maya couldn't understand her as she continued her conversation with her grandmother, even pausing at times as if to hear her grandmother's response.

Doodle Bug dropped her front paws from Hazel's bed and walked over to the creek side windows. She began pacing and sniffing the air. Maya wondered if Doodle Bug could sense the presence of Hazel's grandmother. Maya felt a chill run down her spine and knew she was letting her imagination get the best of her.

She heard a car door slam and stood to head downstairs to let Angela in, happy to have a distraction from her thoughts. Of course, she couldn't forget, she also had a lunch date with Bay at noon. That would certainly be a distraction as Bay had sounded keyed up when they spoke a few minutes ago. She left Doodle Bug lying under the creek side windows and went downstairs.

Maya raced past Toucans marina towards the restaurant. The home health aide had been ten minutes late, throwing her off schedule to meet Bay. Thank goodness for cell phones so Bay knew she was running late. The home health aide would make lunch for Hazel, if she wanted any, and then bathe her in preparation for her son's visit this afternoon.

Maya walked in and headed over to the table by the window where Bay was waiting. She must be feeling a little bit better Maya thought because Bay was well put together with a long sleeve purple wrap dress and pearls on her throat, wrist and ears. Her blond hair was pulled back in a low ponytail setting off her oval face. As Maya sat down she remembered today was Friday and Bay had just had the conference about Holden.

"Sorry I'm late, Bay. So how did it go today? What's the plan for Holden?"

Bay took a breath, looked Maya straight in the eyes and said, "I'm filing for divorce. I'm leaving Holden, and Laura will be responsible for him after the guardianship hearing on Tuesday." Bay left out the event that inspired Laura to file for guardianship.

Maya sat back in her chair, her mouth open. She could tell Bay was carefully gauging her response so tried her best to appear neutral. "Oh, my God, Bay! This is huge. I knew you had thrown divorce around as a hypothetical plan but didn't think you would go through with it. What made you decide to do that?"

Maya was buying time, trying to get a minute to process her thoughts on this before she shared them with Bay. Bay shared her feelings of dread and depression since their Wednesday morning run. When she finished her story, Bay reached across the table and grabbed Maya's arm, "So, what do you think? Do you think I did the right thing?"

The waitress interrupted them to serve their iced teas and Bay released Maya's arm and sat back in her chair, her gaze never leaving Maya's face. When the waitress left, Maya answered, "Bay, I'm proud of you. I know this was a hard decision but really it feels like the only way for you to create your own life and based on what you've told me about your marriage before the stroke, it seems like this may have happened anyway."

Bay's eyes glazed over with tears as she listened to Maya. She exhaled. Maya could tell she was relieved to have at least one person on her side.

"Thank you for understanding. I hoped you would because you're pretty much the only one who could. I'm sure Holden's friends will think I'm a selfish, hard-hearted gold digger and Laura already thought that, so this just confirmed it to her. I'm not sure how my mother will react because she always thought it was a mistake for me to marry Holden. So, thank God I have you."

Maya knew from experience it would take time for Bay to make peace with her decision but was happy she could be there for her. She certainly could identify with the guilt of moving on with your life at the expense of another. "I'm happy I can be here for you."

"Thanks. I hope I'm doing the right thing. I feel like if I took a vote, right here in Toucans, that no one would agree with my choice, but anyway, enough about me. How is Hazel doing? Sorry I've hogged the conversation."

The waitress brought them their salads and Maya stole a look at her watch. She still had 45 minutes before she had to leave so could enjoy her lunch and bring Bay up to date on Hazel. She couldn't help but remember the first time she saw Bay in Toucans and practically ran away from her. She smiled, thinking how unpredictable life can be. She never in a million years would have imagined she and Bay would become such close friends. And, as she shared with Bay the events of the last few days, she was so thankful they had.

Chapter 14

Saturday February 23, 2008

Maya sat in Hazel's office, staring down the driveway and waiting for the women's circle to arrive. It was 9:45 a.m. so they should be here any minute. She leaned her head back against the wall and closed her eyes. Doodle Bug paced back and forth in front of her, aware that something was about to happen but not sure what.

Last night had been emotionally draining. Wynn drove down from New Bern and had stayed a couple of hours. Maya had gone upstairs to check on them several times and each time Wynn was sitting quietly by Hazel as she slept. His tall, lanky frame had looked so out of place in Hazel's delicate bedroom. He still had the physique of a basketball player and his physical presence slightly intimidated her because it reminded her of Steven. Before he left he thanked Maya and Buster for all they had been doing for his mother. He seemed uncomfortable, having trouble finding the right words and his face was frozen into a neutral expression, not giving away any emotion. When he left, Buster had walked him out to the car and

Maya went upstairs to see how it had gone.

"Hazel, how was your visit?"

Hazel, exhausted from the time with her son, kept her eyes

closed as she replied, "It was the same as any other visit. Distance

between us because of years of unexpressed feelings. I appreciate the

fact that he came and know that he loves me the best he can just like

I loved him the best I could, given the circumstances. I just wish my

best had been better."

Maya had sat down in the rocking chair as Hazel continued,

"No Maya, I didn't have the energy or desire to tell him everything.

It felt like too little too late at this point."

"Oh, I know it would have been hard, Hazel, but now he'll

go through the rest of his life thinking there was something wrong

with him that caused you to not love him better." Maya realized her

words may have sounded harsh. "I'm sorry Hazel. I just was

thinking of it from my perspective and how I might feel if I were in

your son's position."

Hazel had reached over and weakly squeezed her arm. "I

know, dear. Could you ask Travis to talk with Wynn after I'm gone?

Travis knows everything and could hopefully help him understand."

The roar of an engine sent Doodle Bug running to the office

door and brought Maya back from her critique of how she handled things with Hazel. She still worried she had been too callous with her comment. Lilith's red Miata was the source of the noise and Maya watched her walking up to the door. Her curly black hair hung to her shoulders and her face was framed with large earrings in the shape of dream catchers. She was carrying a gorgeous pottery vase full of some sort of branches and even though she was arriving for what Maya felt would be a solemn event, Lilith exuded positive energy.

Maya opened the door and without saying a word, Lilith put her vase on Hazel's desk and enveloped Maya in a hug. Maya returned the hug and with no warning, burst into tears. Lilith pulled her in tighter as Maya sobbed. She wasn't really sure what had set her off, probably the culmination of so many weeks of trying to care for Hazel without focusing on the fact she would be gone soon and now there was no more denying it. Maya stepped back from Lilith and grabbed a Kleenex from a box on Hazel's desk.

Before she could say anything, Lilith said, "I know what you're going to say but let me tell you there is no reason to say you're sorry. Women are always apologizing for things they shouldn't and this is one of those times. You have every right to feel exhausted and emotional so why don't you thank me instead of saying you're sorry. After all, I helped you get some of that emotion out."

As Maya blew her nose and her tears stopped, she had to smile at Lilith. She always had a way with words. "Thank you, Lilith. I needed that."

Lilith shook her head in approval. "There you go. That's what to say. You are most certainly welcome." Lilith turned her attention to the vase on Hazel's desk. "I brought this to take up to Hazel. Yesterday I went in my kayak to Hungry Mother Creek and took these small branches from the Mother Tree. I usually don't take live branches off a tree but given the circumstances, made an exception."

"Oh, it's lovely. It will mean a lot to Hazel. Is that a cross in the middle?" Maya asked as she examined the arrangement.

"Yes. I took two branches off the ground and then used some vine to connect them in the shape of a cross."

Maya knew Hazel had been a regular church goer all her life but they'd never been able to discuss her specific beliefs. She understood the meaning the Mother Tree and women's circle had for Hazel, but was less clear about the church. She should have just asked her. Just like those files and visitors, she should have just asked Hazel about that part of her life. Now her life was about to be over and Maya would never have the chance. Lilith must have noticed a puzzled expression on her face.

"Maya, I can see you're questioning how Hazel integrated both the church and the Mother Tree into her spirituality. She and I have talked about this several times over the years. She felt both enriched her life and that one couldn't replace the other. She told me once that the circle around the Mother Tree felt like the feminine divine surrounded by the natural world, with the emphasis on intuition, quiet reflection and egalitarian roles. For her the church represented a more masculine perspective, a hierarchal organization, more directive than intuitive and it provided a linear connection to the past with the repetition of the same words and actions for thousands of years. She also felt a strong connection to church because her family had gone to the Oriental Baptist Church for many generations. Anyway, that's a long explanation of why I have the cross in this arrangement."

Before Maya could ask any more questions, her attention was caught by the sun reflecting off Violet's little Nissan Sentra pulling into the driveway and right behind her was Ella. Maya opened the office door and called to them, "Good morning. You can come on in through this door."

Ella and Violet joined Lilith, Maya and Doodle Bug in Hazel's small office. Doodle Bug was happily greeting everyone but must have picked up on their moods because even her enthusiasm was muted.

"Have you all ever done this sort of thing before with other group members?" Maya asked, directing the question towards Lilith and Violet, knowing Ella had only been a part of the circle for a short time like she.

Violet answered, "No. Our circle has never been in this exact situation before. Of course, other members have died since I've been a part of the circle, but usually it was in their sleep or at the hospital or some circumstance that didn't allow for us to be with them. In the past we would attend the funeral and then honor them at our next gathering at the Mother Tree. I'm at a loss for what to do now. Hazel is so special and has been a friend for so many years." Violet's voice tightened with emotion, "I just want to do what would be most meaningful for her." Violet dabbed at her eyes with the handkerchief she had tucked in the pocket of her wraparound skirt.

"I'm not sure what that would be right now." Maya said. "Hazel is sleeping more and seems to drift in and out of reality when she is awake."

"I'll do whatever you all think is best," Ella said. Since she'd arrived, Maya noticed Ella continued to wrap and un-wrap a strand of her blond hair around her index finger. "This is the first time I've ever been around someone who's this close to death and to be honest I feel a little scared." Violet, standing closest to Ella, put an arm around her and drew her to her side.

"No need to feel scared, dear. We'll all here with you and remember death is a natural event, just like being born and breathing. I was at the side of my mother and my best friend when they died, and although I was devastated by the loss, it was a beautiful, peaceful process to witness."

Maya was glad Ella had spoken up because she was feeling the same way. She tried to sublimate these feelings as she immersed herself in the day-to-day care of Hazel. It was comforting to hear Violet's experiences with death but she found it hard to believe this was always the case. She had wondered a million times about the exact moment that Steven died. Did he suffer beforehand? Did he know he was going into a diabetic coma because he'd run out of insulin? Was he all alone under that bridge outside of town? Before Maya could get lost in the what-ifs around Steven's death, Doodle Bug brought her back to the moment by licking her hand. Maya petted her, silently thanking her for not letting her get caught up in that line of thought when they were here today to honor Hazel.

"I think just our presence will be a comfort to Hazel, "Lilith said. "From what Maya has said, it feels like too much talking or listening would be overwhelming for her. Why don't, after we've each said hello to her, we hold hands and breathe together? We can focus our thoughts on how much Hazel has meant to us and I imagine that with the state she's is in now, it will be easier for her to feel our energy rather than listening to any words we could say."

Everyone agreed so Lilith took the vase and the women silently followed Maya down the hall to the staircase. Maya could feel the weight of emotion surrounding them and imagined each was thinking the same thing; this would be the last time they all would gather together in a circle. Maya swallowed hard to hold back the tears and led the others up to Hazel's bedroom. She could hear Doodle Bug's toe nails on the hardwood steps, slowly following Violet who was at the end.

Maya had told Hazel this morning that the group would be coming but wasn't sure if Hazel had grasped that. She was lethargic and confused this morning, no wonder since she hadn't eaten anything in the past two days. Maya had put on Hazel's favorite white bed jacket with the purple ribbon. She had fixed her hair the best she could but it was hard to hide the tangle at the back of her head where she'd laid on the pillow for so long.

Doodle Bug shot past the women and bounded to the bed. She put her front paws on the mattress, trying to arouse Hazel. Hazel's eyelids fluttered, but she didn't seem to have the strength to pet Doodle Bug. Maya said, "Down, Doodle Bug," and Doodle Bug dropped her paws to the floor and headed over to the creek side windows where she paced and sniffed the air again before lying down.

Each woman went over to say hello and kiss Hazel on the check. Her eyes finally opened when Lilith said in a booming voice, "Hazel, I gathered some branches from our Mother Tree to have here with us. I thought it would be a good reminder of all the meaningful experiences you've had at the Mother Tree and also to represent the spirits of those women in our circle who have passed on before you." Hazel didn't move her head but her eyes followed Lilith's hand to look at the branches of the Mother Tree in the vase. Hazel looked back at Lilith and Lilith said, "Yes. I also made a cross out of some branches on the ground to represent what the church meant to you." Maya thought she noticed a flicker of a smile on Hazel's lips.

Maya and Violet walked around to the right side of the bed and on her way there, Maya cracked the window behind her to let in some fresh air and the sounds of the birds. The buds on the trees outside the window were beginning to fill with the potential of new leaves. Lilith and Maya were on either side of Hazel's head and each took one of her hands, then the others all clasped hands, closing the circle.

Lilith said, "Hazel, We're going to keep this simple and just be with you."

Maya's mind jumped ahead. How long will we do this? When will we know it's time to stop? She caught Ella's eye across the bed and knew she was thinking the same thing. Taking her lead from

Lilith, Maya closed her eyes and began to focus her thoughts on her breath, letting go of those distracting thoughts. It didn't take long for their breath to become synchronized, even Hazel's breathing sounded more even. As directed earlier by Lilith, Maya began reflecting on what Hazel had meant to her in the past eight months. She thought of Hazel at her door with the tuna casserole, their conversations over coffee, playing with Doodle Bug outside, cleaning out her living room.

Maya realized the greatest gift Hazel had shared with her was simply the gift of her life experiences and her honesty about her challenges and successes. Hearing Hazel's stories had helped her better understand parts of her own life, question other areas and inspired her to make choices different from Hazel's.

Maya became overwhelmed with the implications of these thoughts and a sob escaped her lips. Her heart flooded with gratitude and sadness at the same time. Tears were now flowing down her cheeks and her chest was heaving. Maya felt a slight squeeze in her right hand and opened her eyes. Hazel was looking right at her and her eyes were clear and alert. Maya smiled at Hazel and returned the squeeze. While her eyes were open, Maya looked around the circle and saw similar intensity of emotion in the faces of the others. She closed her eyes, feeling as if she was intruding on their privacy and tried to focus on her breath again.

The women continued to hold hands and breathe. After her crying spell, Maya became peaceful and felt a strong connection, not just to the women in the room, but to everything. She wasn't sure why and had never felt this way before, maybe it was being in the presence of someone dying. If she were able to visualize this feeling, Maya imagined it would look like a swirl of white light in the middle of their circle, growing stronger with each of their breaths, until it left the confines of the house and spread out to the world.

Suddenly the spell was broken as Doodle Bug stood from her resting place under the windows and gave a low growl, the hair on her back standing. Maya looked her way and whispered, "Quiet girl. It's all right."

The other women opened their eyes and Lilith smiled. "I guess that is our sign to end the silence." Maya gave Violet's and Hazel's hands a squeeze and then let go. Hazel's eyes were open too and she seemed alert but until this point she had not spoken.

"Thank you." Hazel said weakly, looking closely at each one. "Thank you for being here and for all you have meant to me. You have been my sisters, mothers, daughters and friends. You have enriched my life and helped me be a better person." Hazel now looked past the women gathered around her bed and seemed to focus on the space between her bed and the creek windows where Doodle Bug was nervously pacing. Maya wondered what she saw in that empty space. Hazel began to speak again, still looking towards the windows, but her voice was so soft and slurred no one understood what she said.

Maya could see Ella nervously shifting on her feet, her eyes darting to look at the others. "It's okay," Maya said. "Hazel's been doing this off and on for the past few days. The hospice nurse said it's normal and she thinks Hazel may be talking to people she's loved who have already died."

Lilith put her arm around Ella and said, "Sometimes death comes quickly out of nowhere and other times it is a slower process like with Hazel. I can say it's an honor to be such a close witness to a sacred part of the life cycle." Ella seemed to relax with Lilith's arm around her.

Hazel had stopped talking and seemed to be asleep again. Her breaths were now irregular and labored. The women kept standing vigil, no one seeming to want to be the first to make a move. Maya absorbed the feeling of them all being together. Finally, Lilith leaned down to hug Hazel and the others followed her lead. They all filed out of the room silently and headed back downstairs, except Doodle Bug who continued to pace under the creek side windows.

Violet, Lilith, Ella and Maya all hugged one another in Hazel's office but few words were spoken. As she watched them drive away, Maya suddenly felt scared and alone. What if Hazel died right now, when she was here alone? What should she do? Maya felt

unprepared to be the one with Hazel when she died. Lilith would be

much better. She walked back to the kitchen to get a bottle of water

and then checked her watch. It was almost noon and Angela, the

hospice nurse, should be here any minute. She'd ask her again to run

through what to do when Hazel died. Maya left the door unlocked

for Angela and then went back upstairs to sit by Hazel.

***

It was now just past four o'clock and the late afternoon sun

was streaming through the windows behind Hazel's bed. Maya's

back was stiff from sitting in the wicker rocking chair for most of the

day. She was grateful that Buster had showed up earlier than usual

and brought her a cup of chowder from M & M's for lunch. He was

sitting on the trunk at the foot of Hazel's bed. Doodle Bug hadn't

left the room all day and was sitting at attention under the windows,

her ears alert.

"Maya," Buster said. "Why don't you take Doodle Bug out

for a short walk? You've been sitting in that chair too long. I'll stay

here with Hazel."

"Thanks. I've tried to get Doodle Bug to go out and potty

but she won't leave. I guess I understand because I feel the same way.

I hate to leave, especially after what Angela said. I think she

thinks…" Maya didn't want to finish her sentence in front of Hazel.

They all sat there in the deepening shadows as the sun dipped below the trees, Maya slowly rocking in the wicker rocking chair, Buster sitting on the trunk and staring out the creek windows and Doodle Bug watching over them all. Hazel had not woken since the women's circle had been there. Her breath had become more irregular and slow and Maya had even counted twenty seconds between her breaths a couple of times.

Maya wasn't sure how long they'd been sitting there when something just felt different. Buster must have felt it too because he stood and walked to the other side of the bed and Doodle Bug left her station under the windows and laid her head on the mattress by Hazel's hand. Maya stood too and stepped closer to the bed.

She realized the silence in the room was what changed. It was profound now, without the interruption of Hazel's breath. Maya met Buster's eyes across the bed and saw they were filled with tears. She looked back at Hazel and saw her face was relaxed, peaceful and no longer pinched with the effort of breathing. Doodle Bug stood silently too, her brown eyes looking up at Hazel. The three of them stood there for several minutes, not moving and barely breathing themselves. Suddenly, Doodle Bug turned, ran to the creek windows and putting her paws on the window sill let out a whimper. Maya imagined Hazel's spirit was sweeping down the creek at sunset, heading home.

Epilogue

Friday March 21, 2008

Maya stood on the front porch of a small ranch style house that had been converted into an office. William D. Hudson, Attorney at Law was spelled out in brass letters on the front door. She took a step towards the front door and her normal stride was halted by the circumference of the pencil skirt. Maya had never had to meet with an attorney and for some reason felt she needed to dress up, but now wished she hadn't. Her white dress shirt felt stiff and her skirt had slid around her waist in the car so now the small slit was at the top of her right knee instead of in the back. She grabbed the waist band and moved the skirt back in alignment. Then, taking a step within the range of her navy blue skirt, she opened the door.

Maya nodded politely to Wynn as she walked into the small lobby of the attorney's office. He was sitting in an over-stuffed chair in the corner, next to a closed door that must be Mr. Hudson's office. Wynn was dressed in a business suit and with a blue and white striped tie and had a pair of reading glasses pushed up to the edge of his receding hairline. Maya sat down awkwardly at the edge of a folding chair that was right next to the receptionist's desk. No one was at this desk, though it was almost ten o'clock. There must be a receptionist because of the picture frames crowding one corner and an empty diet Coke can by the phone. Maybe she lived by Oriental time and just hadn't gotten to work yet.

Maya wondered if Wynn knew she would be here too. She watched him out of the corner of her eye punching busily away on his Blackberry. She had spent the last three weeks wondering why she needed to be here. Bill Hudson, who she now knew was Hazel's attorney, had called her a week after the funeral and asked her to come to his office today. He said Hazel had requested her presence when he read the will. She hadn't mentioned this to anyone except Kate, not sure exactly what to make of it. She wondered if anyone else would be here besides her and Wynn.

Her question was answered when she saw Travis walk through the door in his usual attire of jeans, a Columbia fishing shirt and Teva sandals. Their eyes locked and both looked surprised to see the other. Neither of them had mentioned coming to this meeting when they'd been together. Travis had been very supportive since Hazel's death and had taken her to lunch twice since the funeral. Travis and Wynn nodded to one another and just before the silence was about to be uncomfortable, Mr. Hudson opened his office door.

"Ah. Looks like everyone is here. Thanks for being on time. Come on in," he said opening his door wider. Mr. Hudson was shorter than Maya, had a pot belly and appeared to be only be a few years younger than Hazel had been. She realized she missed the mark with her attire as Mr. Hudson was casual in his khakis, a light blue golf shirt that was un-tucked and a pair of topsider boat shoes. Well, at least she hadn't worn pantyhose.

There were three chairs arranged in front of Mr. Hudson's desk. Maya took the one at the far end, Wynn took the one closest to the door and Travis sat in the middle. The air was heavy with the unknown and the anticipation of finding that out.

Mr. Hudson began, "I am sorry we have to gather under these circumstances. I've know Hazel since she moved back to Oriental after her husband died, and have been her attorney for about twenty years or so. She was also a good friend. We worked almost ten years together planning the CroakerFest we have here over July fourth. Hazel stopped by just before Christmas and told me about her diagnosis and wanted to update her will. Her death is a personal loss for me and a loss to the town of Oriental as well. Anyway, let's move on with why we're here, to disperse her assets."

Maya flinched at these words. They seemed so empty compared to who Hazel was. Her assets had nothing to do with what was written in her will and everything to do with who she was as a person. Maya adjusted herself in the chair and put her attention back on Mr. Hudson.

"Travis, I asked you to be here today to represent the First Baptist Church. Hazel would like $25,000 of her liquid assets to be donated to your church." Both Travis' and Maya's mouths must have flown open. Neither could have guessed from Hazel's lifestyle that she had that much money to give away. Mr. Hudson continued, "As executor of her estate, Travis, I will make sure you receive these funds. It may take some time so don't start spending it yet, but you should have it by the summer."

Travis nodded, still appearing stunned by the amount of the donation and Hazel's generosity. "Now, Wynn, as her son, you will get the bulk of her estate, all the remaining monies in her checking and savings account and her life insurance. She would like you to have any of the contents in the house you would like as well as her cars and three boats." Wynn nodded and didn't seem fazed by this information. Maybe Hazel had discussed it with him Maya thought.

"And Maya. I imagine you're wondering why you're here. Well, from what Hazel has shared with me, you were very special to her and became an important part of her life in a short time. I'm not sure if you caught this when I was addressing Wynn, but she left him the contents of her home and has left you her house, the boathouse and the ten acres that make up the property."

Maya grabbed the arms of the chair and tried to remember to breathe as she processed what she had just heard. She looked at Mr. Hudson, then Wynn and finally Travis in disbelief. She wasn't going to have to move. She could stay right there on that beautiful creekside property. Then it hit her, she could move into the big house. Maya felt Travis rubbing her left arm.

"Maya, are you okay? You look like you are going to faint."

Maya took several breaths, "Thanks. I'm fine. I just wasn't expecting this and am in total shock. I'd been keeping my eye out for other places to live thinking Wynn might sell the property. It feels unreal that now it's mine."

Wynn, who hadn't said anything yet, leaned forward and addressed Maya. "Mom and I talked about this over Christmas because she didn't want me to be hurt by her decision. I was at first, but after seeing what good care you gave her over the last three months, I understand why she did this. Anyway, Oriental has never been my home so I don't have much emotional attachment to her place and I know I could never convince Emily, my wife, to live down here so far away from a mall." He smiled at Maya and sat back in his chair. She could see him resisting the urge to look at his Blackberry that had just beeped with an incoming text message.

Maya continued to sit at the edge of her chair, her mind overwhelmed with this information. She needed to call her sister right away to let her know. She could fix up the guest bedroom for her and Worth and they could stay there during the summers when Kate was off from school. Maya's planning was interrupted by Mr. Hudson. "Now, there is one more thing. It just involves Maya so, Travis and Wynn, you are free to leave."

Both of them stood and Wynn was already pulling his Blackberry out of his pocket to check his text messages and email. Travis hesitated and looked questioningly at Maya. With his back to Mr. Hudson, he mouthed to Maya, "The Bean." She nodded and then turned her attention back to Mr. Hudson.

When the door closed behind Travis he said, "Maya, I'm glad you have a strong heart because you've had a lot to deal with in the last few minutes. Now brace yourself because there is more. At Hazel's request, please keep this information confidential. Besides her mother and grandmother, I'm the only other person who knows this."

Maya couldn't imagine what he was going to share and why Hazel had wanted her to know.

"Now, Maya, I'm sure since you've lived on Hazel's property you have noticed that periodically people from out of town came to visit."

Maya leaned forward, very interested now. "Yes. Yes. I have wondered about that. Hazel never told me and would just say she had an appointment and leave it at that."

"Well, Hazel has a trust fund that is used for philanthropic work. Her grandmother created this fund from money she inherited from her father. From what Hazel told me, her great grandfather was a blockade runner in the Civil War and made huge amounts of money. When Hazel's grandmother, Sadie, inherited her father's money, she took the bulk of it and put it in a trust fund to be used only to help others. She left the responsibility of the fund to Hazel's mother when she died, then Hazel took over when her mother died, and now Hazel would like you to manage this money. She told me that her grandmother's intent was to pass this from mother to daughter, but since she didn't have a biological daughter, she wanted you to be the one to have it."

Maya let this sink in. It all seemed to make some sense now. She guessed the visitors were from agencies that had applied for money from this fund and the files she always wondered about where the proposals from all the different agencies.

Mr. Hudson continued, "There are no guidelines for how you spend this money but Hazel did ask me to tell you to support causes that are close to your heart. She also wanted me to share with you that her focus had been on supporting programs for unwed mothers and adoption agencies. She mostly donated to local and state organizations, but occasionally she would even donate to agencies outside of North Carolina if someone submitted a strong application." Mr. Hudson pushed some papers towards her. "You'll need to meet with Tridet Investments since they manage the account so that it continues to grow. They'll help you with how much you can give each year while still growing the principal."

Finally, Maya found enough saliva in her dry mouth to speak, "So, Mr. Hudson, do you know how much Hazel would donate each year?" She thought it must be at least $1000 at a time to warrant people driving from all over the state to see her.

"Last year, Hazel donated right around $100,000. She would usually give anywhere between $2500 and $10,000 depending on the needs and focus of the agency. I'm sure if you look through her files you'll get a better understanding of what she looked for in an agency."

"One hundred thousand dollars, is that what you said?" Maya had never seen $100,000 all in one place before. She made about $3000 a month and had about $1500 in her savings but that was it.

"Yes, $100,000."

"Then what is the value of the fund if she could spend $100,000 and still have it grow?"

"You can look at the balance on that paperwork I gave you, but if I remember correctly, the fund is worth about 4.5 million right now."

Maya left Mr. Hudson's office and had walked for five minutes before she realized her car was parked in the opposite direction. She turned, walked back to Mr. Hudson's office, and found her car, just a couple of spaces away from his front door. She got in her Saturn and sat there trying to digest the shift her life had just taken in the matter of 45 minutes. She still gripped Mr. Hudson's card, knowing she would be calling him with more questions as all this sank in.

She finally started the car and drove slowly down Broad Street towards home. She knew she was leaving Travis at The Bean, but Mr. Hudson had told her that she couldn't talk about this fund with anyone and she needed time alone to figure out how to integrate this new role into her life before she could be around others. She might have to tell her sister though. She'd always told her everything and had never kept a secret from Kate before.

Maya turned into Hazel's driveway and parked in her usual spot. She gathered her purse and the stack of papers Mr. Hudson had given her and slammed the car door. She slowed her normal pace to the boathouse because of the low heeled pumps she had worn to this morning's meeting and then stopped halfway and took in her surroundings.

She looked towards the creek and the water sparkled with thousands of tiny diamonds created by the late morning sun. A gentle breeze rattled the halyards on Hazel's sailboat. A couple of dogwood trees by the creek bank were in full bloom, their flowers a herald of Easter, just a few days away. Maya's heels began sinking into the ground softened by last night's rain, so she took her shoes off and stood there on the dirt path in her bare feet. Her gaze moved up the hill, through the grove of trees to Hazel's home. Some daffodils were blooming by the back porch steps. The hydrangea bushes were starting to fill in with leaves, just as they had been the first time she saw this place from her kayak, almost a year ago.

It was hard to grasp that all this was hers now. This was all hers, the house, the trees, the dirt, everything. Her heart swelled with gratitude and it felt like it might pop out of her chest. She'd always be connected to Hazel by her property and her money flowing out to do good.

Maya turned and began a slow jog to the boathouse. She couldn't wait any longer and had to call Kate and tell her everything. She opened the front door and Doodle Bug raced out to meet her doing her usual happy dance all around Maya. Maya rubbed her head and then, for the first time ever, joined Doodle Bug in her own version of a happy dance. The two of them circled and wiggled on the small front porch of the boathouse. Some red winged blackbirds sang their applause from the river grasses beside the creek.

Book Club Guide for
Hungry Mother Creek

1. Maya immediately feels a sense of connection to the town of Oriental and the water around it. How does being close to the water and more connected to nature contribute to Maya's healing? Discuss the role nature plays in the plot of *Hungry Mother Creek*.

2. Maya is nervous about sharing her story at the fall equinox gathering and then surprised how powerful that experience is. Why do you think Maya chose to talk about her marriage and Steven's death with the women in the circle, after having just met some of them? When Maya first met Bay at lunch in Toucans, Bay asked her about her husband and why she was in Oriental. Maya didn't want to share her story with Bay even though she'd already done so in the circle. Why do you think she initially decided not to talk about her past with Bay?

3. Maya wasn't brought up in a religious or spiritual home so doesn't have a basic foundation to help her make sense of life. As Hungry Mother Creek progresses, Maya begins to feel a connection to something greater than herself when running, kayaking and sitting in the circle of women at the Mother Tree. How does Maya's increased spirituality contribute to her healing?

What questions are raised for Maya as she becomes more aware of her spirituality?

4. Throughout the novel, Maya and Violet struggle to stay focused on the present moment.   Maya is analyzing her past and Violet is worrying about her future. What helps them stay more connected to the present? How does being more mindful help Violet and Maya?

5. Maya initially judges Bay as arrogant and self centered but by the end of the novel Maya and Bay have developed a supportive friendship. Why did Maya's feelings change towards Bay?   In what ways did her relationship with Bay help Maya?

6. Maya and Travis begin a relationship based on fun, being in the moment, and mutual physical attraction. When Maya finds out the truth about Travis and sees how this opens up old wounds from her marriage, she ends the relationship. Was this the best choice? Could staying in the relationship have helped Maya in her healing process? Do you think she would have made a different choice if they'd had sex?

7. Bay is faced with the choice of doing the "right" thing and fulfilling others expectations or following a path she feels will lead to her ultimate fulfillment. Do you think Bay made the right choice to divorce Holden and leave him in Laura's care? What

other options could she have chosen? Why do you think Maya supports Bay's decision?

8. Maya has a perception that if a woman is physically beautiful somehow her life should be easier. As she gets to know Ella, Maya sees the burden that outer beauty can bring. How does Ella's beauty interfere with creating meaningful relationships? What could Ella do differently to make friends? Compare and contrast the role outer beauty plays in the lives of Ella and Bay.

9. Buster and Lilith seem to show up just when they are needed. Discuss the ways they both support Maya and Hazel.

10. When the women gather around Hazel's bed as she is dying, they hold hands and stand silently, reflecting on what she meant to them. Do you think this was the right choice or should they have done something different to honor Hazel? Do you think Hazel had made peace with her life decisions before she died?

11. Were you surprised at the contents of Hazel's will? What ideas did you have about Hazel's neat office, file cabinet and out of town visitors? Maya now has the responsibility of managing Hazel's philanthropic trust fund. If you were in Maya's position, what causes and organizations would you support?

12. What theme or storyline could you most identify with in the book? Why?

Women's Circle Guide for
Hungry Mother Creek

The following questions are deeper, more personal questions related to the characters and themes of *Hungry Mother Creek*. Please use these questions if you would like to create an experience similar to the women's circle portrayed in the novel. Use these questions in a group where you feel safe and respected. It may be your book club, or you may want to create a new group to read *Hungry Mother Creek*, and then answer these questions together. Depending on the size of your group, you may want to select just one or two questions to use for your circle discussion.

1. Maya felt a strong connection to the town and Oriental and the water surrounding it. Is there a location that you feel a strong connection to? Why? Where is it? Do you think your connection is because of the physical surroundings or your state of mind when you are there? How do your physical surroundings influence your mood and perspective?

2. The women's circle has a positive impact on Maya's healing and personal growth. She is surprised how powerful it is to share her story and how much wisdom she gains by listening to the stories of others. Have you ever shared your challenges, joys and experiences with a group of women you respected and trusted? If

no, how do you think you would feel in that situation? If yes, how was this different from telling just one other person?

3. As *Hungry Mother Creek* progresses, Maya begins to feel a connection to something greater than herself when running, kayaking and sitting in the circle of women at the Mother Tree. What places, activities or people provide you with a spiritual connection? Do you have a daily spiritual practice that connects you with a power greater than yourself? How does your spirituality help you deal with life's challenges?

4. Being mindful and fully present in the moment is a skill Maya works on throughout the novel. Are you able to live in the present? Do you ever find yourself missing out on the present by overly focusing on the past or future? What practices help keep you fully present? Are there mindfulness practices you plan to add to your life?

5. Maya initially judges Bay as arrogant and self centered but by the end of the novel Maya and Bay have developed a supportive friendship. Do you ever judge people based on their appearance or their initial behavior? If your first reaction to someone is negative, do you give them another chance? Have you ever become friends with someone you initially didn't like?

6. Maya ends the relationship with Travis because she doesn't feel either of them is ready for intimacy and because it had become a

distraction from making peace with her marriage and Stephen's death. When you are dealing with a difficult time in life do you find an intimate relationship assists or hinders your growth and healing? How so? Does it depend on what issue you are facing?

7. After Holden's stroke Bay feels resentment growing at the prospect of giving up her own dreams to care long term for him. She knows, as his wife, the right thing to do is to be Holden's primary caregiver but ultimately chooses to divorce him and let his daughter care for him. What would you do if faced with circumstances similar to Bay's? Have you ever made a decision that was based on your needs and desires but went against society's expectations? What was the outcome of making that choice? Have you ever done what was expected of you when you would have rather made a different choice? What was the end result in that situation?

8. Maya has a perception that if a woman is physically beautiful somehow her life should be easier. As she gets to know Ella, Maya sees the burden that outer beauty can bring. Do you have a stereotype of what life is like for someone who is beautiful? How do you deal with the emphasis our culture places on outer beauty?

9. Both Maya and Hazel are disappointed in decisions they had made in the past, Maya for staying in an abusive relationship and Hazel for having an abortion and neglecting her son. During the

course of the novel, both realize that forgiving themselves is the most important step in their healing. Have you ever had to forgive yourself for choices you regretted? Is there something you need to forgive yourself for now? How does someone forgive herself?

10. The women's circle hold hands and stand silently as Hazel is dying, reflecting on what she meant to them. Hazel, Lilith and Violet all refer to death as a natural part of life's cycle while Maya and Ella are more uncomfortable with being so close to death. Have you ever been with someone who is dying? How was that experience for you?

11. What theme or storyline could you most identify with in the book? Why?

Resources

Books Maya read

- The Power of Intention – Wayne Dyer
- Power of Now – Eckhart Tolle
- Heal Your Life – Louise Hay

Oriental, North Carolina

- www.townoforiental.com
- www.orientalmarina.com
- www.towndock.net

Kayaking

- www.pamlicochamber.com\kayak
- www.paddling.net
- www.americancanoe.org

Women's Circles

- The Millionth Circle – Jean Shinoda Bolen
- www.millionthcircle.com
- Sacred Circles: A Guide to Creating Your Own Women's Spirituality Group – Robin Carnes and Sally Craig
- Calling the Circle: The First and Future Culture – Christina Baldwin
- The Circle Way: A Leader in Every Chair – Christina Baldwin
- www.peerspirit.com

Made in the USA
Lexington, KY
15 July 2014